P9-BBN-923

REVOLVER
ROAD

ALSO BY CHRISTI DAUGHERTY

THE ECHO KILLING

A BEAUTIFUL CORPSE

REVOLVER

ROAD

CHRISTI DAUGHERTY

MINOTAUR BOOKS
NEW YORK

First published in the United States by Minotaur Books, an imprint of St. Martin's Publishing Group

REVOLVER ROAD. Copyright © 2020 by Christi Daugherty. All rights reserved. Printed in the United States of America. For information, address St. Martin's Publishing Group, 120 Broadway, New York, NY 10271.

www.minotaurbooks.com

Designed by Anna Gorovoy

Library of Congress Cataloging-in-Publication Data

Names: Daugherty, Christi, author.
Title: Revolver road: a Harper McClain mystery / Christi Daugherty.
Description: First edition. | New York: Minotaur Books, 2020. |
    Series: Harper McClain mysteries; 3
Identifiers: LCCN 2019039542 | ISBN 9781250235886 (hardcover) |
    ISBN 9781250235893 (ebook)
Subjects: GSAFD: Mystery fiction.
Classification: LCC PS3604.A883 R48 2020 | DDC 813/.6—dc23
LC record available at https://lccn.loc.gov/2019039542

Our books may be purchased in bulk for promotional, educational, or business use. Please contact your local bookseller or the Macmillan Corporate and Premium Sales Department at 1-800-221-7945, extension 5442, or by email at MacmillanSpecialMarkets@macmillan.com.

First Edition: March 2020

10 9 8 7 6 5 4 3 2 1

To Jack

Always

REVOLVER

ROAD

1

Holding a police scanner in one hand, Harper McClain stepped out onto the porch of the wood-framed bungalow.

It was unseasonably warm for late February, but the winds were picking up—a storm was moving in. Clouds swept across the moon, sending shifting shadows across the landscape.

The low, steady rumble of ocean waves hitting the shore three blocks away sounded like wind through a forest. Even after months of living out on Tybee Island, she wasn't used to it. It was loud enough to disguise other sounds. A car approaching. Footsteps on the dirt drive.

The sounds she'd hear if someone was coming to kill her.

Muttering under her breath, she held the scanner above her head. Through the crackle and fuzz, she could make out fragments of voices but not enough to understand what was happening. "Two . . . Street . . . Three . . . Sig . . ."

Swearing, she pulled her phone from her pocket and scrolled to a familiar number. It rang twice.

"You've only been home an hour." Photographer Miles Jackson's tone was accusing.

"I can hear something on my scanner but I can't make it out," she told him. "What's going on?"

"A whole lot of nothing's going on. Come on, Harper. You know I'd call you if anything important happened. There's no need for you to keep calling me."

"Something's happening," she insisted, stubbornly. "It's on Broad Street, I think. I couldn't make it out."

"It's a fender bender. Driver appears to be intoxicated. Nothing to get out of bed for." Miles drew a breath, summoning patience. "Harper, I have promised and I will promise again to call you if anything breaks when you are out of signal range. Now, you can call me every ten minutes or you can trust me. It's up to you."

In the background, jazz smoldered from the speakers in his Savannah apartment. She could hear the crackle of his scanner, working just fine.

She was so envious of his normal life it hurt.

Sinking onto the whitewashed wooden armchair next to the door, she gave a small sigh. "I'm sorry. I just hate not knowing what's happening."

"I know." His voice softened. "I get why you're anxious. I would be too, if I were you." He paused. "There's nothing new on that, is there?"

Miles was one of only a handful of people in the world who knew exactly why she'd been forced to move out of Savannah.

Nearly six months ago, she'd decided to leave the city after a single phone call from a man who knew far too much about her mother's murder, sixteen years ago. In that brief conversation, he'd told her someone wanted her dead. Someone who could get the job done. And he'd told her to run.

Since then she'd lived a stranger's life in a house she didn't like, miles from the city that would always be home. Isolated and cut off.

And her damn scanner didn't work.

"There's nothing new," she told Miles, her tone glum.

"I guess that's good news."

Was it, though? She lived like this because of one phone call. One warning. A man she'd never even met telling her that her mother's murderer was coming for her. And she'd had to take it seriously. But after months of silence, she'd started to doubt.

"Miles," she said, voicing a thought she rarely let herself consider, "what if all this was for nothing? What if he lied?"

"But that's the dream, Harper," he reminded her. "If the worst thing that happens is you spend one winter living by the ocean, pretending to be someone else, that sure beats the hell out of dying."

She knew he was trying to help. But there was a cost he didn't know about. She imagined telling him what it was like to live in constant fear. Of explaining that she drove with her eyes fixed on the rearview mirror. That every sudden noise made her twitch. Or how she'd spent every night lying awake, waiting for a killer, for months.

Still, it wasn't his fault. He'd done so much to try it make it easier for her.

"You're good people, Miles," she said, instead. "You know that?"

"Yeah, yeah, yeah." She could hear his smile. "Get some sleep."

John Coltrane disappeared as he hung up, and she was left with only the sound of the ocean for company.

Picking up the scanner, she turned the dial on top, switching it from the channel used by the Savannah police to the one used by the local police department. It was silent, too. Not because of distance. Because nothing ever happened out here.

Tybee Island is a dot on the map eighteen miles east of Savannah. There isn't much to it—a handful of surf shops, a couple of bars, three stoplights, and you're done. But the miles of soft, golden sand fringing the sleepy little town brings tourists flocking in droves. That was why Harper chose it when she needed a place to hide. Nobody here noticed one stranger with so many of them around.

The little community was affluent, small, and quiet. There was so little crime, the local cops spent their days hassling teenagers and handing out speeding tickets. Harper rarely saw a patrol car on the streets after six.

Tonight was no different. Nothing moved. No cars had driven by while she was out here. The only sound was the sea.

Harper dropped her head back against the chair letting her eyes drift shut. She was so tired. If she could just stop worrying for a few hours and rest, she'd feel so much better.

Ten minutes later, she was still sitting there when the scanner burst to life.

"All units, be aware we have a report of shots fired on Cedarwood Drive."

Harper's eyes flew open. She stared at the device as if it had barked.

A male voice crackled from the handset. "This is unit Bravo Alpha nine. Dispatch, can you repeat that?"

He sounded as surprised as Harper felt.

"We have reports of shots fired." At that point, the dispatcher dropped the pretense of radio formality. "I've had three calls so far, two from Cedarwood, and one from the old folks' home on Rosewood." She sounded breathless with excitement. "Everybody says they heard gunshots, Tom. Better get yourself down there."

"Well, all right," the officer said, after a second. "I'll head over. It's probably fireworks, though."

The scanner fell silent, again.

For a second, Harper sat where she was. Then she jumped to her feet and ran back inside. After grabbing her keys off the cheap little table by the door, she hurried across the room to scoop up a notebook and press pass from where she'd tossed them on the sofa when she'd come home from work earlier that night.

She hurried back out, locked the three high-security deadbolts she'd had installed when she first moved in, then ran down the steps to the gravel driveway, and slid into the low-slung Camaro parked under the sprawling branches of a weather-beaten oak tree. The engine started with a velvety rumble.

Who needed to sleep? Just being inside that car made her feel about fifty percent better.

Finding a story out here in the back end of nowhere would do the rest.

2

The streets were empty. Harper didn't pass a single car as she navigated off the wide, ghostly main street onto narrow Cedarwood Drive.

It took only minutes to locate the patrol car, its blue lights flashing steadily on the quiet lane.

She parked a short distance behind it and walked over. The car was empty. The street was just off the beach and the ocean was louder here. The waves sounded angry, hitting the sand so hard she could feel the thud beneath her feet.

The wind whipped her hair into her eyes as she looked around for the driver.

"Can I help you?" The voice came from the shadows behind her.

Harper spun around.

A police officer was walking toward her. He wore the all-black uniform of Tybee Island PD, a silver badge glittering on his chest beneath a name tag that read T. SOUTHBY. He was tall and sturdy, with a thick hipster beard and a quizzical expression.

"Oh, uh . . . Hi," she said, caught off guard. "I'm Harper McClain. From the *Daily News*."

"Right . . ." He still seemed baffled. "You lost or somethin'?"

"I heard the shots fired on my scanner," she explained. "I thought I'd see what was going on."

He slouched closer to her. "I'm sorry to disappoint you, Miss *Daily News,* but you wasted a trip. There's nobody shooting anybody around here." He nodded at the expensive-looking vacation houses behind him, all tall windows and wraparound porches. "As you can see, this isn't exactly a high-crime area."

"The dispatcher said there were multiple calls," she pointed out.

This didn't seem to impress him. "We just don't get shootings out here. What we do get is fireworks." Turning, he gestured at the dark sea at the end of the road, where a scattering of golden lights bobbed on the waves. "I reckon there were fireworks on one of those boats and that's what people heard."

"In February?" she asked, doubtfully.

"It's happened before. It's a warm night." He turned back to her. "Either way, there's no story out here."

Studying her with interest, he leaned against his squad car.

"Now, you tell me, what's a reporter from the *Daily News* doing out on Tybee Island in the middle of the night?"

"I've been staying out here for the winter," she said, unreeling her usual explanation. "Got a good deal on a rental."

He looked interested. "Really? Which one?"

"Spinnaker Cottage."

"Oh, one of Myra Hancock's places. Now, *she's* a character." He folded his arms, watching her knowingly. "I reckon you'll find us all kind of eccentric and strange out here."

"Not at all," she lied. "It's a nice place."

"It is nice," he agreed. "And I'll tell you why. Because we don't have any big-city crime. We haven't had a homicide out here in more than twenty years."

Harper was of the opinion that murder could happen anywhere. But if there hadn't been one here in decades, maybe he had a point. This was his town, not hers.

"No murder is fine with me." She dug in her jacket pocket, unearthing a business card. "Still, if anything does come from this—or if anything else happens out here, for that matter—I'd be grateful if you'd give me a call. I'm always looking for news."

He pulled a long-handled Maglite from his pocket. The beam lit up his face as he examined the lettering. He was younger than Harper had first thought; his skin was smooth and unlined.

"Sure thing, Harper McClain." Turning off the light, he slid the card into the pocket behind his badge. "Might be useful having a reporter out here: about time we had our share of fame." He gave her an ironic grin. "I'm Tom Southby, by the way. If you want to quote me."

"I'll bear that in mind." She smiled.

The police dispatcher's voice boomed from his radio. "BA nine? Y'all still out at the shots fired?"

Pulling the device from his belt, Southby turned the volume down before replying.

"Dispatch, put it down as a false alarm. All quiet here. Unit Bravo Alpha nine back in service."

The dispatcher responded, "Copy that, Bravo Alpha nine. You heading back to base?"

"In a few." He slid the radio back into its holder.

"It was nice to meet you, Harper McClain." Lifting his flashlight, he shined it on the Camaro. "Nice ride, by the way."

Gear rattling, he climbed into his patrol car and slammed the door, switching off the blue lights.

She lifted her hand as he performed a smooth U-turn on the wide, empty street and drove away, taillights glowing red in the darkness.

The next day temperatures dropped. A steady drizzle soaked the trees and sent water dripping from the long strands of moss.

Harper was on the porch locking up the little cottage when she heard a gruff female voice calling her name. Turning, she saw Myra, her landlady, walking down the short driveway, a hood pulled up against the weather, utility belt pinching her middle.

"I wanted to catch you before you left," she said, wiping rain from her face as she stepped onto the porch. "I would have called but I was around the corner anyway, fixing a loose board on the fence. The damn wind keeps trying to tear down everything I put up."

Myra was no more than five feet tall. She had to be in her sixties, but her straight hair was ink black. She wore a heavy layer of dark pencil around her bright, brown eyes, and Harper had never seen her without a screwdriver.

"What's up?" she asked.

The landlady squinted at her. "Look. You've known this was coming but I've got to get this place fixed up, ready for spring break. I hate to ask you to go, given your situation, but I've got no choice. You understand."

Harper's heart sank. Rents out here would quadruple in the summer. She couldn't begin to afford that. But she couldn't argue. They'd agreed at the start she only had the place until spring.

So, she forced a smile. "Sure, no problem. When do you need the place back?"

"Well, you take good care of it, but it'll need to be painted." The landlady tapped a finger against the white bannister where the paint had begun to flake. "Salt air. Give it enough time, it'd strip the fur off a dog." She paused to think. "If you could be out by the fifteenth, that'd be fine."

The fifteenth of March. That was only three weeks away.

"That's fine," Harper said weakly. "I'll start looking right away."

Myra gave her a fierce look. "You find yourself somewhere safe," she told her. "I promise you this—anyone ever comes looking for you, they'll get nothing out of me."

Harper had told her nothing about why she didn't want her real name on the lease or why she wanted three security locks fitted, but the landlady was convinced she was hiding from a bad relationship.

"I know about rough men," she'd confided when Harper moved in. "He comes after you, let me know. I'll bring my shotgun."

Harper had never set her straight. An angry landlady with a shotgun comes in handy.

Now, Myra straightened her hood and looked up at the sky. "I reckon this rain might settle in for a few days. I better go finish that fence."

Harper followed her as far as the Camaro. Damp from the rain, she slid her scanner in a holder on the dashboard and switched it from the Tybee police channel to the Savannah PD. Turning out onto the main highway, she headed west, windshield wipers thumping steadily, her mind going over the conversation she'd just had.

She didn't know where she was going to live now. She'd never imagined she'd still be trapped in this limbo for so long. Some days, she almost wanted the killer to find her. At least that would be the end of it. Even with the precautions she'd taken she wasn't hard to find. Her name was in the paper every week.

And yet, in all these months, there'd been no sign of him.

With effort, she forced herself to focus on the road ahead. Georgia Highway 80 is a silvery strip of civilization running straight through the wild coastal marshes. The drive in from the island has a kind of apocalyptic beauty—nothing but soft gray-brown salt grass stretching as far as you can see in every direction, disappearing into the mist. It was also a communications black hole. Her scanner didn't work out here. Or her cell phone.

It was only when she neared the city that Harper's scanner burst back into life with a litany of car wrecks and cops warning each other of flooded streets and fallen branches.

Five minutes later, she hit Savannah traffic. The roads narrowed, speeds slowed. Huge old oaks spread their branches overhead. Grand, antebellum mansions gazed down imperiously on the cars crawling beneath them.

Harper let out an unconscious breath as the city's familiar beauty wrapped around her like a hug. She'd been born here. Her mother died here. Savannah was in her blood.

The newspaper's rambling, white office building was on Bay Street, near the river. Harper parked in the crowded lot behind it, and dashed through the rain to the back door. She pushed the button to be let in, waving at the CCTV camera above her head until the lock released and the door swayed open.

The guard at the front desk made a note in his computer as she walked in.

Over the last few months the paper had tightened its security. The editors were taking the threat against her seriously.

"Thanks," Harper told him, running up the wide staircase to the newsroom, where twelve reporters sat at desks scattered across five rows divided by sturdy, white columns. Tall windows let in watery light.

Managing editor Emma Baxter sat in a glass-walled office at the far end. Her head was bent over an open laptop, and her dark, blunt-cut hair swung forward, hiding her face as Harper tapped her knuckles against the glass and pushed the door open without waiting to be invited.

"There was almost a shooting on Tybee last night," she announced. "Would have been the story of the year given how little happens out there."

Baxter glanced up at her. "But?"

"But it was only fireworks, cops think. No body. No blood."

"Terrific," Baxter said, dourly. "I'll hold the front page."

There were dark shadows under her eyes. Harper dropped into one of the chairs facing her desk. "You look worn out."

"Thanks." Baxter closed the laptop. "I'd be fine if one of my reporters would bring me a big story. Actually, I'd accept anything at this point. The newspaper building burning down, for instance. That would work."

She leaned back in a black leather executive chair that had been hers since Paul Dells, the previous managing editor, had been fired last summer. Baxter, the night editor, had been doing both their jobs since he left, and the strain showed. But she had little choice. MaryAnne Charlton, the paper's mercurial owner, was demanding more work done by fewer staff. The paper was profitable but there was no such thing as enough for the Charlton family.

"There was that shooting last week," Harper reminded her. "That should've calmed Charlton down for a while."

Baxter dismissed that. "It was a one-day story. Charlton's a thorn in my side but she's right about this—we haven't broken anything big in weeks." She picked up that day's paper with its front-page image of bumper-to-bumper cars. "What gets people subscribing are crooked politicians and crime. All we've got is traffic. I need something big before Charlton throws us all out and opens a boutique hotel in my newsroom."

Standing, she yanked her blazer from the back of her chair and stabbed her hands into the sleeves. "I need a cigarette."

Harper followed her through the door into the newsroom bustle. The editor didn't make it far.

"Hey, Baxter. Could you take a look at this?" Ed Lasterson, the court reporter, waved her over. As she turned toward him, Harper headed to her desk.

Education reporter DJ Gonzales spun his chair around as she passed.

"You're early." His tone was accusing. "You're not supposed to be here until four."

Harper smiled sweetly. "I couldn't wait to see you . . . to tell you to mind your own business." She switched on her computer and logged in with motions so automatic her brain hardly knew it had happened.

Unbothered by her sarcasm, DJ rolled closer to her. "What's up with Baxter? She looks rough."

"She's tired," Harper told him, quietly. "I don't know if she can handle the pace much longer."

DJ grew sober. "If she goes, who the hell will run this place?"

Harper didn't reply. She didn't have to. They both knew Baxter was the glue holding the newspaper together. The editor's joke about Charlton converting it into a hotel was too close to reality to be funny.

"She'll be fine," she said, shortly. "All we need is a good story."

"We'll get one," DJ said, without hesitation. "We always do." He spun his chair back to his computer, somehow ending up with his hands on the keyboard.

He was right. But Harper wasn't willing to just wait for a story to fall into her lap. Her beat was the one that sold the most papers. There was nothing people liked more with their cornflakes in the morning than a juicy glass of homicide, and the criminals of Savannah had been too quiet lately.

Or maybe she'd missed something.

Yanking open the top right-hand drawer of her desk, she pulled out a handful of reporter's notebooks and began riffling through them for a crime she could follow up on. Something she'd overlooked.

The slim, wire-bound pages were filled with hasty scribbles that had made sense at the time.

"Nine-millimeter hollow-point shells fired six times. Casings recovered."

"Three males last seen running west on Broad. One bleeding from the shoulder . . ."

"Bags tested positive for cocaine . . ."

When her phone rang, she picked it up absently. "McClain," she said, not looking up from the notes in front of her.

"Um. Hi." The voice on the phone was cautious. Gruff. "This is Officer Tom Southby from Tybee. We met last night?"

"Oh, hey," Harper straightened. "What's up? Is there news on the shots fired?"

"It's not that," he said. "I'm sorry to bother you, this might be nothing, but you did say for me to call if anything happened out here. And, well . . . Someone on the island's gone missing."

In Harper's experience, most missing people were teenagers running away from home. Generally they came back before the news story was published. Still, it was unusual enough for a street cop like Southby to tip her off, that she pushed the old notebooks out of the way, and dug out a new one.

"Tell me about it," she said. "Is it a juvenile? How long have they been missing?"

Southby must have been in his car—she could hear the sound of traffic during the brief pause before he spoke. "That's the reason I'm calling you. The missing man's kind of famous. A musician. Name of Xavier Rayne."

Frowning, Harper summoned a vague mental image of a handsome young man with high cheekbones and light brown skin.

"I've heard of him. So, he's gone AWOL?"

"So, it seems," Southby said. "His friends called this morning. They say he hasn't been seen since last night."

Harper was puzzled. Normally the police didn't consider someone truly missing until they'd been gone twenty-four hours.

"They don't think he just went to someone's house and crashed for a while?" she asked.

"Here's the thing," Southby said. "Last time his friends saw him, he was walking out to the beach with his guitar in his hand." He paused. "We found his guitar this morning. But there's no sign of Xavier Rayne."

3

Now Harper was intrigued.

"You say he was at home?" She was scribbling notes as she talked. "Where's his house?"

"On the north side of the island, not far from the lighthouse," Southby said. "He lives right off the beach."

"What time was he last seen?"

"Just after two in the morning," he said.

Harper's pen stopped moving.

"That was the same time people reported gunshots," she said. "Do you think that's connected?"

"Now, hold on." Southby's voice grew stern. "Don't go writing anything about that. We've got no evidence that there even *were* gunshots. We've also got no crime scene. No blood was found. No sign of an altercation. All we've got is a missing person. His housemates are clear that they saw no intruders and heard nothing suspicious. They didn't even notice he hadn't come home until this morning."

"And they say he walked down to the beach alone at two in the morning?" Harper's tone was doubtful. "The storm was coming in around then. The winds were pretty high."

"His friends say he does it all the time. They say he likes to 'connect to the ocean.'" He sounded more bemused than concerned.

"Does it seem suspicious to you?" Harper pressed. "Rayne's been getting a lot of press lately. Could it be a kidnapping?"

There was a telltale pause before he responded. "I wouldn't go on the record with any theories right now. But I will say this much—currents are unpredictable on the north side of the island, especially at this time of year. His friends say he'd been drinking. Drunks make bad swimmers. But, right now, we don't know if he ever went in the water. The wind blew the sand around all night, leaving no footprints, and then there's the rain." She could almost hear him scratching his head. "Basically, we don't have much to work with. At the moment, he's a missing person. And we need to spread the word in case anyone out there knows where he is. That's why I'm calling."

"I'll do whatever I can to help," Harper said. "Let me know if he turns up. And thanks for the tip. I owe you one."

As soon as she set the phone down, she typed "Xavier Rayne" into a search engine. Dozens of headlines opened—many of them in national newspapers and online magazines. As she scanned them, Harper's eyes widened.

Here's your front-page story, Baxter, she thought.

The editor was no longer talking to Lasterson. Nor was she in her office. She must have finally made it outside for that cigarette.

Putting her notebook and scanner in her bag, she grabbed her jacket, still damp from the rain, and sped across the newsroom and raced down the stairs. At the bottom, she hit the green button to unlock the door.

Baxter stood on the front steps under an overhang that shielded her from the rain. Her back was to the whitewashed wall, a Marlboro Gold was between her lips. Her eyes were closed as she absorbed the smoke like oxygen. Her blazer hung loose on her bony shoulders. She wasn't yet fifty, but right now she looked ten years older than that.

As if she sensed someone watching her, Baxter opened her eyes.

"Missing-person case," Harper began.

"Oh terrific." She blew out a long stream of disinterested smoke.

"The missing guy is a musician named Xavier Rayne," Harper continued, undaunted.

The cigarette, which had been swooping back toward the editor's mouth, stopped in midair. "You're kidding."

"I just looked him up." Harper could barely contain her excitement. "His album came out this week and it's in the top ten already. He's supposed to go on tour in three days. And, as of right now, no one knows where the hell he is."

The editor's exhaustion seemed to evaporate. She stood straighter, her eyes sharpening. "How much have you got?"

Harper recapped what Southby had told her. When she finished, Baxter dropped the remains of her cigarette on the sidewalk and ground it down with the toe of her low-heeled shoe.

"Get out there right now," she ordered. "Get your hands on the missing-persons report. Take Miles. Talk to Rayne's friends, find out what they have to say. I'll leave space on the front page."

"On it." Leaving her there, Harper ran around the building to the back lot, boots splashing in the puddles. By the time she reached the Camaro, she was soaked but she barely noticed.

She pulled out her phone and dialed Miles's number. It only rang once.

"Nothing's happening," the photographer said, instead of hello.

"I'm in the city," she told him, starting the engine. "How would you feel about a trip to the beach?"

"Please tell me you mean Bermuda."

Harper smiled. "Not exactly."

She picked Miles up in front of his apartment building ten minutes later. He lived at the dicey end of River Street—far from the paddlewheel boats and praline shops that were hallmarks of tourist Savannah. The warehouse conversion was surrounded by industrial buildings and empty lots. Harper hated going there at night—it sent her crime radar off the charts. But it had a hell of a view and he'd got it for a song.

Miles set his camera bag carefully in the back and climbed into the passenger seat. Harper was soaked, her hair in wet tangles. By contrast, he looked pristine in a snazzy black raincoat over a crisp button-down shirt with a burgundy print. He kept his dark hair cropped short, and he was always clean shaven. He brought style to every crime scene.

"How much do we know?" he asked, buckling up.

On the way out to the island, she filled him in. She had to take it slow: the road was nearly flooded in places.

When she'd given him the basics, he fell silent for a moment before saying, "Tell you what, if Xavier Rayne's dead it's a goddamn shame."

Harper glanced at him, surprised. "Do you know him?"

"Not personally," he said. "But I've been following his career since he started out, singing at open-mic nights around town when he was a teenager. He always had talent but, in the last couple of years, he found his voice." He sounded almost reverent. "He's the real deal. Two years at Juilliard on a full scholarship. Dropped out to go pro. His new album is something else."

She should have known Miles would be all over this. He loved music, and had a professional's affinity for spotting new talent in the area.

"He's probably just passed out on someone's couch," she told him.

"Maybe." Still morose, he looked out the window at the marshes. "Or else he's feeding crabs."

The Tybee Island police headquarters was a low clapboard structure near the beach. The street was quiet as the two of them hurried up the wide sidewalk to the front door. The rain had eased a little, but a cool breeze blew in hard off the ocean. The air smelled of brine.

Inside, pale light flooded through wide picture windows into an airy, open-plan space that felt for all the world like a luxury real-estate office. There was no one in the lobby. The reception desk was unmanned.

Harper looked around, bewildered. She'd never seen a police station that wasn't teeming with activity at this time of day.

She stood on her toes, calling into the office behind the front desk. "Hello?"

A chair, which she'd assumed to be empty, twitched before it rolled back, revealing a woman in her thirties with short, blond hair.

"Oh my heavens," the woman said, getting up. "You startled me. I didn't realize anyone was there." Her apologetic smile was outlined in pink lipstick, matching her pink cardigan. Her gaze swung from Harper to Miles and back again. "Can I help you?"

"We're from the *Savannah Daily News*." Harper held out her press pass. "We'd like to see the crime report on Xavier Rayne."

"Oh yes." The woman grew serious. "Tom Southby told me you might come in. I've got it right here." She picked a folder up off the desk and slid it across to them, already open to reveal an official form. "It's such a shame. That poor young man. I hope he's okay."

Harper and Miles bent over the document, which set out the case in stark, emotionless terms.

Missing person: Michael Xavier Rayne.

Age: 24

Height: 6ft

Weight: 160

Race: Mixed

Hair: Black

Eyes: Hazel

Last seen: Approx. 0200 hours

Last known location: 6 Admiral's Row

Last seen: Individual had been drinking heavily at his residence for several hours. Individual announced he was going to the beach to write music. Housemates report seeing him walk to the beach with guitar and bottle of Jack Daniel's. Housemates say they fell asleep after that point. When they awoke, individual had not slept in his bed. When he did not answer his phone or respond to messages, they searched the house and nearby beach. At approximately 1200 hours they contacted PD to report missing person.

Page two had a few additional details: basic information about the scene—house in good repair, no sign of forced entry, no evidence of a struggle.

At the end was a final entry.

Reporting persons: Hunter Carlson, Cara Brand, Allegra Hanson.

All of them listed the Admiral's Row address as their home. Harper wrote down all three names before handing the file back to the receptionist.

"Have you had any calls at all about him this afternoon?" Miles asked. "Any sightings?"

"Nothing at all." The receptionist looked past them out the glass wall to the swirling clouds and falling rain. "I sure hope he turns up. This is no kind of weather to be out in."

Harper couldn't argue with that. But all she said was, "Can you tell us how to get to Admiral's Row?"

The receptionist's directions took them to a short, leafy street of six grand, two-story Victorian mansions on a low bluff overlooking the ocean. The houses were identical and magnificent—each had a high, peaked roof and a spacious wraparound porch on both floors.

Number 6 was the last house on the lane.

Harper parked at the end of the street, and killed the engine.

"Nice place," Miles observed, looking up at the huge windows. "I guess music pays."

The low, menacing growl of the ocean was clear in the distance as they got out of the car.

Harper turned around, trying to get her bearings. She thought the lane was probably a mile from Spinnaker Cottage. And maybe half a mile or more from where gunshots had been reported the night before. But it was hard to tell without looking at a map. The island's winding roads were confusing.

"What's up?" Miles asked, glancing back at her.

"Oh it's nothing," she said, after a second. "Just thinking."

It was too early to make any guesses about what was going on here. She had nothing substantial to connect this missing-person case with the gunshots. And the police didn't believe there had even been any gunshots at all.

She didn't want to blow a good story by hoping for a better one.

She glanced at Miles. "You want to come inside or head straight down to the beach?"

His eyes swept the impressive house. "I'll come with you. I want to get a feel for the place."

The front door was broad and sturdy, painted the same white as the house, with a fan-shaped transom window above it that looked as old as the building.

Harper took the lead, knocking firmly. A long silence followed. She was thinking of knocking again when the door was yanked open so unexpectedly she jumped back, bumping hard into Miles.

A man in his twenties glared at them. "What the hell do you want?"

He was tall and slim. His sandy-brown hair stood up as if he'd just raked his fingers through it. He wore a faded band T-shirt for a group called the Lumineers.

Remembering the names on the report, Harper said, "We're sorry to bother you. Are you Hunter?"

His brow creased. "Who's asking?"

He had a Northern accent—New England, maybe. He was trying to sound intimidating, but Harper could hear the nervousness that lay beneath his words.

"My name is Harper." She kept her voice measured. "This is Miles. We heard about what happened with Xavier Rayne. We work for the *Savannah Daily News*." At the mention of the newspaper, he flinched, and she hurried to finish. "The police have asked us to write about it. To spread the word. In case someone's seen him or knows where he might be." She took a step forward, keeping her eyes steady. "We just want to help."

"Oh, man." He rubbed the back of his hand across his forehead. "I didn't think the press would find out so soon."

His eyes were bloodshot. His shoulders sagged a little, as if the day pushed down on him. There was something boyish and vulnerable about him that Harper instinctively liked.

"Who is it, Hunter?" A woman about his age appeared just behind him. Resting a hand on his shoulder, she moved him aside gently.

She was stunningly beautiful. Long, honey-blond hair hung across one shoulder; her makeup-free face was fine-boned and poreless. She wore a flowing white skirt so long the hem brushed the tops of her small, bare feet. A white cotton sweater exposed one narrow shoulder.

This had to be the actress, Harper thought. Cara something.

"They're from the newspaper in Savannah." There was an unspoken warning in Hunter's voice. "They want to know about Xavier."

"We just want to spread the word," Miles interjected. "To get people looking out for him."

"He hasn't even been missing a day," Hunter began to argue, but Cara cut him off.

"He's been gone since two A.M. We can't assume he's okay. Someone could have kidnapped him or drugged him. . . ." Her eyes filled with tears and she stopped, biting her lip. After a second, she stepped back and motioned for them to follow her.

"Please come in. We'll tell you whatever you need to know."

4

Inside, the house seemed bigger than it had from outside and, if possible, more impressive. A wide central hallway led in a straight line from the front door to the back. Harper could see the angry gray ocean through the window at the end. The air was cool and dry, and carried the scent of some exotic incense with a faint and not unpleasant hint of cigarette smoke.

As she followed Cara and Hunter, she caught glimpses of rooms, each a blur of bohemian elegance: a large kitchen with towering white cabinets and a wide-board floor, a dining room with silk wallpaper in delft blue, a long oak table bearing candelabra dripping wax. A curved, stately staircase with a heavy oak bannister that drew her eyes upward to a light-filled corridor above.

Gradually, she became aware of music. Somewhere in the house, a woman was singing mournfully. The ghostly sound made the fine hairs on the back of her neck rise.

The living room was at the back of the house. When they entered, all the curtains were closed, shrouding it in gloom. Cara hurried to open them—ripping the fabric aside with quick, impatient movements, revealing a room as perfectly disheveled as a spread from a design magazine.

Beneath soaring ceilings, sofas and deep armchairs covered in white linen faced each other across a glass-topped coffee table littered with cigarette packs, melted candles, and empty glasses.

"Hunter"—Cara turned to where he had stopped in the doorway, his hands hanging limp at his sides—"could you get some coffee? I'm so tired I think I might pass out."

He pivoted instantly, as if relieved to have an excuse to leave the room.

Harper and Miles perched stiffly on a sofa. Cara placed herself across from them. Her skirts billowed as she sat, a cloud of gauzy fabric.

It was hard not to stare at her. She was as delicate as a fawn. Her long slim wrists looked breakable. She was too thin to be healthy—every bone seemed to stand out in relief beneath skin tanned pale gold. But the overall effect was striking.

"I'm sorry about that," she apologized disarmingly. "None of us slept much. It's been chaos since we noticed Zay . . . since Xavier was gone."

She stumbled over what Harper presumed was his nickname.

"I guess I should start with the obvious question." She kept her tone gentle, unthreatening. "Do you have any idea where Xavier might have gone?"

Cara shook her head. "We only know a few people on the island. Most of his friends are in Savannah or Atlanta. We've called his agent, his manager, his mom . . . no one has seen him."

She had a pleasant voice—soft, with a curiously flat accent that seemed to come from nowhere in particular.

Before Harper could ask another question, Miles noticed an acoustic guitar leaning near a spindly music stand.

"Is that Xavier's guitar?" he asked. "The one he left on the beach?"

Cara turned to look at it, her chin trembling. Her reply was a whisper. "Yes."

"Do you mind if I take a look?"

When she didn't object, he walked over, picking it up to examine it. "This is a limited-edition Gibson." His voice held something like wonder. "It's a beautiful instrument. It's hard to believe he'd leave it behind voluntarily."

Cara tried to speak but no words emerged. She brushed a tear from her cheek with a quick, unconscious gesture. "I'm sorry," she said. "I keep doing this. I just want him to come back."

"Don't apologize," Harper told her. "We understand."

Setting the guitar down as carefully as if it were made of glass, Miles returned to the couch. "Is there anything you can think of that might have caused him to run away?" he asked.

She shook her head. "None of this makes any sense."

The singing had stopped at some point. In the quiet, Harper could hear the clatter of cups from the kitchen, water running. The house was big, but sound carried through it. If something had happened to Xavier in this house, they would all have been able to hear it.

She decided to wait to ask more questions until Hunter was back in the room. There was an angry edge to him—she had a feeling he'd reveal more than Cara, who was giving them nothing but tragic fragility.

"This is a beautiful house," she said, stalling. "How long have you lived here?"

Cara looked around as if she'd never thought about it. "It's really Zay's place. He rents it."

"He doesn't own it?" Miles asked.

"He wants to buy it." Cara gave a sad smile. "It's the main thing we disagree on. I want him to move to LA, where I live. He wants to stay here."

"Why doesn't he want to move?" Harper asked.

Cara straightened her skirt with a nervous swish of her fingers. "He says LA is filled with cheats and fakers."

Her lips were tight—this was clearly a sensitive subject.

"Didn't he grow up in Savannah?" Miles asked.

Cara nodded. "His dad was from here. He died when Zay was ten. After that, he and his mom moved to Atlanta. Zay moved back after he left Juilliard."

Harper scribbled quick notes in a pad resting on her knee. Cara's gaze glanced off it like rain bouncing off a stone.

"Who else lives in the house?" Harper asked.

"Hunter." Cara gestured vaguely at the kitchen. "He plays keyboards in Zay's band. They're very close."

That was where Harper had seen him. He was in some of the photos she'd come across earlier that day, standing onstage harshly lit by the spotlight.

"Don't forget Allegra." Hunter stood in the doorway, holding four mugs by the handles, some leaning perilously.

"Yes," Cara glanced at him before turning back to Harper and Miles. "You haven't met her yet. She sings backup on his new album."

While she talked, Hunter set the coffee down on the low table, moving candle holders and ashtrays to make space.

When he finished, he dropped down onto an overstuffed chair and lit a cigarette.

Reaching out gracefully for a cup, Cara gestured for Harper and Miles to do the same. "I can't be the only one who needs caffeine."

Hunter blew out a stream of smoke and made a dismissive sound. "Nobody sleeps when Xavier's pulling one of his acts."

Holding her coffee with both hands, Cara pretended not to hear him. But this was what Harper had been waiting for. She turned to Hunter. "What do you mean by 'one of his acts'? Has Xavier disappeared before?"

"He's always taking off without telling us." His voice was clipped. "He's a drama queen, like all the best artists."

"Hunter, that's not fair." Cara fired a look at him, but he didn't back down.

"Come on. New York six months ago. He walked out of a recording session and checked out of his hotel and disappeared. Stu was furious."

"That was different," Cara insisted, but he waved his cigarette at her, smoke trailing.

"It's exactly the same." His voice rose. "Xavier does this shit, Cara. He *does*. New Mexico, last year. Walked off the stage because he didn't like the sound he was getting. Got on a plane and left. Stu spent two days trying to get him to come back."

"I'm sorry, who's Stu?" Harper interrupted.

There was a pause as the two of them exchanged a simmering look. It was Cara who replied. "Stuart Dillon. The band's manager."

"He's getting a flight back from Paris tonight," Hunter cut in. "I'm sure he'll be thrilled to abandon his vacation to look for Xavier."

"You have to stop comparing this with other times." Cara looked increasingly tense. "Every other time he was working, and he got upset about something in the music. This time he's not working. This is down-time. He doesn't feel ignored. Everything was *fine*."

Hunter gave her a weighted look Harper couldn't read. Her face red-dened, but she said nothing, turning instead to Harper and Miles and insisting, "I know Xavier. I love him. He wouldn't run away like this."

"He'll come back." A pixieish young woman stood in the doorway from the hall. She was tiny—under five feet tall—with short, glossy dark hair and huge eyes. Like Cara, she wore no shoes. "Stop talking like he won't come back."

With a frustrated sound, Hunter leaped to his feet and stalked to the window.

Cara, though, calmed down. "Of course he will." She patted the sofa next to her. "Come here, Legs. Do you want some coffee?"

"No caffeine," the girl said. "I already can't sleep." She walked across, taking a seat next to Cara on the sofa. Her gaze was disconcertingly di-rect as she glanced from Miles to Harper. "I'm sorry—I don't know who you are."

A South Carolina accent, thick as cane syrup, lay on every word. Harper knew where she'd grown up without even asking her.

"They're from the Savannah newspaper," Cara explained. "They want to write about Xavier. To help us find him."

"I think he's just gone to be with friends," Allegra announced. "He does this kind of thing sometimes."

"Could you tell me in your own words what happened last night? When and why he left?" Harper included them all in the question, but it was Cara who spoke first.

"Nothing happened. That's what's so strange. I came in from LA around six o'clock. We had some wine. Allegra cooked dinner." She rested a hand on the girl's arm—an almost maternal gesture. "Xavier was fine. Tired, maybe. But in a good mood."

Out of the corner of her eye, Harper saw Hunter turn from the win-dow to watch as she continued. "Zay and Hunter played the new music they've been working on. We talked for hours, the way we always do when we're all together. I was tired after traveling so I went to bed around one. Hunter and Legs both stayed up."

"After Cara went to bed, we talked some more," Hunter said, picking up the story. "Drank some more. At about two in the morning, we were all going to bed, but Xavier said he was too wired to sleep and he wanted to go down to the beach. That's the last time I saw him."

"Was this unusual?" Harper glanced at the three of them. "Going to the beach in the middle of the night? Even in February?"

"He loves it there," Allegra explained. "He says he takes strength from the ocean. It inspires him."

As if this irritated her, Cara set her coffee mug down a little hard. "Zay has insomnia," she said, simply. "He says watching the sea helps him relax."

"So none of you thought anything about it until . . . ?" Harper glanced back and forth between them.

"Until this morning." Hunter walked back to sit down, picking up his cigarettes again, but not lighting one. "He wasn't in his room. It didn't look like he'd slept in his bed. There'd been a storm overnight. We went looking for him outside, on the beach—he wasn't there."

"I hate to ask this but, have there been any signs of trouble?" Miles asked, delicately. "Any sign that he's depressed? Has he been using drugs at all?"

Cara dropped her eyes, the resigned set to her shoulders said she'd expected this question. Allegra looked outraged. "He doesn't touch drugs," she insisted. "He wouldn't."

"And he isn't depressed." Hunter's voice was firm. "Our album just came out. Things are looking good."

Miles considered this. "I just keep thinking about how he left that guitar behind," he said. "I've never met a musician who wasn't protective of his instrument. Was it like Xavier to leave his guitar out there all night, exposed to the sand and salt water?"

Hunter and Cara exchanged a long look.

"He just forgot," Allegra insisted.

But Cara shook her head.

"Xavier would cut off his right arm before he'd leave that guitar behind." She looked from Harper to Miles, her eyes filling with anguished tears. "Please help us. I think something terrible might have happened to him."

5

Miles and Harper caught rush-hour traffic on the way back, and it was after six o'clock when they walked into the newsroom. By then, most of the day-shift reporters had gone home. Only DJ was still at his desk, headphones on.

The second she sat down, he ripped them off and spun around to face her. "Tell me Xavier Rayne isn't dead," he demanded. "I've got tickets for his show next month and I don't think I can get a refund."

"Maybe he's lost." She plugged her scanner in to charge. "People get lost."

"Seriously, though. What do you think happened?" He rolled closer. "Has he gone on a bender or something? Is he a junkie?"

"I'm not sure yet," she admitted. She thought about that guitar. "But I'm not getting a good feeling."

"Ah, dammit. It's always the talented ones." DJ sighed. "His new album was going to put Savannah on the map."

"Savannah's already on maps," she said.

"Yeah, but he was going to make us look cool." His tone was doleful.

Across the room, Baxter appeared in the doorway of the glass office.

Spotting Harper, she hurried across, her navy blazer fluttering behind her. "What've you got?"

"All anyone knows is he got drunk, walked down to the beach, and disappeared," Harper said. "There are a few possibilities but drowning is the obvious one."

Miles, who was uploading his pictures at a desk nearby, walked over to join them. "He could have had a breakdown—the housemates implied he was emotionally fragile." He glanced at Harper. "Also, I don't know about you but I wasn't buying their 'everything was fine until he disappeared' act."

"They definitely weren't telling us everything," Harper said. "I got the feeling they were protecting him somehow."

"Whatever happened to him, if he doesn't show up by morning we'll have the national press on this," Miles said.

"Were there any TV crews out there?" Baxter asked.

Harper gave her a significant look. "Not a single one."

The editor gave a thin smile. "Call the island cops—find out what kind of search they're doing. If they've got boats out looking for him, we run it on the front page. I'll pull some images from the wire. Let's put together a package—who he is, his music. What's his story? Was he an alcoholic? A druggie?"

DJ, who had been pretending not to listen, couldn't take it anymore. He spun his chair around. "His new album is all about his dad," he informed them, eagerly. "I think he was shot to death in Savannah when Xavier was a kid."

Harper made a mental note to look through the old files.

Baxter pointed a finger at DJ. "Drop whatever you're working on and help Harper with this. I want a front-page spread ready to go by ten o'clock."

As everyone got to work, she headed to her office, her last words floating across the rows of empty desks: "I'm going home to get some rest. I'll be back at ten. Call me if a body turns up."

This was the system that had been developed since she took over for Paul Dells. She came in at nine, worked all day, went home for a quick break, then returned to work until midnight.

DJ rolled his chair closer to Harper's, not bothering to hide his eagerness. "How should we divide this up?"

He covered education, but often got roped into helping her on bigger stories. He rarely objected. His own beat wasn't, he freely admitted, as sexy as hers.

"You know Rayne's music better than I do—why don't you write about that: his career, his new album. Anything you don't know, ask Miles," she told him. "I'll handle all the cop stuff."

"Sounds like a plan." He spun back around as she logged into her computer.

There was something that had been bothering her since she first saw Admiral's Row. Opening an internet map, she located the lane—a tiny dash, next to the sea—and traced the island's edge until she located Cedarwood Drive, where she'd first run into Tom Southby.

She stared at the map for a long time, and then she picked up the phone.

The Tybee officer who'd tipped her off about Rayne's disappearance answered on the first ring. "Tom Southby."

"This is Harper McClain," she said. "Sorry to bother you, but I'm checking in on the Rayne case—is there any news?"

"Nothing so far. We've contacted family and friends, checked with hospitals and all the morgues in the area. No sign of him, dead or alive."

Harper tucked her phone under her chin and picked up her pen. "You got people out there looking for him—the Coast Guard?"

"We've had boats out all day. They called it off an hour ago when we lost the light. We'll pick up the search in the morning."

"I've got one more question," Harper said. "Those gunshots people reported last night. Are you still certain those two things aren't related?"

"I can't find anything to connect them," he said. "Besides, Cedarwood's a good distance from Admiral's Row."

"It is by road." She glanced at the map still open on her screen. "By beach, it's much closer. No more than a few hundred yards. And if the wind was blowing the right way, it could have carried the sound down there easily." She drew a breath. "I just think it's a hell of a coincidence that he disappeared when people heard shots."

There was a long pause.

"Now look, I know why you're thinking this." His tone was placating. "Over there in Savannah, you've got a lot of crime. You hear gunshots, you've got yourself some trouble. We hear gunshots out here?

We've got duck hunters out in the marshes. We've got a boat with a bad mix in its fuel line. We don't have a murder."

"Duck hunters at two in the morning?" Harper couldn't keep the skepticism out of her voice, and Southby obviously noticed it, because when he spoke again his voice was noticeably cooler.

"Miss McClain, if he was shot, where's the crime scene? I've got no blood, no viscera. I've got no *body*. I've got nothing, Miss McClain, except a man who went for a walk and didn't come home. Speculation is entertainment. I am not in the entertainment business. What I know for a fact is that riptides off that beach kill people every year. And sound carries strangely over water. Are we clear on this?"

Harper didn't miss the warning underlying his words.

"Crystal clear," she said.

"Good," he said. "What's important right now is that we find out what happened to Mr. Rayne and we are working on that day and night. We are making no assumptions about what has occurred, and neither should you."

After they both hung up, Harper sat for a moment, thinking, before leaning forward and tapping DJ on the shoulder.

"DJ, did you say you thought Rayne's dad was murdered? I can't find anything about that online."

He spun around, blinking at her from behind smudged glasses. His dark, wavy hair was even more unruly than usual. "I don't know for sure. But the album has lines in it that make it sound that way. Hold on a minute."

Spinning back, he typed something into his computer.

"There's one line in particular in the song 'Revolver Road.'" After a second, he half turned so she could see he was looking at lyrics online. He pointed at the screen. "'I don't want to go out like my daddy done. Live by the gun, die by the gun . . .'" He looked up at her. "I mean, maybe he was singing about someone else, but . . ."

"But it sounds autobiographical." Harper finished the thought for him. "His girlfriend said he died when Xavier was ten. That would have been fourteen years ago." She stood up. "I'm going to go see what I can find in the morgue."

She ran across the empty newsroom, beneath the silently flickering television screens. She passed the cramped little break room and pushed through the double doors into the stairwell. Her footsteps echoed as she hurried up to the next floor. There, a hallway led past a series of offices for marketing, classified ads, and admin.

Harper stopped in front of a plain white door. The sign on the door read RECORDS.

Inside, the windowless room was pitch black. Harper felt the smooth wall for the light switch. When she found it, the harsh fluorescent strips lit up with a buzz, illuminating a small, utilitarian room filled with rows of metal filing cabinets.

Just over a decade ago, the paper had gone fully digital. Every article written was automatically logged and filed on the system. But there'd never been any money to go back and scan in the old articles. Anything before then was stored in here.

All the articles were filed by year and within the year by subject or name in a somewhat haphazard system that depended on whose job it had been to file.

She'd been in here not all that long ago researching her own mother's murder. The unsolved crime that was at the heart of everything happening to her now. And some part of her drew her to that particular file, filled with terrible memories. At twelve years old, she had been the one to find her mother's body on the floor, naked and cold, surrounded by blood.

Her father would be the first suspect, but with an alibi provided by his mistress, he would walk free. And nobody else was ever charged. Harper's own investigations had found little new information, until the phone call last year that told her the murderer was still out there, looking for her.

Today, though, she walked by that filing cabinet, and turned to the first row on the right, making her way to the cabinets dated fourteen years back. Focusing on the crime at hand, she pulled a drawer open with a rattle and flipped through the overstuffed manila folders until she found the "R"s.

"Raccoon." "Racing." "Randall." "Reptiles" . . .

No "Rayne."

Just to be sure, she opened another drawer and looked under "M," for "Murder," but finding four thick folders with that label, she sighed. It would take an hour to go through it all.

After a moment's thought, she slid them back into the drawer, and walked farther down the row to drawers marked for the year before that. Fifteen years ago. Again, she searched through the "R"s.

Right in the middle, she found what she was looking for. "Rayne, Michael James."

She pulled the folder out. Inside, a small stack of articles was carefully folded. She opened the first, the paper soft beneath her fingers. There was a faint scent of dust to it.

Man Killed in Suspected Drug Deal Gone Wrong
By Tom Lane

Two people were injured and one killed in a shoot-out on 19th Street last night.

Twenty-nine-year-old Michael James Rayne was pronounced dead at the scene.

Detectives believed the shooting was drug-related. Bags of crack cocaine were found in Rayne's pockets, along with a considerable amount of cash.

Witnesses said a large group of men had met on the corner. The meeting started amicably but soon deteriorated into an argument and then gunshots.

Police said Rayne was shot three times with a high-caliber handgun. He died almost instantly.

Detectives declined to comment on whether there are suspects in the case. At this time, no arrests have been made.

She folded the article away, and checked the next item in the folder. It was Rayne's obituary. She read it, looking for one name in particular. She found it in the last paragraph.

"Mr. Rayne is survived by his wife, Lyla, and his son, Michael Xavier."

She scribbled hurried notes as she flipped through the few remaining articles. One had been written a few days later, when two men were arrested in the shooting—both were known for their involvement in drug gangs.

When Harper had read through it all, she put the file away and closed the drawer slowly. The more she learned, the more twisted this story became.

She had a bad feeling about Xavier Rayne.

6

By the time Baxter returned at ten, Harper and DJ had finished writing and Miles, who had submitted his photos hours ago, had gone home.

The main article walked a fine line between exploitation and straight-forward reporting. Baxter read it with a crease between her eyes.

Local Music Star Disappears
By Harper McClain and DJ Gonzales

Michael Xavier Rayne, a singer and guitarist, disappeared from his Tybee Island home in the early hours of Thursday after a night of drinking with friends.

He was last seen walking down to the beach from Admiral's Row on the north side of the island just after two in the morning.

His guitar was found on the sand early Thursday, but there was no sign of Rayne.

Police and Coast Guard searches failed to locate him and were called off at sunset.

At press time, his whereabouts were unknown.

The 24-year-old Savannah native, who performs as Xavier Rayne, recently released his first full album, "Revolver Road." The first single off the record, "The Lying Game," was one of the top streamed songs in the country this week.

Rayne is due to begin a national tour on Monday. His record company declined to comment on the situation or what his absence might mean to those plans.

His manager was rushing home from a trip to Paris, and could not be reached.

Hunter Carlson, keyboardist in Rayne's band, was one of the friends with him that night, but said he went to bed when Rayne walked out to the beach, and had no idea what happened after that.

Rayne's backup singer, Allegra Hanson, said no one noticed Rayne hadn't returned until nearly midday, when he didn't come down from his room. Only then, did they begin searching for him.

The actress Cara Brand, Rayne's girlfriend, was also at his house when he disappeared. She said she wasn't worried at first. It was only as time passed and he did not return that she became concerned.

"Xavier often went down to the beach at night," she said. "He had insomnia. He said watching the sea helped him relax. The only difference is, this time he didn't come back."

"This is good," Baxter murmured, tapping the last line with the blunt tip of her nail. "Gets everything across."

When she'd finished reading both articles, she turned to Harper and DJ. "Good work, both of you. I'm sending this to the copy desk." She gestured at DJ, who had propped his feet up on his desk, his arms pillowed behind his head. "Go home. Or wherever it is you go when you're not here."

Knowing better than to wait for a second invitation, he leaped from his chair and pulled on his jacket. "I'll be at Rosie's if anyone needs me," he said. Rosie Malone's was a downtown dive favored by Savannah's media.

"Don't get drunk and tell your friends from Channel Five what we've been working on," Baxter barked as he disappeared down the stairs. "This is exclusive."

His reply floated back to them from the stairwell. "I won't."

When he was gone, the editor walked over to where Harper still sat at her desk. "First thing tomorrow, I need you to go back to Rayne's house and talk to the girlfriend. But no interviews. Just work on her. And all of them. Get them to trust you."

"Okay. . . ." Harper didn't hide her puzzlement.

"You've never covered a real missing-person story, have you?" Baxter gave her an assessing look.

Harper shook her head.

People had gone missing in Savannah before, of course. The police had asked the paper to run pictures of runaways now and then, usually teenagers on the verge of adulthood from difficult homes. A grown man vanishing in the night, though—this was new to her.

"This isn't like a murder investigation." Folding her arms, Baxter leaned against DJ's empty desk. "After today, there won't be much to get from the police because they won't know any more than you do. Your information will come from the people who know Rayne personally. As soon as this breaks in the morning, you'll have to compete with not just the local TV stations but stations from Atlanta and Charleston. But you got there first and you know everybody involved already, so you have an advantage." Her dark eyes had a predatory gleam. "If Rayne's friends trust you before the shit hits the fan, they'll want to talk to you over all the outsiders. Convince them you're someone they can trust. Make sure the story stays ours."

She lowered her voice, although they were alone in the room.

"We need this, Harper. This story could keep Charlton off our backs."

When her shift ended at midnight, Harper was too wired to think about going home, sitting on that little porch, watching the driveway for monsters.

She could have gone to Rosie's with DJ, but she didn't want to deal with the TV news crowd. In the end, it always turned into a competition—everyone acting tough, comparing war stories.

She wanted to talk to someone who really knew her.

She drove across the historic district, tires thumping on cobblestones as she made her way around the city's picturesque garden squares, with their statues of stalwart generals. The elegant old buildings were beautiful in the pale amber glow of the streetlights, but she kept her eyes on the rearview mirror. Every time she turned a corner, she waited to see if anyone would appear behind her. But the streets were still.

Only when she was certain no one was following her did she turn down a short, scrubby lane not far from the Savannah College of Art and Design.

There were only two businesses on this street—a clothing shop popular with art students, and the Library Bar.

She pulled into an empty space at the end of the street, well away from the lights.

Before getting out, she checked her face hurriedly in the mirror, smoothing her tousled auburn hair and rubbing smeared mascara from the corner of her eye. When she was presentable, she climbed out.

She could hear music thumping as she approached the bar. The air held a faint, sweet hint of marijuana smoke. Harper smiled. To her, the scene was as familiar and comforting as home cooking.

For months now, she'd been carefully avoiding her old routine. She rarely went to Pangaea, her favorite coffee shop. And she only came to the bar now and then, when she was feeling lonely.

Junior, the bar's hulking bouncer, grinned when she walked up, revealing a jeweler's array of silver and gold teeth.

"Harper McClain. You're a sight for sore eyes."

"Right back at you."

Perched on a tall stool just inside the front door, he tilted his large head as he contemplated her. "Where've you been? You hiding?"

"A little," she admitted.

"Bonnie said you might have some trouble." A calculating look entered his usually warm brown eyes. That look told her Junior had seen his own trouble. "Well, you won't have any problems in the Library. If you need anyone taken care of I know people who can do it. You got me?" He held up a fist the size of a brick for her to bump. "No one messes with my people."

She was touched. It wasn't every day someone threatened to have her enemies killed.

Inside, the place was packed. The sickly sweet smell of spilled beer hung in the humid air.

She'd forgotten today was Thursday. Ever since the bar's owner had instituted a two-for-one drinks night, Thursdays had done massive business. Three bartenders were on hand to deal with the young and very drunk crowd. Andi was newest: she had glossy, raven-black hair and wore a swoosh of eyeliner above fake lashes as long as butterfly wings. Tony (buffed, with dimples that earned him huge tips) had been working the late shift for nearly six weeks now. He was the strong, should-be-silent type.

The shift manager was Bonnie Larson. She wore a miniskirt and cowboy boots, topped by a black T-shirt that read THE LIBRARY BAR: LAST OF THE MOJITOS. Her long, white-blond hair was streaked with hot pink and pulled up into a high ponytail that swirled behind her as she swung four Bud Lights onto the counter and popped the tops.

"Here you go, kittens," she shouted above the music as she slid them across. "These are so cheap they're practically free."

Harper stood at the back of the crowd, waiting her turn.

When she reached the counter, Bonnie had her head down, wiping spilled tequila from the bar.

"What can I get you?" she asked, without looking up.

"Margarita on the rocks," Harper said, raising her voice to be heard above the music. "Don't go crazy with the salt."

Bonnie's head shot up, a grin spreading across her face. "Harper!" Ignoring the other customers, she hopped up onto the bar to give her a hug. "What are you doing here?"

Harper breathed in Bonnie's comforting scent of cool, lemony cologne and the turpentine she used to remove oil paints from her hands.

An artist in reality, Bonnie supported herself tending bar and teaching part-time at SCAD. The two had been friends since they were six years old. Bonnie was the closest thing to family Harper had these days.

"It's good to see you, too," Harper said, as Bonnie released her and dropped down behind the bar. "I just needed to see a friendly face."

"I'm as friendly as they get," Bonnie assured her, dropping back behind the bar. She turned to a man in his twenties who was slumped on a barstool, watching the two of them with drunken fascination.

"Get up, Neil." She snapped her fingers. "Give the lady your seat."

Startled, he hopped up so quickly he nearly fell over. "I . . . yes." He looked confused about the order and his own actions but shuffled back obediently as Harper took the pilfered barstool, still warm from his backside.

For a second, he stood there wavering. But then, giving the two of them an awkward bow, he retreated unsteadily.

"You're mean," Harper chided.

Bonnie waved that away. "He's been sitting there for an hour, drunk as a coot and staring at me like a sick calf." Standing on her toes, she turned toward the door and yelled, "JUNIOR!"

Across the room, he stood and gave her an inquiring look.

Bonnie pointed at the retreating figure. "Grab Neil and send him home. He's wasted."

Snapping a salute, the hulking bouncer stalked off across the bar in search of his prey.

"You really want a margarita?" Bonnie asked Harper, holding up the cocktail shaker. "Be aware: If I make you more than one of these I have to steal your keys."

"Just one," Harper told her. "I can drive on one."

Bonnie narrowed her eyes. "I'll make it weak." She reached for the lime-juice bottle beneath the bar. "But tasty."

Harper turned to check on Neil. Junior had found him. He rested a thick arm across the young man's shoulders and spoke to him amiably. Neil seemed resigned to his fate. The two of them ambled to the door.

Bonnie placed a full cocktail glass on a napkin. "I've got to deal with all this," she said, gesturing at the crowd pressing in around Harper. "But don't you dare leave. We need to talk."

Before turning away, she reached across the bar and grabbed Harper's cheeks with cool fingers. "Damn, girl. I've missed your *face*."

While she hurried to work, Harper settled in to people-watch, sipping the tart drink, the tequila making her tongue curl.

The crowd was the usual mix of mostly young, mostly beautiful grad students and other local twentysomethings. Many, like Bonnie, had brightly dyed hair. The women all seemed to have long, glossy manes. The men favored ironic T-shirts. Aside from the bartenders and Junior, Harper didn't know anyone. Cops wouldn't be caught dead in this bar. The other reporters didn't know it existed. And that was the whole attraction. Here, she could relax.

An hour passed before things calmed down enough for Bonnie to leave Andi and Tony in charge and take a break. She headed around the bar, a beer in one hand, and motioned for Harper to follow.

By then, the dance floor was mostly empty, although a crowd lingered at the tables around the edges.

The bar still looked very much like the library it had once been. The walls were covered in old bookshelves, filled with a free lending library of well-thumbed paperbacks and textbooks. The old reading rooms, reached through arched doorways, were dubbed Poetry, Prose, and Pool, respectively. Pool and Poetry were both occupied, so the two of them settled on the faux-leather couches in Prose, where the smudged white walls were painted with the opening lines of famous novels in inky black.

Bonnie propped one foot up on the scarred coffee table and studied her. "So, how's it going? Are things getting any better out there?"

Harper wished more than anything that she had good news.

"There's nothing new," she admitted. "Sometimes I feel like I'm hiding from a ghost."

"Nothing at all from that guy who called you?" Bonnie asked.

Harper shook her head. "Not a peep."

Bonnie took a ruminative sip of beer, and then unexpectedly asked, "What if he's dead?"

Harper blinked. "Excuse me?"

"Seriously." Bonnie eyed her steadily. "What if since that guy told you someone wanted to kill you, one or both of them died? You'd never know. You'd just be hiding in the middle of nowhere forever, waiting for a dead man to call."

In the long hours staring at the driveway, Harper had considered this possibility more than once. After all, there'd only been the one phone call. What if he *was* dead?

It couldn't be true. Surely if he was dead someone would tell her. She'd know.

Besides, every word the caller had said was seared on her mind as if it had been written with a blade: *"The person who killed your mother is looking for you. He's been in prison for a long time and he's about to get out. And he's going to come for you."*

"I don't know," she said, after a long pause. "I trust my gut. And my gut says lay low. I need to keep digging. He's out there somewhere. And if he won't come to me, I need to find him. Somehow."

She knew how unconvincing that sounded, but Bonnie knew her well enough not to argue. "Well, you do what you have to," she said, tactfully. "I just miss normal you, you know? Coming in here all the time. Talking about crime."

Harper gave her a melancholy smile. "I miss normal me, too. More than you know."

In the main bar, the music changed to a soulful song. The singer's voice reminded her of the story that had filled her day.

"Oh, I almost forgot to tell you," she said. "That singer, Xavier Rayne. He disappeared today."

Bonnie, who'd been about to take a sip from her beer, stopped with the bottle midway to her lips. "What do you mean 'disappeared'?"

"He walked out of his house in the middle of the night and never came back."

"Well, shit." Bonnie looked shocked. "What do they think happened? Is it drugs? It's usually drugs." Before Harper could reply, she added, "Did you know I met him once? At SCAD. He was thinking about enrolling. Came up for a tour. But then he got into Juilliard, and that was the end of that."

Bonnie was an artist, supporting herself by bartending and teaching at the Savannah College of Art and Design, or SCAD as everyone called it.

"I didn't know that. What was he like?" Harper asked.

"Beautiful," Bonnie said. "And so soft-spoken I had to lean close to hear him but, *man,* did he have a powerful presence. He walked into a room and everyone looked up—he's that kind of a guy. Gorgeous eyes. Kind of amber. And my God. That new album. Have you heard it?"

Harper shook her head. She'd meant to listen to it but she hadn't had time today. DJ had been the one writing about his music, anyway.

Setting the beer down, Bonnie jumped to her feet. "Wait here."

She ran into the main bar. A minute later, the song cut off in mid-verse. After a few seconds, a new, fast-driving tune filled the air. A distinctive melody, led by keyboard and guitar. A low, smooth voice flowed over it, weaving through the chords, rising high and then sinking to sudden, shivering lows.

Bonnie returned and dropped back into her seat. "Just listen to that." She reached for the bottle. "What a talent."

A beautiful female voice rose behind his on the chorus, and Harper guessed it had to be Allegra's. The two voices together were pure gold. She could see why everyone was obsessed with this album.

It was hypnotic and chilling—a musical cry of pain.

From the speakers, Xavier Rayne's voice growled, "Revolver Road, don't take me down Revolver Road . . ."

7

The next morning, Harper's phone rang just after nine. She woke to find herself lying on top of the bed with her clothes from the night before still on, her legs tangled in a blanket. Zuzu was sound asleep beside her, curved into a perfect silver-gray circle.

It was Baxter, who sounded like she either hadn't slept at all or had injected herself with amphetamine. "Get yourself over to the Rayne house," she barked. "The story's out and Channel Five is going to make a beeline for the place. Be there first."

Her eyes still closed, Harper mumbled, "On my way."

This must not have been convincing, because Baxter added sharply, "Make them your friends before ten o'clock this morning, McClain. That's an order."

Grumbling, Harper dragged herself out of bed. It had been nearly three in the morning when she got home, and it had taken a couple of hours to get to sleep.

A shower and a quick cup of coffee woke her up, though. And soon, she was in the car.

Despite Baxter's urgency, she made two stops on the way to the musician's mansion. The first was at the Tybee PD headquarters. "I've got nothing new," the harried receptionist told her breathlessly as the phone on her desk rang unanswered. "The boats went out again just after seven. I must have said that twenty times already today." She gave a nervous giggle. "Reporters are calling from all over. I just had a call from New York!"

Baxter was right. The media had found out about Xavier Rayne.

When she pulled up on Admiral's Row a short while later, she was relieved to see no media circus had assembled yet outside the row of grand, columned houses. Everything was cool and quiet. Yesterday's rain had passed, but the skies remained gray. The only sound came from the seabirds that wheeled overhead, their mournful cries rising above the breeze as she got out of the car and grabbed a tray holding four cardboard cups and a bag of warm doughnuts from the passenger seat.

It was the oldest trick in the world. But the old ones are the best.

When she climbed the front steps, she observed no signs of life. The huge windows were sealed tight, all the curtains closed. If she didn't know better she'd think the house was empty—locked up for the season.

She tucked the bag under her arm and knocked briskly on the door.

It was Hunter who answered, cracking the door cautiously to peer out. As soon as he saw her, he blanched.

"Oh shit." A sharp edge of fear entered his voice. "Is there news?"

"No—I'm sorry," she said, hurriedly. "The police haven't found him—I just talked to them. There's nothing new."

She noted and filed away the information that he'd assumed the news would be bad.

Behind the smudged lenses of his trendy glasses, exhausted, red-rimmed eyes skated from her face to the cups in her hand and back again, uncomprehendingly. He was wearing the same T-shirt and jeans he'd had on the day before, both considerably more rumpled now. His jaw was shadowed with stubble. His caramel-brown hair, tangled.

She held the tray of drinks out to him. "Look, I know it's not much but I brought coffee. I thought you guys might need it."

She was prepared for him to reject the offering. If he sent her away, she'd come back with sandwiches. Food figured heavily in her plan to ingratiate herself with them.

To her relief, though, he took the tray and stepped aside. "You might as well come in," he said. "The others are just waking up."

Holding the coffees, he headed down the hall, gesturing for her to follow him.

The house had a hushed, sleeping feel to it. Harper found herself walking softly across the polished oak floors. She couldn't have said why but it felt good to be back in this elegantly bohemian mansion. The half-melted candles on the long dining room table, the art on the walls, the exotic scent of incense and cigarette smoke hanging tantalizingly in the air—it was like something out of a dream.

"Have you slept?" she asked, keeping her voice low.

"I wouldn't call it sleep," he said, bleakly. "Every sound I heard . . . I thought it might be him, coming home."

The living room looked less perfect today. The cushions on the sofas were out of place and compressed from use. One huge sash window that faced the side of the house had been opened, letting in a cold sea breeze that made the white curtains sway.

Hunter set the cardboard tray down on the coffee table and dropped into a chair. Picking up a battered pack of cigarettes, he lit one with a chunky Zippo lighter.

Harper put the bag of doughnuts down and sat on the sofa across from him.

"I stopped by the police station this morning and all they'll say is nobody's heard from Xavier and he hasn't been spotted," she told him. "There's a statewide alert. But there have been no sightings."

Hunter absorbed this with heavy silence. The cigarette smoldered, already half forgotten between his long fingers.

"What does that mean, do you think?" he asked. "The fact that no one's seen him, I mean."

Harper hesitated, wondering how much truth he could take. "It's not great," she said, finally.

He nodded, slowly. As if he'd expected her to say that.

She couldn't get over the change in his demeanor. The animated, angry bandmate from the day before was gone. Behind his smudged glasses, his face had the stunned look of someone who'd been punched.

Lifting a cup from the tray, she held it out to him. "Drink this. I think you need it."

When he leaned forward to take it, his eyes—brown with specks of gold—met hers. "It was nice of you to do this. None of us has left the house since . . . Well. Since yesterday. I haven't even showered." He looked down at his rumpled band T-shirt with distaste. "I can't seem to do anything. My phone keeps ringing—managers, journalists, lawyers. Everyone but Zay."

His cigarette had grown a long tail of ash. He tapped it into an overfull ashtray at his feet. "At least if I get cancer now I deserve it," he muttered. "I must have smoked a hundred cigarettes in the last twenty-four hours." With a sigh, he straightened. "Do you know what happens now?"

"They'll keep looking for him." She kept her tone calm. "Boats went out again this morning just after seven." Seeing a spark of panic in his expression, she added hastily, "It's just a precaution."

His eyes fluttered shut and he whispered, "I hate this so much."

Soft sounds from upstairs—a thudding of footsteps, a faint murmur of voices—indicated the others were coming down. Hunter must have heard it, too, because his eyes flew open. "Listen, don't tell them what you just told me," he said with quiet urgency. "Tell them there's no news. But nothing else."

Harper didn't know how she felt about that. Before she could make up her mind, though, Cara walked into the living room talking over her shoulder. "Could someone turn the coffeemaker on? I'm so tired, I . . ." Spotting Harper, she stopped abruptly.

Allegra, who was right behind her, looked around her shoulder and brightened.

"You're back." She said it like it was no big deal, and bounced into the room.

Cara remained frozen in the doorway, watching Harper like a dog might observe a rattlesnake.

Uncertain of how to handle this, Harper found herself rising, awkwardly. "I'm sorry to show up out of the blue. I'll leave if you want me to."

"She brought coffee." Hunter pointed at the cups. "And food."

"Oh thank God." Snatching the bag off the coffee table, Allegra opened it and peered inside. "Doughnuts!" She looked up at Harper, gratefully. "There's no food at all in this house. I was about to eat my own *hair.*"

As she spoke, Cara moved slowly into the room. Out of the corner of her eye, Harper saw her give Hunter a look that was part question, part accusation. His response was a very slight shrug. It could have been apology or rebellion.

It made sense that Cara would be the most suspicious of a journalist, Harper supposed, given what she'd learned the night before when she'd researched all three of them.

She knew Hunter had met Xavier at Juilliard. He was a classical pianist before the two formed a band. There was nothing in the articles about his background, but something told her he came from money. He had the confidence a wealthy childhood brings. The polished sheen of a worry-free life.

Her research had turned up almost nothing about Allegra. It was unclear how Xavier had discovered her, although her voice made it obvious why he'd chosen her.

Cara had the most interesting history. She'd started modeling while in her teens, doing the usual round of commercials, music videos, and voice-overs before being cast in a hit TV series playing a teenager at a haunted boarding school. The series had run for four years. By then, she was in all the celebrity magazines. She developed a substantial following.

Last year, though, there'd been a minor scandal when she was accused by the tabloids of cheating on her boyfriend—her costar from the TV series—with Xavier. One publication in particular—a tabloid blog called *L.A. Beat* (or *L.A.B.*, as its logo would have it)—had gone for her viciously, running numerous attack articles and unflattering paparazzi photos of her covering her face, hiding behind her bag, ducking into a car. It seemed to Harper the blog had gone out of its way to destroy her. The articles were filled with innuendo about drug use and sleaze, with few facts and no evidence.

It was easy to understand why Cara approached her with such caution.

"I don't want to sound rude," the actress said, as she settled stiffly onto the sofa, "but why are you here?"

"I stopped by the police station this morning," Harper said, not answering the question. "They told me there's no news. No one has seen him."

"No news is good news," Hunter told the others with false cheer. "That's what I'm telling myself, anyway."

"Yes." Allegra brushed doughnut sugar from her fingertips. "He'll come home when he wants to. He just needs time."

Hunter turned to Harper. "I've been meaning to ask—what are the odds that he could have been attacked on the beach? He'd had so much press. What if someone kidnapped him? They could be holding him somewhere. Waiting until we're desperate, and then they'll ask for money."

"The police are looking for any sign of that," she assured him. "Did he owe anybody money? Was he in some kind of trouble? Was he in debt?"

"Zay never spent money." Cara pointed at the guitar still leaning against the wall. "Even that guitar was given to him by the record company. He grew up with nothing, and he lived like he was still poor, always."

Harper tried another tack. "Can you think of any reason anyone would have wanted to harm him? Maybe someone from his past? Someone who knew his father?"

Cara's head snapped up, and she fixed Harper with a penetrating stare.

"His father died when he was ten," Allegra pointed out. "You can't make enemies at ten."

"He didn't have any enemies at Juilliard." Hunter reached for his cigarette pack but didn't pull one out. "It's not that kind of world."

"Then what?" Cara demanded, suddenly angry. "Where has he gone? Why would he just walk away from us without a word?"

"He wouldn't," Allegra said. "He didn't. I keep telling you—"

"Oh, shut up, Legs," Cara snapped, cutting her off. "I can't listen to that anymore."

Allegra recoiled as if she'd been slapped.

Instantly repentant, Cara pressed her fingertips against her lips. "Oh God. I'm sorry. I didn't mean . . ."

But Allegra didn't wait to hear the apology. She fled the room, disappearing into the hallway.

"Oh hell." Cara looked at Hunter. "Why did I do that?"

Shrugging, he pulled a cigarette from the pack before tossing the pack to her.

"She's being irrational." He lit the cigarette with his Zippo and took a drag, blowing out a stream of smoke. "It's exhausting. Don't sweat it. She'll get over it."

"I shouldn't yell at her, though." Kicking off her flats, Cara pulled her feet up onto the sofa and lit one for herself. "We're all stressed."

Harper, who had never seen her smoke before, watched, fascinated as she blew out a long stream of smoke as pale as the fine knit of her top.

"She's not dealing," Hunter said, "and that makes it harder for us. It's time we quit babying her." He paused, glancing at Harper. "She's not a bad person. She's just young. And she's hung up on Xavier."

Cara suddenly remembered who they were talking to. "Don't write any of this," she ordered, abruptly. "This is all off the record, agreed?"

"Absolutely," Harper held up her hands. "I'm not taking notes."

Cara took another drag and considered her with new curiosity. "I hope I don't seem unfriendly," she said, after a second. "I don't like journalists."

"I don't blame you. There are bad reporters out there," Harper said. "But there are good reporters, too. I'm just a crime reporter. I stick to the facts."

"Do that," Cara said crisply, "and we'll be fine."

"She's helping us, Cara," Hunter reminded her.

She waved the cigarette at him, dismissively. But the tension passed.

As the two of them began to talk again, Harper decided to take advantage of their distraction. Maybe Baxter wanted her to make friends, but she couldn't be here and not investigate.

Looking at Hunter apologetically, she said, "Do you mind if I use the bathroom? I had a lot of coffee."

"Oh, sure." He pointed down the long hallway. "It's the door near the dining room."

Neither of them got up to follow as she walked down the long hallway to the foot of the curved staircase.

She paused there, glancing around to make sure Allegra wasn't anywhere near. Then she hurried up the stairs, the rubber soles of her shoes soft against the wood.

At the top, the stairs gave onto a long, bright hallway—a mirror image of the one below. At the far end, a glass door led onto the wraparound balcony. Through it, she could see the dark blue sea.

Before that, a series of heavy oak doors opened off it, three on each side. Most were open.

Holding her breath, Harper tiptoed to the first one. It was a large room, dominated by a bed with a modern, black frame. It was unmade—blankets thrown to one side as if the person had kicked them off. A keyboard on a stand stood nearby, with sheet music piled on the floor beneath it. A guitar leaned against the wall, propped against two Converse sneakers.

It was obviously Hunter's room.

The door across from his was closed, and Harper crept past, in case Allegra was in there.

Conscious that she didn't have much time, she hurried to the next open door. She stepped into a spacious room flooded with light.

The walls were clean white. The floors, bare boards. There was no bed—just a mattress on the floor, covered in bright fabrics. A framed black-and-white poster of Jimi Hendrix leaned against one wall. A large mirror was propped against another.

Aside from a pair of worn leather shoes left incongruously at the foot of the bed, there was nothing else in the room. It was a simple, almost ascetic space. The scent of incense she'd noticed downstairs was heavier here. It clung to the air. Sandalwood. Patchouli.

There were no instruments. No stereo or speakers. No computers. It was a room from another time.

"This is Zay's room."

Harper spun around to see Allegra standing in the doorway behind her, dark eyes somber.

She held up her hands. "I'm sorry. I just—"

"It's fine." Allegra didn't seem angry. In fact, she looked almost pleased. "You should see it."

Harper turned back to the clean, mostly empty room.

"There are no guitars." Her voice echoed off the bare walls.

"There's a practice room across the hall with all his equipment in it," Allegra explained. "This is his private space. He meditates a lot here."

She gestured at an incense burner on the windowsill. Next to it sat a small matchbox and an ashtray that held four used matches.

"He needs a clear space to empty his mind." Allegra looked out the window at the beach in the distance. "I wish he'd come home."

The simple phrase was so melancholy and heartfelt—the look of worry on her face so raw—Harper turned away.

Over the years, she'd trained herself to feel nothing for victims of crime and those who loved them. It was necessary if she was going to do her job. For some reason, though, her heart twisted for Allegra—for all of them. Their pain was so near the surface.

"I'm really sorry this is happening," she told her. "It must be torture for you." She paused before asking, "How did you meet him?"

The girl brightened. "I grew up in a small town outside Spartanburg," she explained. "I moved to Savannah the day I turned seventeen. Packed everything I could fit in the car and drove straight down here. Got a job waiting tables." She leaned against the wall. "I had no money but I loved music and I thought I could find a band to join in a town like this. I saw a notice at a coffee shop one day for a backup singer, so I went and auditioned." She smiled at the memory. "I was scared to death—it was my first real audition. But when I walked in Xavier was sitting at the piano playing a song and Hunter was there, messing around on the guitar. They were so nice I forgot to stay scared. And, well. We started singing and we never stopped."

"What's going on?" Hunter's voice made them both jump. They hadn't heard him walking up the stairs. But now he stood in the hallway, watching the two of them through the open door.

Allegra stiffened. "We're just talking." She sounded defensive.

Hunter's accusing gaze swung to Harper, who felt instantly guilty.

"She was showing me around," she explained, heat rising to her face.

He walked into the room, his eyes dark with grief and anger. "I suppose if you're going to write about him, you might as well see it all," he said, with some bitterness. "The police have already stomped all over it. You might as well do the same."

She'd pushed things too far. She'd lost them. She retreated to the door. "I'm sorry," she said. "I shouldn't have come up here. I didn't mean to intrude."

Hunter let out a long breath and looked around Xavier's room, as if ensuring nothing had moved.

"It's so hard," he said, not meeting her eyes. "We're so tired. We keep answering questions from the police. The same questions over and over. And they don't have any answers for us. All we want to know is where he is and what happened. We tell them everything and they tell us *nothing.*"

Pivoting, he pounded one fist hard against the wall with a sound like a piece of meat hitting the floor.

Caught completely by surprise, Harper and Allegra stared at him, openmouthed.

He raised his fist as if to punch it again.

"Stop it, Hunter!" Allegra ran to his side, grabbing his wrist in both her hands. "Stop hurting yourself."

All his muscles tensed as he tried to free his arm. He looked so angry and lost, for a split second Harper thought he might punch her.

"Allegra?" Cara's voice rose from downstairs. "What's going on?"

All the fight left him. Dazed, he cradled his hand. His knuckles were torn and bleeding.

"You idiot," Allegra said, still holding his wrist gently. "Look what you've done."

Cara raced into the room, her face white. "What happened? Hunter?"

"It's nothing," he told her, calming down. "I decided the wall was my enemy."

Cara glanced from the blood on his hand to the faint, red mark he'd left on the pristine wall. She gave him a long searching look, but all she said was, "We should put ice on this."

Hunter didn't argue. They trooped down the stairs, Cara and Allegra both talking at the same time about whether he should go to the doctor, or wait and see if it started to swell. The scene was, in its own way, a glimpse of what life had been like in this house before Xavier walked out to the beach on Wednesday night.

Harper trailed behind. She was conscious she shouldn't stay much longer. She wanted them to see her as someone they could call on when they needed her. Not someone who hung around and got in the way.

As the three of them made their way into the kitchen, she stopped in the doorway.

"Look, I should probably go," she said. "You need your space."

They looked up at her with surprise, and something like disappointment.

"Could you come back with more food?" Allegra asked.

"Allegra . . ." Cara chided.

She didn't back down. "We're out of food. I'm starving."

Harper pulled three business cards from her pocket and set them on the table by the door. "I'll come back later if you want," she promised. "I don't mind bringing you anything you need. Give me a call."

Hunter walked over to her, his wounded hand wrapped in a towel. The scattering of freckles on his nose gave him a boyish look that was nothing like the angry man she'd glimpsed a few seconds ago.

"I'm sorry about this." He held up his hand. "I'm just tired and frustrated. You're the only person telling us what's really going on. Thank you for coming over."

"You're welcome," she said. "I'm glad I could help." She looked past him to the other two. "I can show myself out."

Leaving the three of them in the kitchen, she walked down the grand hallway. She was nearly to the door when someone knocked on it, hard.

"Who is it?" Allegra called from the kitchen.

"I don't know," she called back.

The knocking came again, harder this time.

"Hunter, are you in there?" an angry male voice demanded. "Cara? Wake up."

Bang, bang, bang.

Hunter appeared behind her. "Oh crap. It's Stu."

It took Harper a second to figure out who he was talking about. Stuart Dillon—the band's manager, who'd flown back from Paris.

Hunter moved past her to the door, letting out a breath before grasping the handle with his good hand and opening it.

"Stuart," he said, without enthusiasm. "You're back."

On the porch stood a tall, athletic man, with a tanned face and suspicious eyes. The sun gleamed on his smooth head. He wore jeans with glossy, expensive-looking boots, and a dark cashmere sweater. "I came straight from the airport," he said, pushing his way in without waiting for an invitation. "Tell me he's back."

"He's not," Hunter said.

"Well, where the hell is he? He's supposed to be on tour tomorrow. The record company's asking questions I can't answer." Stuart's eyes skimmed the hallway, stopping on Harper. "Who the hell are you?"

"I'm—" she began to explain, but Cara stepped between them before she could get the words out.

"Stuart," she exclaimed, holding out her arms. "Thank God. We've been desperate for you to get here."

Harper had a feeling every word was a lie. But Stuart didn't appear to have the same sense as he gave her a tight, emotionless hug. "Cara, how are you holding up? You must be losing your mind."

While Cara distracted him, Hunter motioned urgently for Harper to go out the open door. Clearly, none of them wanted the manager to figure out that they'd invited a reporter into their house.

"We don't know what to do," Cara was saying as Harper slipped outside. "The police are useless."

"Don't worry," Stuart assured her, something threatening in his tone. "I'm here now. I'll get their asses in gear."

It was the last thing Harper heard before Hunter closed the door.

8

When Harper walked into the Savannah police headquarters
later that afternoon, the first thing she noticed was that it was colder
inside than it was outside. Darlene, the daytime desk officer, wore a coat
over her dark blue uniform.

"What's going on?" Harper asked, looking up at the air vents. "It's
freezing."

Darlene gave her a gloomy look. "The air conditioner's blowing instead of the heating and nobody can get it to turn off. Thank God it's
Friday, is all I can say. I can't wait to get out of this crazy place."

Without waiting to be asked, she slid a binder containing the day's
crime reports across the desk. "Supposed to work in a snowstorm, I
guess," she grumbled.

Harper, her mind still on the Xavier Rayne story, flipped disinter-
estedly through the pages. *Burglary, burglary, burglary, larceny, assault,
burglary.* Nothing newsworthy except a minor stabbing.

Finishing in record time, she handed the binder back across. "I wanted
to grab the lieutenant for a second. Is he in?"

Instead of answering, Darlene leaned one elbow on the counter. "You and the lieutenant are getting to be regular friends now." She lifted one eyebrow suggestively.

"Oh, come on. The man hates me like a burning sensation in his nether regions," Harper said, horrified. "I just need to consult with him about a story."

"Maybe." Darlene, who loved gossip more than air, didn't reach for the phone. "Seems to me y'all are getting along better than you used to at least. It's nice. That's all."

"*Darlene.*" Harper gave her a stern look.

"I'm calling him." Smiling, the desk officer picked up the receiver and dialed three numbers. When Blazer answered, she used her sweetest voice. "Lieutenant, Harper McClain would like to speak with you. Can I send her back? Thank you." As she hung up, she gave Harper a pleased look. "He says come on back. Didn't even ask what you wanted."

Ignoring the insinuation, Harper crossed to the security door leading to the back offices. Darlene hit the button that unlocked the door with a shrill warning buzz.

Beyond the door the narrow hallway was busy with officers, detectives, dispatchers, and support staff. Harper weaved through them, nodding to familiar faces. She knew this building even better than the newspaper offices. In some ways she'd grown up here.

After her mother was murdered, when Harper was twelve, the detective on the case had taken her under his wing. Somehow he'd known there was no one else to pick up the pieces of her life and he'd stepped into that role as if it were a perfectly natural thing for a homicide detective to do.

She'd stayed close with Lieutenant Robert Smith all her life—even after she became a reporter and found herself at odds with him from time to time. They'd made it work.

But that all fell apart eighteen months ago when Smith murdered a woman he'd been having an affair with. He was now serving life in prison. For months after his arrest, she'd found these halls unwelcoming and foreign. Gradually, though, she was beginning to feel at home again in the long corridors and small, windowless offices. The faint smell of dust and bleach that seemed to permeate the brick comforted her the way baking cookies might make an ordinary person feel happy.

Lieutenant Larry Blazer, though, had never been part of that feeling for her. He hadn't approved of Smith's decision to become so close to her, and he'd never trusted her as a reporter. They grated on each other's nerves. Still, Darlene wasn't wrong. Lately, Harper was figuring out how to work with him now that he was head of the homicide unit. And he was learning to trust her, just a little bit.

His office was the last on the hallway. Harper tapped her knuckles against the frosted window where his name was painted in glossy black.

"Enter." He fired the word like a gunshot.

When she walked in, the lieutenant sat at the blond-wood table that acted as his desk, a laptop open in front of him. He was not a bad-looking man, if you liked the chilly, Nordic type. Tall and thin, he had high cheekbones, graying blond hair, and narrow blue eyes that missed nothing.

The office, which she would always think of as Smith's, was large and sparsely furnished. Two chrome-and-black leather chairs faced his desk, above which a poster-sized street map of Savannah had been fixed to the wall. Red pins marked the site of every murder in the last twelve months. Harper knew without counting that there would be around forty of them. It had been a bad year.

Blazer peered at her over the top of a pair of reading glasses. "You can have five minutes. I've got a budget meeting this afternoon and God himself couldn't get me out of it."

Harper got straight to the point. "I'm covering this missing-person case out at Tybee. Are you guys working on it yet? He's been gone a day and a half and I'm not sure the local cops have it under control."

"The Tybee Police Department is professional and highly rated," Blazer said, coolly.

"They found his guitar on the beach and gave it back to his housemates without printing it," she told him.

There was a pause before he said, "Get out your notebook."

Smiling, Harper pulled out a pen.

"I received a call this morning from the island's chief of police. He asked us to take the lead. A Savannah detective team has been assigned to the case as of today."

Harper looked up at him in surprise. Nobody at Tybee PD had

whispered a word about that. "Does that mean you're treating this as a potential homicide?"

"We're treating it like a missing-person investigation, McClain," he said. "We don't know where he is. We intend to find him. There's not much else I can tell you."

"Tybee PD thinks he went swimming and got caught in a riptide," she said. "But it seems strange to me that he'd swim in February. The water's freezing."

"Nothing musicians do surprise me." His tone was dry.

"I wouldn't put my toe in that water," she said.

"That is irrelevant to my case."

He obviously wasn't going to give her any more to work with. Harper slid her pen back into her pocket as she asked, "Who's lead detective?"

Only she would have noticed the infinitesimal hesitation before he replied. "Julie Daltrey and Luke Walker have this one."

She didn't react. Still, he fixed her with a look. "Don't you go bothering Luke for information."

"I won't bug them any more than I bug you," she said.

"In that case, God help them." With a glance at his watch, he stood up. "I've got to get going or they'll decide we can live without heat all winter." He headed for the door, motioning for her to follow him into the crowded hallway. "Look, McClain, go slow on this. Don't write a murder where there isn't one. Give us time to do our jobs."

Leaving that as his good-bye, he ran up the stairs, back stiff, laptop clutched firmly in one hand.

After he'd gone, Harper lingered in the hallway, pretending to check her cell phone. Really, she was watching the clock on the screen. She waited four minutes, until she was certain Blazer must be in his meeting; then she ran up the same stairs he'd taken and down a long hallway at the top.

The detectives' office was a few doors from the end. When she reached the unmarked door, she stopped, steeling herself. There is nothing on the planet more intimidating than walking into a room full of detectives.

She knocked on the door briskly, opening it without waiting for a response.

The room was crowded and badly in need of a paint job. The chilly air had a permanent smell of sweat and stale coffee. Eight desks were arranged along scuffed walls that had once been white. Only three were occupied.

Detective Roy Davenport gawked at her from the nearest desk. Detective Shumaker, the most senior detective in the room, sat a few seats away. Next to him was Luke Walker.

"Well, hell. I didn't know we were due a visit from the fourth estate," Shumaker drawled. His voice sounded amused but his eyes were alert.

"Sorry to intrude," Harper said. "I was hoping to find Julie Daltrey." She glanced fleetingly at Luke, who watched her with a guarded expression.

"She's out," Davenport offered. Tall and angular, with a heavy country accent, he was the newest detective on the team. "Won't be back for an hour at least."

"Damn." Harper sighed. "I don't suppose any of you know anything about that missing-musician case out at Tybee?" She let her gaze fall again on Luke, but he was looking away.

"Nobody here knows anything about anything," Shumaker assured her. "We are the dumbest people in this building. I'd have thought you'd have gathered that by now, McClain."

He was a bearlike man with a beer belly that peeked through the buttons of his short-sleeved shirt. The fluorescent lighting glinted over the pale pate visible beneath his comb-over.

Harper didn't like him at all, but she forced an easy tone. "Well, I'm sorry to intrude. If you see Daltrey, would you tell her I came by? I'm just looking to touch base."

"Ooh, now, I don't need to know anything about what you've been touching." Shumaker wrinkled his nose. "What you ladies get up to is no business of mine."

Swallowing a sarcastic response, she left hurriedly, closing the door behind her. As she did, she heard Shumaker say something quietly and give a mean laugh.

Harper couldn't care less what Shumaker thought. As she walked downstairs her thoughts were about Luke. And whether the rumors she'd been hearing were true and he had a new girlfriend.

The thought was an empty chasm she didn't want to walk into.

The two of them had known each other since they were twenty. They'd been friends first, and then lovers. Now, she didn't know what they were. For months, they'd hardly spoken—ever since he'd told her he wanted to get back together, and she'd declined. She didn't like life without him but the on-again, off-again roller coaster they'd been on was too painful. She couldn't see a way for them to keep trying and not damage each other.

Reporters and cops were oil and water. Police were forbidden from dating journalists, and vice versa. It all made sense to her. And yet she still thought about kissing him every time she saw him.

Downstairs, she stopped to say good-bye to Darlene before heading out to her car. She was nearly to the Camaro when someone called her name.

Luke was loping across the parking lot toward her.

He was tall and rangy, with broad shoulders and sandy-brown hair that tended to get too long. He had eyes the color of the midnight sky. She wondered if she would ever be able to look at him without feeling like someone just punched her in the chest.

"Hey," she said. "What's up?"

"I'm working on that missing-musician case." He stopped next to her car, hands in his pockets. "I couldn't say anything in front of Shumaker. What'd you want to talk to Julie about?"

"Oh, nothing much. I wondered if there was anything new." She kept her tone as casual as his. "Tybee Police don't know much. Are the boats still out? Have they found anything?"

"We haven't really had a chance to get to work on it yet," he said, not answering her question. "We only picked the case up this morning."

"What're you thinking?" she asked. "Was he just drunk and stupid? Or did something else happen? Drug deal gone wrong?"

He paused as if he wanted to tell her something, but all he said in the end was, "That's what we're trying to find out."

She didn't hide her exasperation. "Come on, Luke. I got more out of Blazer. Give me a break."

He had the grace to look sheepish. "I'm sorry. When Julie comes back I'll find out more. If there's anything to talk about, I promise I'll give you a call."

He leaned against the car, watching her with those eyes. "So how's it going, anyway? I haven't seen you in a while."

"Yeah." Suddenly awkward, she glanced down at her dusty boots. "Oh, you know. The usual."

Have you got a girlfriend now? She imagined asking him. But she couldn't. Because, what if he said yes?

"You still out on Tybee?" he asked.

"For now. I've got to move in a few weeks. The landlady needs the house."

"Where're you going to go?"

She shrugged. "No idea. It's just weird, you know? I don't know if it's safe to have my life back. Or if I should stay scared forever."

His phone beeped and he glanced at the screen.

"We should talk about this before you do anything," he said, turning his attention back to her. "I've got to get back right now—I'm working on about five cases. Can I call you later?"

"Sure," she said. "I'd like that."

As he headed back toward the station, she called after him, "And let me know about that musician." He lifted a hand in acknowledgment without turning around.

She got into the car and ordered herself not to watch him go. She hated how happy his offer to call her made her. It was stupid to be happy. Nothing would ever work between them. They'd tried twice and all that came of it was pain and confusion. She knew she'd hurt him when she'd refused to get back together. And she knew she didn't have the right to miss him.

But she missed him all the same.

With a sigh, she shifted into gear, pulling out of the parking space. She was almost to the exit when her phone buzzed in the dashboard holder. The message was from an unrecognized number. She stopped the car so she could read it.

> Dig into the Southern Mafia. Look back seventeen years for
> the name Martin Dowell. His lawyer might be of interest.

Harper's brow creased. What the hell was that about?

She turned the phone over as if it might reveal answers.

Maybe it was a wrong number. But she didn't think so. That phrase "dig into." That was for a reporter. That was for her.

She quickly typed, *Who is this?*

She waited for several minutes, but no one replied. It was probably nothing. Her number was on the newspaper website and she often received tips. Most of them were bogus.

If she had the time, she'd look into it later. Seventeen years ago made this an old story.

Still, as she pulled out onto Habersham Street, something about the text bothered her. It was so specific. But there wasn't any time to think about it. Right now, she had a missing musician to find.

9

Back in the newsroom, she wrote quickly, but with the cops refusing to give her more than a few skimpy quotes, she didn't have enough information for a front-page story good enough for Baxter.

She was digging through old articles about Rayne, looking for anything she could use, when her phone rang. She grabbed it impatiently.

"McClain,"

"Harper?" The voice was male. It sounded tentative and familiar, but she couldn't quite place it.

"Who's this?"

"It's Hunter. From this morning?"

Her eyebrows rose. "Hey, Hunter. What's going on?"

"Yeah . . ." He hesitated. "Look, I'm sorry to bug you. This'll sound weird but, would you mind coming back out here?" There was a nervous edge to his voice. "Things are getting kind of crazy—there are TV vans all over the street. People keep knocking on the door. Cara's about to lose her shit, and the cops won't tell us what's going on."

This was just what she needed.

Harper stood and glanced at her watch. It was nearly seven o'clock. She had time.

She swept her jacket off the back of the chair and pulled it on one-handed.

"I'm on my way," she told him, as she headed across the newsroom. "Don't open the door to anyone."

When she reached Admiral's Row twenty minutes later, the narrow tree-shaded street was lit up like a film set. Television satellite vans the size of RVs were parked bumper-to-bumper in the dirt at the side of the short lane and around the corner on the adjacent street.

Harper parked behind a nursing home a couple of blocks away. As she climbed out of the car, she pulled a heavy tote bag from the back seat and swung it over her shoulder. She'd made a stop on the way, gambling that food and cigarettes would seal the deal between her and Rayne's housemates. The bag thumped against her hip as she jogged toward the house.

The reporters gathered in small clusters looked out of place on the quiet lane in sharply tailored suits or pencil skirts tight enough to make breathing unfeasible. Most of their faces were unfamiliar—the out-of-town media had arrived.

"Harper!"

Catching her eye, Natalie Swanson, the reporter from Channel 12, motioned for her. She stood in the bright glow of TV lights—her blond hair and makeup mystifyingly perfect despite the damp ocean breeze, a white wool coat wrapped tightly around her narrow waist. A camera mounted on a tripod stood next to her. A microphone with ten feet of black cabling was looped loosely around the van's side mirror.

"I can't believe you're only just getting here," Natalie chided. "I figured you'd be out here all day."

"I was here this morning." Harper glanced past her to number 6, which was still and shuttered against the glare of the spotlight. "Has anyone talked to them?"

"Only neighbors. And they're not what I'd call welcoming. No one in the house will come out. We keep asking the cops if they'll give a statement but they aren't talking either. My editor's screaming." She gave Harper a curious look. "How did you get so much out of them yesterday?"

"Oh, you know." Harper made a vague gesture. "Right place; right time."

Natalie barked a laugh. "Please don't tell my boss that." Her eyes fell on Harper's bag. "What's that? Supplies? You planning to be out here all night?"

Shifting her posture so the bag hung out of view, Harper took a step away. "It's just a few things Miles asked me to pick up." She glanced around. "Speaking of him, I better go track him down."

Miles was still in Savannah, but Natalie couldn't know that.

"Hey, do me a favor," Natalie called, as she hurried away. "Don't make me look bad."

Harper laughed. "You always look good, Natalie."

She waited until she was out of earshot before slipping her phone from her pocket and dialing Hunter's number. "I'm here," she told him quietly.

"Come around to the side gate. The lock code is 0924." She could hear the relief in his voice.

Out of the blinding circle of TV lights, it was easy to fade into the darkness. The backs of the houses on the row were shielded by high hedges and tall, locked gates. Privacy was obviously important to the residents—small, tasteful signs warned of CCTV cameras and alarms.

Slowing her steps, Harper glanced over her shoulder. Natalie was deep in conversation with Josh Leonard from Channel 5. No one was watching.

Unobserved, she slipped down the walkway between number 5 and number 6. The path was dark and narrow, hemmed in by oleander bushes. Harper was looking for the gate when a small, wiry man rounded the corner ahead of her.

She couldn't make out his features in the shadows, but she didn't think she'd seen him before. For a second, his presence made her uneasy. Then she noticed the camera in his hand.

He had to be part of the out-of-town press.

For some reason the realization made her bristle. What the hell was he doing, trespassing?

She avoided his eyes as they neared each other, but he spoke as he passed.

"Don't bother. It's all fenced in. There's a gate, but it's locked. I've been all the way around."

How he knew she was a journalist she had no idea. She didn't like being so obvious.

"Thanks," she muttered, keeping her head turned away.

The gate he'd mentioned was an arched door, artfully tucked into the greenery. A lighted electronic combination lock glowed blue. The sound of the ocean was closer here—the footpath must continue on to the beach.

She typed in the number Hunter had given her, and the lock released. She slipped through, latching the gate behind her.

In the sheltered garden, the night felt different, somehow. More peaceful. Overhead, the clouds were dissipating. Stars glittered silver against a velvet sky. From where she stood she could see the white, columned house in all its glory. Out front, the curtains were all closed. Back here they were open, the windows ablaze with light.

Sliding the tote-bag strap back up her shoulder, she crossed the lawn. As she neared the raised veranda, she could hear the faint hum of voices, then music. Someone was playing a guitar with real skill. It sounded like they were outside.

"Hello?" she called, as she reached the foot of the wide wooden back steps.

The music stopped.

"Harper!" Allegra's voice came from the porch above. "Come up."

When she reached the top, the three housemates were sitting on white wicker chairs arranged around a low table. Hunter, cupping a wineglass in one hand. Cara, her beautiful face watchful. Allegra, curled up like a kitten with her feet tucked under her—dark eyes gleaming in the porch light.

Harper held out the shopping bag to Hunter, who had invited her. "I thought you might need supplies."

"You star." He pulled out two cartons of cigarettes, relief suffusing his features. "We can live without food but not without smokes."

"Please tell me there's food in there." Jumping from her seat, Allegra ran over to kneel next to him to root through the supplies.

Cara watched the other two with faint disapproval. "We could just order online."

"I tried, but they can't come until tomorrow," Hunter told her. "Anyway, I don't know how they'll get past the circus in the front yard."

"Pasta!" Allegra held up the bag delightedly.

"It's not fair to make her bring us things," Cara chided.

"She doesn't mind." Allegra looked at Harper. "Do you?"

"I don't mind." Far from minding, Harper was grateful for this excuse to win them over.

She hovered near the seats, trying to gauge their mood. Hunter had sounded desperate on the phone, but they seemed almost relaxed. Cara in particular seemed less suspicious of her, as she motioned for her to sit. "Have a seat. Someone give her wine."

Harper perched on a soft cushion that smelled of salt air and shook her head. "No wine, thanks. I've got to go back to work soon. Has there been any news?"

The actress gave her a wan smile. "We're right where we were before—sitting around knowing absolutely nothing. We hoped you could help."

"Haven't you heard from the Savannah police?" Harper asked, surprised.

Hunter, who'd been tearing the cellophane from a pack of cigarettes, looked up sharply. "No. Why?"

"They've assigned detectives to the case," she told him. "It's not just the local cops anymore."

"Why would do they do that?" Cara kept her voice neutral, but her fingers tightened around her glass.

"The Tybee force is very small," Harper explained. "They could use the extra hands on this case."

"But why do they need a detective?" Hunter seemed to have forgotten the pack of cigarettes in his hand. "What do they think's happened to him?"

"Nothing's happened to him. He's fine." Allegra raised her voice.

"He's *not* fine," Cara snapped. "He's been gone for *days*. He hasn't called. He hasn't texted. Something happened. And you need to accept that, Legs. We all do."

"Cara." Hunter's voice was soft but meaningful.

She let out a breath. "I'm sorry," she said, with instant regret. "I keep yelling at you."

But Allegra, her face red and wounded, kept her eyes on the package of spaghetti in her hands.

They'd clearly spent all day working themselves up until their tempers were at the breaking point. Harper needed to calm them down.

"I know this is hard," she said, "but you have to be patient. They're looking everywhere."

Hunter blinked at her through his glasses. "You still think there's hope? That he might be out there?"

In truth, Harper did not believe there was much hope, but the three of them were looking at her with so much need she couldn't say that.

"Of course there's hope," she assured them.

Taking this as evidence that she'd been right all along, Allegra leaped up from the floor. "That's all I've been saying. We don't know for sure that anything bad has happened." She picked up the grocery bag. "I'm going to make food." Pointing at Harper, she said, "And you're having wine whether you like it or not." She turned to Hunter. "Make her drink wine."

She disappeared into the house with one hand raised, saying, "Everyone must drink wine!"

In the quiet that followed, Cara and Hunter seemed deflated. Allegra's determination that everything had to be okay was exhausting them.

After a second Hunter squared his shoulders and reached for the bottle of wine. He filled a glass, holding it out to Harper.

"Everyone must drink wine," he said.

She took it. One drink wouldn't hurt.

He raised his glass, his expression somber. "To Xavier. May he come home soon."

"Yes please," Cara whispered.

Harper took a sip. The wine was cold and crisp. "That is delicious," she said, surprised.

Cara gave her a rueful half smile. "Careful. We'll corrupt you."

Harper found herself smiling back.

It struck her that sitting in the cool ocean breeze on the beautiful veranda she could easily forget why she was here. It would be so nice to live like this. To have friends like these. To be talented and young. Harper was still only twenty-eight, but she hadn't felt young in a long time. She wondered if she would have had a life like this if her mother had never been killed—if, instead, she'd lived long enough to worry about gray hair and smile wrinkles around her eyes.

Hunter lit a cigarette and held the pack out to Harper, with an inquiring raised eyebrow. When she declined, he said, "How do you manage to have so few vices?"

"Harper's a good girl." Cara sounded amused.

Hunter turned the pack to her and she slid one thin cigarette out, bending forward for a light. He flicked the glittering silver Zippo. The flame danced across her delicate features. Leaning back in her chair, she blew out a plume of white smoke that floated into the moonlight and hung there, ghostlike.

They'd clearly been drinking for quite a while. Harper thought that could work in her favor. "How did things go with Stuart today?" she asked. "Did he talk to the police?"

"Until they hung up on him." Hunter's tone was dry. "Because he's such a dick."

"The problem with Stuart is he wants to control everything, and he hates being told no," Cara explained. "Xavier and he tend to end up fighting because Stu pushes him until Zay just snaps."

"Is that why you think he might have run away? He snapped?" Harper asked.

Neither of them answered. Hunter focused his attention on his cigarette.

"Have you thought any more about where he might have gone?" Harper tried again.

It was Cara who replied quietly, "He wouldn't stay away for so long without calling us. He should be in touch by now. He should be home."

In the distance, Harper heard the faint sound of a doorbell. Cara and Hunter both stiffened.

"Christ. Not again," Hunter groaned. Raising his voice, he shouted, "Don't answer it, Legs."

"We put up a sign saying not to ring the bell," Cara told Harper. "But they just keep ringing it."

"Why won't they take a hint . . ." Hunter's voice trailed off and he stared at the door, his body stiffening.

Harper turned to see Allegra emerging from inside the house, her face suddenly serious. Detectives Julie Daltrey and Luke Walker were right behind her.

Daltrey was small, only a few inches taller than Allegra, but she carried seven feet of authority. Her black hair was pulled back, her face tense as she took in the occupants of the veranda. When she spotted Harper, her eyes widened in surprise.

Luke frowned at her, and quickly turned away.

Allegra hurried to the sofa and leaned against Cara as if seeking warmth. "They're detectives," she said, her voice barely above a whisper.

Hunter looked at Harper as if she would explain, but she knew better than to speak right now.

Daltrey stopped at the edge of the circle of chairs. "My name is Julie Daltrey. This is Luke Walker. We're with the Savannah Police Department." She glanced around the group. "I'm guessing you're Cara Brand, and you must be Hunter."

Hunter's foot had begun to jitter. His hands white-knuckled the arms of the chair.

Daltrey turned her attention to Harper. "Perhaps you should leave now, McClain."

There was no point in arguing. She started to stand but Hunter stopped her. "We want her here." His voice was firm.

"This is private information," Daltrey argued, but Hunter shook his head stubbornly.

"Talk to all of us."

The other two nodded their agreement.

With obvious reluctance, Daltrey gave in. She motioned for Luke to take over.

"I'm afraid we don't have good news." He stepped closer to them, his voice somber. "A body was found this afternoon by a fishing boat off the coast. I'm sorry to tell you, we believe it's Xavier Rayne."

10

The night descended into chaos.

"It's not true," Allegra kept saying, looking plaintively from Cara to Hunter. "It's not true."

Hunter stood, knocking the guitar over. It hit the floor with a crash as he rounded on the two detectives, his face red, every muscle tense with shock. "How do you know it's him?"

Cara was the only one who didn't speak. She stared at Luke, as pale and still as a church statue.

"His mother is on her way now from Atlanta to identify the body." Daltrey's voice was steady. "But based on the pictures and descriptions we've received of markings and tattoos, we are confident."

Cara gave a low moan.

Deprived of more objections, Hunter fell silent, his expression suddenly empty.

Allegra appealed to Harper, her huge eyes swimming with tears. "How is this happening?"

All Harper could think of to say was, "I'm very sorry."

Jumping to her feet, Cara shoved past the detectives and fled into the house, her filmy white top floating behind her like wings.

Abandoned, Allegra ran to Hunter. He pulled her into his arms, holding her like a child. Harper heard her say something that sounded like, "I'm so scared."

She wanted out of here. Watching them go through this was excruciating. They'd invited her in to talk, not to watch their lives shatter into a million jagged pieces.

As if he were thinking the same thing, Luke stepped closer and spoke to her, his voice low. "Come with me."

Relieved, she hurried after him through the double glass doors into the hallway.

The house still looked as magical and perfect as it had that first day, but the feel of the place was already changing. A solemn chill permeated the huge, bohemian rooms.

"You need to go." Luke's voice was low but firm. "Right now."

Harper ignored that. "You knew this afternoon, didn't you?" she whispered accusingly as she hurried to keep up with him. "That's where Daltrey was when I saw you. She was with the coroner."

They'd reached the front door. He turned back to face her. "You know I couldn't tell you what was going on right then. Anyway, we weren't sure it was him yet."

"Well, if you had told me, I wouldn't have come in here tonight, asking them idiotic questions about where they thought he was hiding," she said. "What the hell happened to him, anyway? Did he drown?"

His face closed.

For some reason, this got to her. There'd been a time when he wouldn't have hesitated to trust her.

"Oh, fine, Luke," she snapped. "Thanks for nothing."

But when she tried to open the door, he pressed his hand against it, stopping her.

"Jesus, Harper. Could you just give me a second?" He raked his fingers through his sandy-brown hair, his brow knitting. "What I was trying to say is Julie would kill me if she found out I told you. I don't want to piss her off. That's all."

"Give me a break, Luke. You know I won't identify you. I never have before. Besides, Miles and I have a bet. I've got twenty dollars says he drowned."

For a long second he held her eyes. Then he said, "Where did Miles put his money?"

"Overdose."

He glanced around to make sure no one was near, then stepped close enough that she could smell the clean, sandalwood scent of him, and lowered his voice. "You both lose. Someone shot him."

Harper's jaw dropped. "You're shitting me."

"I am not, in fact, shitting you. This is a homicide investigation." He reached past her for the door, his arm brushing hers as he pulled it open. "Now, get going before the forensic team gets here, unless you want to spend the night in an interrogation room."

She had her front-page story. "Thanks, Luke."

"No idea why you're thanking me," he said, deadpan. "I told you nothing except that there's a press conference in an hour."

Racing from the beachfront mansion into the glare of the TV lights, she pulled her phone from her pocket, dialing without slowing down.

It rang three times before Baxter answered. "This better be good."

"Oh, it's very good." Harper's voice shook with each step. "Someone shot Xavier Rayne to death. They found his body."

"Fuck me." All the tiredness left Baxter's voice. "When?"

"Just now. I was there when the police informed his housemates." Breathless, Harper glanced to where the TV vans were parked. Natalie was watching her with a suspicious expression. She lowered her voice to a whisper. "No one else knows."

"Is Miles out there?" Baxter asked.

"Not yet."

"Call him. Get him to meet you. I'm heading back to the office. What time is it?"

Harper looked at her watch. "Eight o'clock. Listen, there's going to be a press conference within the hour, but I got all this from a detective off the record. No names."

"A well-placed detective?"

"Extremely."

"That's good enough for me." Baxter sounded impatient. "Write something for the website right now citing an unidentified police source. I'll rejig the front page. You and Miles get everything you can out there then get your asses back here. Break the speed limit. I'll pay your tickets."

The line went dead.

Without missing a beat, Harper called Miles. He answered on the first ring. "What's up?"

She gave him the same information she'd just told their editor. "Baxter wants you here. Press conference within the hour."

All he said was, "On my way."

Nothing ever surprised Miles.

Harper jogged to where she'd parked the Camaro and popped the trunk to get her laptop and into the driver's seat to write.

She was waiting impatiently for the mobile Wi-Fi to connect when two dark sedans drove down the narrow lane, followed by a van. Harper spotted Lieutenant Blazer in the passenger seat of one of the cars.

If Blazer was already here, there wasn't much time. The cops would be eager to get the message out—to show that they were on top of it. Soon the forensics team would descend on the house and turn it inside out.

Harper kept replaying the moment Luke and Daltrey stepped out on the porch. The way Hunter had turned pale. And Cara's hope shattered like glass.

She could kick herself for caring. But for some reason, the three people in that house had gotten under her skin.

When the connection screen finally opened, she gave a relieved sigh and put them out of her mind as she got down to work. The story came together quickly.

Missing Musician Xavier Rayne Found Dead
By Harper McClain

Up-and-coming Savannah singer and guitarist Xavier Rayne has been found shot to death, a police source told the *Daily News.*

Rayne, 24, had been missing for three days. He was last seen at 2 A.M. Thursday morning, walking from his Tybee Island mansion to the beach.

He was never seen alive again. Police and Coast Guard
have been looking for him ever since. Tonight, his body
was found by a fishing boat, off the coast.

Police are now investigating the case as a homicide.

She was just wrapping up when Miles pulled in next to her, the engine of his Mustang a rumble of power. He must have driven a hundred miles an hour to get out here so fast.

After hastily sending the article through to the newsroom, Harper slid the laptop under the seat. When she climbed out, Miles was standing next to the Camaro, camera in his hand, gazing at the TV lights ahead. "I see the circus has arrived," he observed.

"Murder always attracts a crowd," she said.

As they walked down the dark street, she told him everything she'd learned in the last hour. When she finished, his expression was gloomy.

"I almost wish it was drugs," he confessed. "Such a talent, wasted."

"It's wasted either way," Harper said. "There's no good way to die at twenty-four."

A minute later, they walked into the harsh media glare. Word of the upcoming press conference had spread. Portable lights were being lugged from the vans and aimed so that the white house was vividly illuminated. Microphone stands sprouted like saplings at the foot of the front steps.

In the blur of sudden activity, Natalie sidled up to Harper and grabbed her elbow with long fingers. "Don't think I didn't see you scuttling out of there earlier, you cheat. What'd you find out?"

Harper hesitated, but her story would go up on the website any second. Besides, everyone was about to learn what she already knew.

"A fishing boat found Rayne's body," she whispered.

"I *knew it*." The TV reporter's voice held quiet triumph. "I had five dollars on drowned."

Harper gave her a long look, and her expression changed.

"Not drowned?"

Harper leaned closer. "Murdered."

Natalie swore. "Josh had murdered. He's going to clean up."

She spoke too loudly. Josh Leonard, the Channel 5 reporter, who was standing nearby, glanced up. "Did I hear my name?" He glanced back and forth between them. "What am I cleaning up?"

Harper gave Natalie a condemning look.

"I know." Natalie winced. "Inside voice."

Before either of them could explain, the door of Rayne's house opened. The reporters surged forward. Harper had to elbow her way between Natalie and Josh to see what was happening.

In the glare of the TV lights, Luke stood next to Julie Daltrey. Blazer was at her other elbow. A fresh-faced police press officer hovered nearby. At the edge of the group, Tom Southby looked uncomfortable in his black Tybee PD uniform, as if he'd been invited to a party where he didn't know anyone.

Somehow, Harper doubted he still believed the gunshots reported the night they met were fireworks.

Blazer stepped up to the bank of microphones and began to read a statement. "Just after fourteen hundred hours this afternoon, crew on the *Rocky Road,* a fishing vessel from St. Simons Island, discovered the body of a man about a mile off the Georgia coast. The body has been identified as that of Michael Xavier Rayne." Building the drama, he paused, looking at the assembled cameras. "It is clear from preliminary examination by the coroner's office that he suffered two gunshot wounds."

There was a collective intake of breath from the assembled journalists. Blazer spoke over it, his face absolutely expressionless. "This investigation is now being treated as a homicide. At the request of the Tybee Island Police Department, Savannah PD will lead on the investigation from this point on. A full autopsy will be held tomorrow to determine the cause of death." He folded his notes and put them in his pocket. "We will now take questions."

The press erupted.

"Did the gunshots kill him?" Harper asked, raising her voice to be heard above the others shouting around her.

Blazer looked at her. "We will learn the cause of death in the autopsy tomorrow. Until then, I don't want to speculate."

"How long had he been in the water?" someone shouted.

"We'll know more after the autopsy," Blazer repeated, "but I can say the body bears the hallmarks of several days in the water. Those of you who have covered floaters before will know what that means."

"Crabs go for the eyes first," Harper heard a cameraman say behind her. All around her, the reporters were leaning forward, eagerly. She could feel their excitement like heat.

"Is there any indication that the gunshots could have been self-inflicted?" Natalie asked.

It was a good question. Blazer gave her a glance of dark approval. "We saw no obvious indications of that in the preliminary, but we'll know more tomorrow."

Harper doubted it. Shooting yourself once is hard enough. But twice? That would take determination.

"Are there any suspects?" a man asked.

The lieutenant squinted into the lights. "None I can tell you about at this time."

"What about Cara Brand, Rayne's girlfriend?" the same man pressed in a flat West Coast accent. "Is she a suspect?"

Harper twisted around to see him. He was short and wiry, with dark, unruly hair and an unshaven jaw. She recognized him instantly as the man she'd passed on the footpath earlier trying to find a way into the house.

She turned back, waiting for Blazer to shut him down.

"I'm not prepared to comment on suspects at this time." The lieutenant's tone was measured.

Harper stared at the lieutenant, stunned.

Everyone else accepted his statement at face value, and the questions resumed. But she'd covered the police long enough to know what he wasn't saying. He wasn't saying no.

Cara was a murder suspect. And so was everyone in that house.

11

The press conference continued for a few more minutes, but Harper tuned out. She kept thinking about the way Cara's face had crumpled earlier tonight—those thin shoulders trembling. It had been picture-perfect grief. But, perhaps, too perfect?

After all, a voice in her head reminded her, *she's an actress.*

On the front steps, the lieutenant was wrapping things up. "That's all I have at the moment. Call the press office in the morning for updates."

With the reporters shouting questions at them, the detectives trooped back to the house. Luke got there first, holding the door open for the others. For a brief moment, in the glow of the chandelier, Harper glimpsed Allegra at the foot of the stairs, looking tiny and trapped.

Then the door closed, shutting them all inside.

As soon as the detectives were gone, the TV reporters raced back to their vans. Miles walked up to Harper, his camera in one hand. "I'm going to get a few shots of the house. I'll meet you in the newsroom."

"Baxter wants us there faster than physically possible," she told him. He just nodded and kept going.

She headed toward the Camaro. She was just passing the last TV vans when the small wiry reporter suddenly appeared at her side.

"You're Harper McClain, aren't you?" In the dark, his eyes glinted. "I'm told you're the one who knows everything when it comes to Savannah cops."

"I wouldn't go that far," she said.

"I would." He held up his phone. It displayed the story she'd filed earlier. "If the time on this is right, you wrote this *before* the press conference. Is that where you were going when I passed you earlier? Who tipped you off?"

Harper stopped walking. "Look, who are you and what do you want? No offense, but I'm on deadline."

"No offense taken." He had a predatory smile. "I'm Jon Graff. I work for the blog, *L.A. Beat*—maybe you've heard of it?"

For a second Harper drew a blank. Then she remembered the tabloid that had covered Cara's love life with obsessive interest.

"I'm looking for juice on this case," he continued. "Anything you've got on Cara Brand. We pay good money for tips. I know reporters in cities like these don't make much." He paused, still smiling. "No offense."

She fixed him with a withering glare. "No thanks." She resumed the walk toward her car, but Graff stuck to her heels. He seemed amused.

"Hey, wait. I thought Southerners were supposed to be *friendly*. How'd you get the story before everyone else, Harper? I saw you come out of the house. You pretty friendly with the Xavier disciples in there? What'd they tell you?"

Gritting her teeth, she kept moving, but it was like trying to ignore a wasp buzzing around her head.

When they neared the Camaro, he gave a low whistle. "Nice car."

She wheeled on him. "Look, Graff, why don't you try doing your own reporting for a change? It's easier than begging for scraps."

Her tone was scalding, but his unpleasant smile only broadened. "I like you, Harper McClain. I can see why people talk about you like they do. You want to get a drink later?"

She gave him a look of pure disbelief. "You must be out of your mind."

Without waiting for him to reply, she climbed into the Camaro and slammed the door. She started the engine with a roar, and backed out, tires spinning.

There wasn't time to think much about Jon Graff.

Baxter was waiting when she got back to the newsroom, already redesigning the front page to leave a huge space for Harper's story.

In the end, the whole spread was electric: Above the fold, a large picture of Xavier standing onstage, a guitar loose in one hand. The glow of the lights brought out the amber in his soulful eyes. Beneath that, a shot of dark-clad detectives standing in front of the white beachfront mansion.

The headline read:

Musician's Body Found—Foul Play Suspected

Inside were pictures of Cara, Allegra, and Hunter, and explanations of their relationships with Xavier, but Harper wrote nothing about Cara being a suspect. She told herself her reasons were strategic. Everyone inside that house trusted her. If she wrote about that, she'd lose them all as sources.

And friends, a small voice in her head warned.

She did tell the editor about Graff. Baxter checked the blog and found that he had already posted an article about Xavier that night. It was more or less Harper's first article, without attribution, including lines he'd taken word-for-word.

Guess he decided he didn't need to pay me for it after all, Harper thought.

"Plagiarism," the editor groused. "If this paper could still afford a lawyer, we'd sue." Closing the browser in disgust, she headed back to check the final layout with the copy desk.

Miles had gone home some time ago and, alone in the newsroom, Harper stared out the window at the river. A small boat—visible only by the red light in its bow—churned against the current to heaven knew where.

It was nearing midnight. She didn't want to think any more about dead musicians and their friends. She wanted a drink and some conversation with someone she trusted. She called Bonnie, hoping she'd be working at the bar. But when she answered, there was no sound of music or the usual Library hubbub.

"Hey, hon. Hang on a minute." There was the sound of muffled talking and then a door opening. "Sorry about that," Bonnie said. "What's up?"

"You're not working." Harper rocked back in her seat, planting her feet on the desk. "You want to go get a drink?"

"Can't. I'm on a date."

"Who is it?"

"He's new. An installation artist. Very intense." Bonnie yawned. "Too intense, actually. He's been explaining his work to me for hours."

Bemused, Harper asked, "Can he hear you saying this?"

"He's in the bathroom. I'm not *that* cruel." Bonnie's tone changed. "Hey, tomorrow's Saturday and I've got the weekend off for once. I was thinking of coming out to your beach house for some sun and fun. Would I cramp your style?"

"Never," Harper said. "But I'm working on a big story at the moment. You probably haven't seen the news . . . Xavier Rayne was murdered."

"Oh, hell." Bonnie sounded somber but not surprised. "Do they know who did it?"

"Not yet. And I'm going to be covering that story all weekend. If you don't mind having the house to yourself most of the time, you're more than welcome."

"Perfect!" Bonnie said, serenely. "It's supposed to be sunny. I'll be there tomorrow with my bikini."

"It's February, Bonnie," Harper said. "Bring a sweater."

"It's February in *Georgia*," Bonnie corrected her. "I'm bringing SPF thirty."

A male voice rumbled in the background.

Bonnie whispered. "I've got to go. Loverboy's back and getting offended. See you tomorrow."

In the quiet that followed the call, Harper scrolled through her contacts, looking for someone else to go out for a drink with. She was about to give up and go home when she suddenly remembered the text she'd received that afternoon.

She read it again.

Dig into the Southern Mafia. Look back seventeen years for the name Martin Dowell. His lawyer might be of interest.

In the rush of work, she'd forgotten all about it. On a whim, she pulled the keyboard closer and typed "Southern Mafia" "Martin Dowell" into LexisNexis, tapping her fingers on the desk as the system churned.

Anonymous tips were often dubious—people settling old scores, looking for trouble. So she expected nothing much. When the system spit out two hundred hits, her eyebrows shot up.

She leaned forward, scanning the long list of articles. It was old stuff—the most recent piece had been written thirteen years ago in the Atlanta paper.

It was a straightforward article about a man named Martin Dowell who had lost an appeal of his conviction for murder and racketeering. By that point, he'd already been in jail for several years.

There was, it seemed to her, nothing special in the piece. She read it again, looking for anything she might have missed. Any connection to her work, or even to Savannah.

But there was nothing. Dowell was based in Atlanta. All his crimes had been committed there.

She almost closed the window at that point. Only her innate curiosity stopped her. After all, the message had specifically told her to read articles from seventeen years ago.

She changed the search terms, adding the specific year.

This time, fifty articles came back.

The first one she opened had run in the Atlanta paper seventeen years ago.

Alleged Boss of the Southern Mafia Charged with Murder
By Christina Steel

Martin Dowell, 55, who the state police allege is head of the so-called Southern Mafia—a loose alliance of drug gangs and organized criminals based outside Atlanta—was arrested last night at his Marietta home, and charged with murder and racketeering in the death of Paul Johnson, a convicted drug dealer.

Johnson's body was found in February, inside an oil barrel

at the Halerson Refinery outside Atlanta. The gagged and bound corpse had been shot twenty-seven times. By then, Johnson, who had a long record of arrests and convictions related to robbery and drug crimes, had been missing for six weeks.

Police sources say they believe the murder was revenge over a drug deal gone wrong. Dowell and Johnson were known associates, and Dowell had been a suspect since Johnson disappeared.

Police declined to reveal the evidence behind the arrest. And Dowell's attorney said this showed the arrest was groundless.

"This is a fishing expedition," attorney Peter McClain said, outside the courthouse where Dowell was arraigned. "The police have wanted to bring my client down for years. They'd do anything to get a conviction. We will fight this all the way."

As soon as she saw her father's name, Harper stopped breathing.

Her mind scrambled for excuses. It couldn't be her dad. It had to be another Peter McClain. After all, her dad had done most of his work in Savannah. His office had been a few blocks from where she was sitting right now.

She scrambled to close the article and bring back the list of news stories from that year. But she was moving too fast in her panic, fingers gripping the mouse too tightly, and she managed to close the entire list by mistake.

Swearing under her breath, she typed in the search words again, fumbling with the keys. And then waiting impatiently for the articles to reappear.

Finally, the list was in front of her again, and she clicked on article after article, scrutinizing the images at the top of each story. It took a few minutes to find what she was looking for.

The caption read, "Accused murderer Martin Dowell, leaving the courthouse with his lawyer, Peter McClain."

The two men stood side by side in front of the cold, stone edifice of the Fulton County Courthouse. Both of them stared straight at the camera. Dowell's blunt nose and round, pugnacious face were instantly recognizable. He looked at the photographer like he'd enjoy punching him.

Next to him was a young version of Harper's father. No salt-and-pepper hair yet, just that straight dark hair her mother was always complaining needed a trim. His face was unlined; his eyes clear and youthful. And he stood with one hand on the shoulder of a murdering drug kingpin.

Harper stared at her father, barely breathing.

One year after this was taken, his wife would be stabbed to death in the kitchen of their modest home in Savannah. His twelve-year-old daughter would find the body when she returned from school.

The murder would never be solved.

"Are you still here?" Baxter walked back into the newsroom, her low-heeled shoes tapping against the floor. "Don't you have a home to go to?"

With effort, Harper forced herself to look up. "I'm going in a second." Her voice sounded small and far away.

Distracted, Baxter didn't notice. She typed something into her computer, mumbled to herself, and left the room again. The whole time, Harper sat frozen, trying to process exactly what she was learning.

Her father had never once mentioned his connection to Dowell. Not when her mother was newly dead and the police were using words like "professional" to describe the killing. And not years later when the case grew cold.

With his record, Dowell would have made an obvious suspect if police had been aware of his connections to her father. But there was little chance they'd have discovered it on their own. Her father was a busy criminal lawyer. They would never have the time to go through every case he'd represented. This case hadn't even been reported in the Savannah paper.

Besides, her father had been the suspect, not his clients. Until his mistress provided his alibi.

At that point, the police had moved on, looking for drifters, or ex-cons living nearby. Someone her mother might have had the bad luck to run into that afternoon, sixteen years ago.

Besides, if these articles were right, Dowell was already in prison when the killing happened.

The ultimate alibi.

Still, her father's entanglement with organized crime mattered. He must have known that. But he'd never once brought it up. Why would that be?

Grabbing a writing pad, she began taking notes. Clicking through article after article, she pieced together a story of murder.

A month after that photo was taken on the front steps of the court-house in Atlanta, Martin Dowell was found guilty by a jury, whose identi-ties were zealously protected for fear of reprisals, and sentenced to twenty years for murder and racketeering.

Dowell appealed but the conviction held.

Harper's father didn't represent him on appeal. By then, he was liv-ing in Connecticut with his new wife.

At some point as she worked, Baxter went home, complaining that Harper was crazy to still be there. In the quiet that followed, she went back through older articles, discovering that her father had been Dowell's attorney for several years before the trial that sent him to prison, repre-senting him on drug cases and assault allegations. He'd fought for Dowell like a pit bull—countersuing prosecutors, making allegations in the At-lanta press about personal vendettas and police failings.

"A victim of the system," he called Dowell once in an interview. "A businessman under attack by a government gone mad."

When she'd finally had enough, she closed the notepad and leaned back in her chair, her head throbbing.

She wasn't sure what to think. Dowell was a killer, she had no doubt of that. But he'd been locked up when her mother died. How could it have been him? Besides, what would his motive have been? Her father had kept him out of jail for years.

It was one in the morning but still she didn't go home. Snatching her phone up off the desk, she scrolled to the text that had tipped her off. No name. The number had an area code she didn't recognize. She knew if she asked a cop to trace it, it would be a cheap burner phone.

But she thought she knew who'd sent it.

There was only one person who knew enough to connect the dots of her life like this. And his anonymous phone call had sent her into hiding six months ago when he'd warned her that her mother's killer was coming for her.

She shivered. Was that killer Martin Dowell?

Typing fast, she sent a short message back:

Why didn't you tell me this sooner?

This time, a reply came almost instantly. It was even briefer than her own:

I'm telling you now.

She stared at the phone for a long time before replying again:

Is Dowell still in prison?

The reply was succinct:

No.

Harper swallowed hard before typing the next question:

Did he kill my mother?

The long pause that followed was excruciating. Finally, her phone buzzed. A message filled the screen:

You already know the answer to that.

Harper drew in a sharp breath. Her hands had started to shake and she squeezed the phone to hold it steady as she typed the next question:

How? He was in jail.

There was no response. She waited five minutes before sending the message again.

Still, nothing.

Desperate, she dialed the number. As she'd known it would, it rang out without going to voice mail.

Swearing, she threw the phone down so hard it bounced.

It was always like this. The man appeared when she didn't expect him. He always gave her just enough information to string her along. But not enough to do any good.

Why should she trust him? Every word he said could be a lie. He could be one of Dowell's goons. For all she knew, he could be the one hunting her.

And yet, her instincts told her to believe him.

Something had happened between Martin Dowell and her father. Something about the case that sent Dowell to prison. It was all connected to her mother's murder. She could sense it. Smell it in the air like blood.

Whatever happened—whatever the man on the phone told her or didn't tell her—she was going to get to the truth. She was going to investigate this case right down to the bone.

12

When she finally left the paper it was nearly two o'clock in the morning. Only a few hours had passed since she'd sat on the veranda at Xavier Rayne's house—it felt like days.

The air was warm and humid but Harper found herself shivering as she unlocked the Camaro. She barely noticed that the security guard had followed her out. "Safe night," he called.

She made a U-turn on the empty street. Her hands navigated the car while her mind worked through all the questions she needed answers to.

Why hadn't her father told the police about Martin Dowell after his wife was murdered? Why would he have kept that information secret when it might have helped find a murderer?

Harper had investigated criminals all her adult life and she knew there was only one logical reason. Her father was protecting Dowell.

Her heart felt like a stone in her chest.

Sixteen years of pain. Sixteen years of not understanding why anyone would kill her mother—a free spirit with strawberry-blond hair and blue eyes, who loved being barefoot on sunny days, who hummed while she painted. Who never in her life hurt a soul. Who was stabbed to death, stripped of her clothes, and left on the cold kitchen floor like a piece of meat.

She'd had no enemies. No drug problem or crazy ex with an axe to grind. Her murder had never made any sense.

Now, though, Harper was beginning to see how it might have worked. Her father had represented Dowell and lost the case that sent him to prison for a long time. The man had lost everything. He must have been furious.

She didn't know how he'd done it from inside jail, but when it came to organized crime, nothing was impossible. He would have had connections on the outside willing to do jobs for him.

She wondered distantly why he hadn't killed her, too. It would have been easy the day her mother died. She was only twelve and all alone. Or any day after that. She'd never known to watch her back. To be afraid.

Harper let out a choked breath, and the sound of it startled her back to awareness.

For a disorienting second, she didn't know where she was. Ahead, a dark stretch of road unfurled in the cold glow of her headlights. Her scanner, which had been burbling a steady stream of information a moment ago, was silent.

She was on the highway heading across the saltwater marshes. The lights of Savannah were far behind.

Isolated and gloomy during the day, the wetlands were worse at night. The flat landscape seemed to absorb light, creating a thick, inky blackness that sprawled in all directions—devoid of any sign of humanity.

Harper tensed, her hands tightening reflexively on the wheel.

How could she be so foolish? She hadn't taken a circuitous route— hadn't made certain no one followed her. For the first time in months she'd just . . . driven. Without thinking about who was behind her.

When she'd first talked to Luke and Blazer about how to live anonymously, they'd both identified this as the obvious weak point. Her home was off the books, and the office was protected by guards with guns and panic buttons and CCTV.

This journey—the one she made every night—this was the chink in her armor. The moment when she was completely alone and cut off.

The lieutenant had been blunt. *"If I was going to kill you, that's where I'd do it."*

She tried to focus on the road ahead, but her eyes kept straying to the rearview mirror.

It was all too easy to imagine a light that started small and far away, but grew closer and closer. A car driven by someone who wanted her dead, all because her dad had gotten mixed up with the mob back when she was eleven years old.

The sole set of headlights behind her were tiny in the distance, visible only because the land was so flat. Still, a trickle of nervous sweat ran down her spine.

She put her foot down. The Camaro responded, powering forward with a growl.

The lights behind her did not close in. Eventually, as she sped away, they disappeared completely. But she didn't lift her foot from the gas until she reached the bridge onto the island.

Gradually, her heart rate returned to normal. The little town's lights glowed reassuringly ahead. There was even a car, passing her the other way. She was safe.

She'd just reached the first red light when her phone rang.

Assuming it was Miles, she answered it on hands-free. "McClain."

"Harper. It's Luke."

She was too tired to hide how glad she was to hear from him, and there was a breathless edge to her voice when she replied. "Hey. What's up?"

"This is going to sound weird but I think I just passed your car. Are you driving into Tybee right now?"

"Just crossed the bridge," she said. "Wait. Was that you going the other way?"

"Pull over," he said. "I'm turning around."

She drove onto the shoulder and put the car in park. As she waited, she hastily checked her face in the mirror, smoothing the tangles from her russet hair.

A minute later, Luke pulled up behind her and killed the engine.

She got out of the car to meet him.

He strode toward her like he was walking across a crime scene. At some point he'd ditched the jacket and tie. The top two buttons of his white shirt were open.

"You just heading home?" she asked.

"Yeah. You too?"

She nodded.

"Guess it's been a hell of a day for both of us." He glanced at his watch. "Look, I know it's late. But do you want to grab a drink? I could use one."

Harper hid her surprise. It had been a long time since they'd had a drink together.

"Sure," she said. "Why not?"

He looked down the empty street. Not a single car had passed while they talked.

"It's a bit late, I guess. You know any place that might be open?"

"How about the Shipwatch?" she suggested. "It's the old white and blue hotel on the main street. It stays open late."

"Sounds good. I'll follow you."

Harper got back into the Camaro and sat still for a second. What were the chances that they'd pass each other like that? There'd been a time when he would have been the first person she called tonight. He was a good cop and, despite everything, one she trusted.

Maybe this was fate.

He stayed behind her as the road curved around the edge of the island to where the Shipwatch sat, just off the main beach. With snow-white walls and nautical blue trim, the 1950s hotel was a blast from the past. Known to everyone in town as "the Shipwreck," it was the island's main late-night hangout.

The parking lot behind the building was half empty. Harper parked at the back, out of habit. Luke pulled up next to her.

"This place is a bit eccentric," she warned him, as they walked across the asphalt to the hotel bar.

"I think I can handle it," he said, with a slight smile.

They could hear the Eagles wailing from the jukebox even before they opened the door. Inside, the cool air smelled of spilled beer. It wasn't crowded, but everyone who'd made it this far was in it for the long haul.

"Fresh blood!" a drunk man cried, pointing as they crossed the empty dance floor to the bar.

Luke gave Harper a raised eyebrow, but all he said was, "Beck's?"

She nodded. "I'll grab a table."

She took a seat near the door and leaned back, scanning the room. There were about ten people left. Most of them were wasted. As the song shifted to another bouncy oldie, the drunk—a red-faced man in an Atlanta Falcons T-shirt—began to dance unsteadily, a beer bottle in his hand.

Luke was chatting with the bartender. She was tiny, with short black hair and a silver hoop in her nose. He said something that made her laugh as she popped the caps off the beers with quick, practiced moves and slid them across, making eye contact.

Harper couldn't blame her. With his rangy good looks and country-boy smile, Luke could charm the fur off a cat.

God, she missed him.

When he reached her a few minutes later and handed her a bottle, he said, "I figured you didn't want a glass."

Shaking her head, she took a sip. The beer was ice cold. She hadn't known how much she needed it until that moment.

"Oh, this was a good idea," she murmured, leaning back in the un-yielding wooden chair, and trying to clear thoughts of her father's past from her mind.

"How'd it go at the Rayne house?" she asked.

He gave a slight shrug. "We didn't find any bodies. It's always harder when they don't leave the corpses lying around."

"So you didn't arrest anyone?" She held up one hand. "Off the record, obviously."

"No. The house was pretty clean." He paused. "Got to say, though, I heard a lot about you tonight."

"Me?" She didn't hide her surprise. "From who?"

"Allegra and Hunter. They kept asking me to call you. Said they'd only talk to me if you were there, too." He gave her a curious look. "What'd you do to convince them that you're their champion?"

"Nothing," she insisted. "I've only met them a couple of times."

She was being disingenuous. After all, she'd spent the last two days trying to win them over. And it had worked.

"Well, they seem pretty hung up on you. Hunter in particular. He kept wanting to call you. We had to take his phone away. Is something going on between you two?"

His tone was elaborately casual, but there was a tension beneath the words.

"*No,*" she said. "Absolutely not."

His doubtful expression didn't change.

"Come on, Luke. They're just kids."

"They're our age." He set his bottle down. "They're not children."

"Well, they're not habitual criminals either," she said. "They didn't understand what was happening. I just tried to explain how it works."

A suspicious look crossed his face. "What exactly did you tell them? This is a criminal investigation. You shouldn't be telling them anything."

"I told them to call the *cops,*" she said, exasperated. "I told them to talk to you guys. I told them everything would be okay. That's it. Give me some credit."

He held her gaze for a long moment before relenting. "I'm sorry if I sounded accusing. I'm just tired."

Harper watched as he took a drink, gazing out across the bar. She didn't know what to make of this. Was he jealous of Hunter? That would be ridiculous. After all, he was the one who had a girlfriend, according to the police station rumor mill.

Either way, they needed to get to safer ground.

"What do you make of Cara?" she asked, after a beat.

"Man." He blew out air from between pursed lips. "That girl is something else. If I choose to believe her, Xavier was a saint, she loved him, a monster snatched him from the beach, and her heart is broken."

"*Do* you believe her?" she asked.

He hesitated, holding his beer halfway to his lips. "I'm not sure, yet."

"You really didn't find anything in the house?" she pressed. "They don't strike me as criminal masterminds."

"Nothing conclusive," he said. "No kill zone. Traces of blood in the kitchen sink but Allegra had cut her finger cooking dinner the night before." He stretched his shoulders as if they ached. "We'll test and see if there's DNA."

"But you still like them for it?"

"They're the closest to him," he said.

He didn't have to say more. Killers rarely come from far away. Except in her mother's case.

The thought jarred her, distracting her instantly from Xavier Rayne.

Pushing her half-empty bottle aside, she leaned forward. "Can I tell you something that happened tonight? It's got nothing to do with the case." She kept her voice low, but he must have heard the change in her tone, because his brow creased.

"Shoot."

"I got a text, from that guy." She didn't have to say which guy she meant.

Luke searched her face. "What did he say?"

Talking fast, she told him what she'd learned. When she mentioned Martin Dowell's name, he held up one hand to stop the flow of words.

"You're not talking about Martin Dowell, as in Southern Mafia Martin Dowell?"

She nodded. "You've heard of him?"

"Your father defended that piece of crap?" His face hardened.

She dug through her bag for the printout of the photo she'd found of her father standing next to Dowell in front of the Atlanta courthouse, and slid it across to him.

Luke studied it with obvious distaste. When he handed it back, his mouth was set in a grim line. "Harper, this is bad news."

"Tell me about it."

"No, I mean, the worst damn news." He angled forward across the table until he was so close she could smell the soap on his skin. "When I worked undercover, I was in Dowell's operation—or what's left of it now." He gave her a weighted look. "You remember the scar on my side?"

Harper thought of her and Luke in bed, her head on his chest, her fingers tracing the angry line of the scar. "I remember."

"Well, it was Dowell's guys who gave it to me. The organization's run by a dirtbag named Rodney Jordan now. A little psychopath. He was Dowell's hit man for years. After the boss went down, the group disbanded, but Jordan brought it back together, a little at a time." His tone was bitter. "Every drug dealer in the state is scared to death of him and the gang of shitheads he's pulled together. They kill ruthlessly, and they leave no evidence." He held her gaze. "They *erase* people, Harper."

Her stomach turned to ice.

"I think they must be the ones who killed my mother," she told him, quietly. "After Dowell went to prison. I think Dowell had her killed to get back at my father for losing that case. I don't know how he did it, but it makes sense."

She could see him working it through in his mind. "You can't know that for certain," he said. "It's speculation." Seeing her expression, he raised one hand. "I get that it's reasonable speculation. But you don't know for certain, and you can't go down that path all the way to deciding it was definitely him."

"But it fits," she argued. "The timing. The fact that the killing looked professional. Dowell's a professional. That guy you mentioned—his hit man. He could have done the job."

Luke fell silent. When he spoke again, his tone was dead serious.

"These guys don't believe in mistakes. They believe in winning and making money. If your dad lost that case, and Dowell blamed him for what happened . . ." His hand tightened around the bottle. "They wouldn't hesitate to kill a woman to send a message. Wouldn't even blink."

Harper's mouth had gone dry. She licked her lips before telling him the last piece of information she had. "Luke, I think Dowell . . . he might be out."

He stared at her. "Are you certain?"

"No," she admitted. "There's nothing about it in any newspaper, and all the offices are closed. But it's been seventeen years. With good behavior . . ."

The worry in his face told her everything.

"I'll need to talk to some people," he said. "See what I can find out. But seventeen years would be about right." The shallow lines on his forehead deepened. He seemed bewildered by this tsunami of bad news. "*Damn,* Harper."

"I know," she said. The knot that had formed in the pit of her stomach earlier had only grown more solid. "The guy thinks Dowell's coming for me. He's the one I'm supposed to be hiding from."

Luke didn't look convinced. "Even if he is out, he'll be on probation," he reminded her. "He'll be monitored. Have to check in every week. Besides, if he wanted to get to you, wouldn't he have had it done it by now? Your name's in the paper every day. You're not impossible to find."

The same question had been puzzling Harper.

"I don't know the answer to that," she admitted. "Maybe Dowell wants to do it himself. Maybe he waited." She held up her hands. "Or maybe the guy's making it all up. I don't know."

He considered this. "What's your gut tell you?"

She held his eyes. "My gut says I'm in trouble."

Suddenly she needed a real drink.

She picked up the bottle of beer, finished it off, and gestured at his. "Want another?"

He started to get up but she motioned for him to stay put and grabbed her wallet, heading to the bar. As she approached, the bartender looked up from putting glasses in the dishwasher. She had unusual blue eyes and a heart-shaped face.

"A Beck's and a shot of Jameson's, please." Harper placed the empties on the bar. "Make the whiskey a double."

The woman plucked a bottle from the shelf. A voice came from just behind Harper's shoulder. "You and the detective look awful cozy. That must come in handy."

Harper spun around.

Jon Graff had shed the light jacket he'd worn earlier that night on Admiral's Row. He held up his glass. "I told you we should have a drink together."

"If I wanted to have a drink with you," she said, icily, "I would have a drink with you."

His grin widened. "You have got such attitude. I like it."

"That's twelve fifty." The bartender was looking back and forth between the two of them with animated curiosity.

Keeping her eyes on Graff, Harper dug a ten and a five out of her wallet and slid them across.

"Keep the change." She picked up the drinks, suppressing the urge to throw them in his face.

"Come on, Harper McClain. Tell me how you got in that house tonight." He followed her across the bar. "Did the handsome young detective let you in?"

"I'm not telling you a thing," she said.

"Sure you are." Glancing to where Luke sat, he said, "You're telling me things you don't even know you're telling me."

Biting back a series of creative suggestions of just what he could do with his questions, Harper tightened her lips and stalked away, holding the drinks in a death grip.

When she reached Luke, his eyes were fixed on Graff. "What was that about?"

"A tabloid reporter from LA looking for trouble." She lowered her voice. "He recognized you."

She didn't have to tell him what this meant. If Graff pushed it, Luke could find himself questioned by Blazer about why he was sitting with her in a bar in the middle of a homicide investigation she was covering.

Luke watched Graff with a murderous expression. "He gave you hassle?"

Harper made a dismissive gesture. "He tried to talk to me out at the house. Followed me to my car talking trash. I didn't like him then. Don't like him now."

She didn't mention that he'd asked her out. The last thing she needed was Luke getting in a macho fight right now. But he seemed to know there was more to it than she was letting on. He pulled out his phone. "Give me his name again. I'll run him through the system tomorrow."

Harper spelled it for him. The whole time, she could feel Graff's eyes burning into her back.

"I think we should go," she said.

He didn't argue. Leaving their full drinks on the table, they headed out. As he held the door for her, Luke fixed the tabloid reporter with an icy stare.

Outside, Harper took a deep breath and let the salt air clear Graff from her lungs.

As they walked back to their cars, she told Luke about Graff's fixation with Cara. "There's something personal there," she said. "He seems obsessed with her."

He shot her a sideways look. "And now he's obsessed with you."

"He's the least of my worries," she said, dismissively.

Harper looked down the empty street. Now that she had some idea what she was up against, living out here was starting to seem like a truly terrible idea. The Tybee police force was too tiny to help her if men like the ones Luke had described came for her.

As if he'd heard her thoughts, Luke said, "I don't like you living out here."

"Yeah," Harper said. "I was just thinking it might be time to move closer to a heavily armed police department."

He didn't smile. "I'm serious. You should think about moving back to town."

"I'm on it," she said. And she was. Tomorrow she would start making calls and see if she could find a new place in the city.

The thought was cheering. Maybe it was worth having a killer after her if it meant she could go home again.

Luke glanced down at the keys in his hand. "Harper. About your mother . . . You're not planning on going after Dowell for revenge, are you?"

There was a long pause. "I don't know what I'm going to do," she said, finally.

He lifted his serious blue eyes to hers. "Well, before you do anything, remember this. I am a police officer with eight years of service. I am over six feet tall and trained in self-defense. And Dowell's thugs nearly killed me." There was a new intensity in his expression. "You're the toughest woman I know. But they would eliminate you. Do me a favor. Don't do anything. Just keep your head down. Pretend you don't know what you know. Give me some time. Let me see what I can find out."

Their eyes locked, and she saw something in his gaze that was more than worry. Something that sent heat into her bloodstream.

"I'll wait to hear from you," she promised.

Suddenly, she felt completely drained. She longed for nothing more than for him to wrap her in his arms, as he once would have done. But that was the past.

"I guess I better go," she said.

He looked almost disappointed—as if he'd hoped she'd suggest something else. But he said, "Yeah, me too," and shifted the keys in his hand. "I'll call you as soon as I know anything."

"Thanks." She opened the driver's-side door. The interior light glowed, illuminating her face.

"Hey," he said. "Watch your back, you hear me?"

It had been a long time since she'd seen that expression on his face—a complex mixture of concern and longing. She felt that look in her stomach.

But there was no point. He had someone else now.

"Don't worry about me," she said, getting into the car. "I'm always careful."

13

That night, Harper dreamed she was speeding across the marshes in the dark. The road unfurled before her, straight as a razor. There were headlights in the rearview mirror. Closing in. The glow grew brighter and brighter until a blinding light filled the car and she couldn't see the road ahead.

There was a bang, and her eyes flew open. She was lying on the couch, her forehead beaded with sweat. Zuzu was asleep at her feet.

Daylight streamed through the open blinds, sending shards of bright sunlight across the dark wood floors.

Bang. Bang. Bang.

Someone was pounding on the door.

She sat up, disturbing Zuzu, who leapt from the sofa in a fluid arc and stalked away with her ears back as the pounding came again.

Still groggy, Harper jumped to her feet, looking around for a baseball bat before remembering that she didn't have one anymore.

"Harper, are you naked?" Bonnie's impatient voice called from outside. "Put some clothes on and open the damned door. These bags are heavy."

She'd forgotten it was Saturday. Bonnie was coming to stay.

"Hang on!" she called hoarsely, grabbing the keys from the coffee table. When she finally got the door open, Bonnie stood on the other side clutching four overstuffed bags, including one that clinked when she stepped inside. "About time," she groused.

"Are you moving in for good?" Harper looked at the overfilled bags doubtfully.

"I need all of this," Bonnie insisted, dropping them by the door. "I know you won't have any food. And the wine is medicinal." She looked from Harper to the rumpled sofa to where Zuzu sat on the floor, blinking at them both disapprovingly. "Did you just get up?"

"It's noon." Harper said it like that explained everything. She was wide awake now, though, and her main thought was that it was not a good idea for Bonnie to be here right now.

She'd invited her before she'd learned about Martin Dowell.

The last thing she wanted was for Bonnie to somehow get caught up in this. But if she explained why she wanted her to leave, she'd insist on staying to protect her.

Utterly unaware of Harper's internal conflict, Bonnie had already picked up the bag of wine and groceries and headed across the living room to the little kitchen, talking nonstop. "Well, as you might have gathered, my date was a disaster."

Harper tried to remember a conversation that now seemed to have happened long ago. "Remind me—who was he?"

"His name is Dylan," Bonnie called over her shoulder, setting bags down in the cramped little kitchen. "He's so good-looking. He does light art."

Harper sat back down on the sofa. "That sounds . . . bright."

"It's *beautiful*. That's why I wanted to go out with him. But, dear lord, he talks about himself more than a homecoming queen." Harper could hear her opening and closing cupboards. Sliding things onto mostly empty shelves. "He has a lot of *thoughts* about his process and art and 'the realized world,' whatever the hell that is, and damn if he doesn't like to talk about it nonstop."

She leaned in the kitchen doorway. Her wavy, white-blond hair was pulled into a side ponytail that hung over one shoulder. The section dyed magenta shimmered in the light. She wore faded jeans rolled up to expose slim ankles, and a black T-shirt that she'd sliced up in places so that it hung loose, revealing the delicate curves of her collarbone. On the front, she'd painted the word "CREATE" in silver, entwined with flowers.

"I'd have sent him home but he's so good-looking." She sighed, leaning her head against the wood frame. "Even when he was boring me, I just thought about how pretty he was and then I felt better about him. He's got this gorgeous hair that falls over his forehead. He kind of peeks out from under it like a little deer."

Harper wasn't impressed. "Did you make an excuse and get out of there?"

Bonnie straightened. "Honey, no. I had sex with him and then I went home before he could talk me into a coma. You want some water? I'll put some coffee on, too."

She talked as if Harper were visiting *her*, instead of the other way around.

"Sure," Harper said. "Was the sex good at least?"

"It was okay when he finally stopped talking. But there won't be a repeat performance." Bonnie's voice floated back from the kitchen. "I'm not as into him as he is." Harper heard the sound of the tap running. "What about you?" Bonnie raised her voice above the water. "Did you go out after work?"

"Sort of."

"Sort of how?" Bonnie walked back in and handed her a glass, before sitting down in a chair.

"I ran into Luke on my way back to town. We went out for a beer."

Harper kept her tone careless but Bonnie fixed her with a knowing blue-eyed stare.

"And what was that like?"

"Like having a beer with the guy who broke my heart," Harper said. Curled up on the sofa, her feet tucked under her, she told her about passing him on the bridge. The way he'd turned his car around.

"I'm sorry but that is sickeningly romantic." Bonnie sighed. "No one ever turned his car around for me. I swear someone up there wants you two together."

Picking up her water, Harper mumbled into her glass, "Well, they'll need to try harder than that."

"So what did you talk about?" Bonnie asked, nudging her with her toes.

"Oh, you know, work," she said. "And this guy from an LA tabloid who's been harassing me. He was in the Shipwreck being a dick. I thought for a second Luke was going to deck him."

"Y'all haven't dated in six months, and he'd still fight for your honor," Bonnie marveled. "If he wasn't a cheating son of a bitch I'd like him."

"Yeah, well," Harper said. "Me too."

"He still got a girlfriend?" Bonnie was as relentless as a pit bull.

"Probably." Harper shrugged. "It didn't come up."

Bonnie's eyes narrowed. "Harper Louise. Have I taught you nothing? You miss him, he obviously misses you, you have to find out—"

"I know, but I *can't*," Harper cut her off, her voice ringing with sudden passion. "Even if he's single, I can't date him again. You know how it was last time. And the time before. We're combustible, Luke and me. I won't get burned again. Even if it means I'm single forever and I live all alone in this stupid little house with no one but the cat."

Bonnie's expression softened. "He'll be sorry one day for blowing this, I promise. And you won't be alone forever. There's no way that's happening." She stood up. "Now, let me get you that coffee."

As she walked back to the kitchen, Harper felt a needle prick of guilt for not telling her what was really going on, but she couldn't. It was bad enough that Bonnie was here now, where anyone looking for Harper might find her.

In the moments before she walked back in with two steaming mugs, Harper decided this would have to be Bonnie's last visit until all of this was settled. For her own sake.

There was a huge amount to do, but Harper couldn't seem to make herself leave the house. Bonnie made an omelet and toast from the supplies she'd brought, and the two of them sat on the sofa, drinking coffee and catching up.

The normality of it was so welcome, Harper allowed herself to relax a little. She told her about the Xavier Rayne case, describing his housemates in detail. Cara's distant beauty. Allegra's exquisite voice.

Bonnie interrupted. "That singer, what did you say her name was? Allegra something?" When Harper nodded, she said, "I think I've heard of her. I think she's got a gig scheduled at the Library later this week." She searched her phone. "Yeah, here we go. Allegra Hanson. She's there on Wednesday." She held it up so Harper could see. On the screen, a blue-tinted Allegra, holding a microphone, looked out at an unseen audience. Written across the image was "The Library Live: Wednesday 8 P.M."

"She hasn't canceled?" Harper asked.

Bonnie shook her head. "It's still on the website."

Harper's phone rang, interrupting them. The number wasn't recognized. She jumped from the sofa so quickly she jarred the coffee table. Bonnie gave her a puzzled look.

She barely got out the word "Sorry" as she ran out onto the porch, her breath tight in her throat. "McClain."

"Harper is this you?" It was Allegra's distinctive voice, her accent thick as honey.

It was as if they'd summoned her by talking about her. Harper was so surprised, it took her a second to reply.

"Hey, Allegra. Is everything okay?"

"No, it really isn't."

In the background, Harper could hear the raised voices. It sounded like an argument.

"Listen, would you mind coming over? I don't know what to do." There was a high, thin nervousness to her voice.

Harper had planned to go in to the office early to dig deeper into Martin Dowell's life. But something was going on over there right now, and she couldn't say no.

"Sure," she said, trying not to sound as reluctant as she felt. "Are you all . . . safe?"

"Just . . . please come," Allegra pleaded, and then the phone went dead.

14

When she reached Admiral's Row, seven TV vans were still parked outside but most of them appeared empty. No reporters leaned against the doors, watching number 6.

Blessedly, there was also no sign of Jon Graff. In fact, Harper passed no one at all until an older woman in low heels walked out of number 5, rolling a Louis Vuitton suitcase with some effort in the direction of a silver Mercedes.

Seeing Harper watching the vans, she stopped. "They've been there all night." Her perfectly made-up face was set in lines of disapproval. "The police won't do a thing."

Harper walked over to her. "This must be a nightmare for you," she said sympathetically.

"You have *no* idea. Reporters knocked on my door at ten o'clock last night trying to interview me. I'm alone in the house. Police were coming and going at all hours." The woman's lips tightened. "I've had enough. My children don't think it's safe for me here until they catch the person who did this." She had the silky patrician accent of old Savannah gentry that elongated every syllable. "I'll stay at the DeSoto until this madness blows over."

The DeSoto was one of Savannah's most stylish and expensive hotels.

"That's probably the right thing to do." Harper kept her tone supportive.

"I think so, too." As if she'd belatedly realized she was talking to a stranger, the woman peered at her. "I'm sorry, who did you say you were visiting?"

Harper gestured vaguely at number 2, where no car was in the drive. "My friends don't seem to be home, though."

"Gerald and Anna? I saw them leave about an hour ago," the woman told her. "I think they're going to stay in the city as well."

This was perfect. She was a veritable one-woman Neighborhood Watch.

"Can I help you with that bag?" Harper offered.

"That's so sweet of you." The woman pushed a button on her key fob, and the trunk lid rose smoothly.

Harper picked up the suitcase, which was considerably heavier than it looked, and maneuvered it in. "There you go," she said, dusting her hands together. As the lid closed, she made no move to leave. "It must be terrible, all of this happening so close to you. Anna's really upset about it."

"It's terrifying." The woman's pencil-lined eyes widened. "The police have no idea where the murder happened; they couldn't even tell me for certain it wasn't on my very *doorstep*."

"I'm so sorry," Harper sympathized. "Did you know Xavier Rayne?"

The woman made a vague gesture. "Enough to say hello. He was a sweet man. Very sensitive. It's *such* a tragedy. He and his girlfriend—that pretty actress—they were a beautiful couple." She leaned forward confidingly. "They had problems, though, I have to tell you. Terrible fights."

This time, Harper didn't have to feign surprise. "Really? They fought?"

"Like *cats*." Mistaking her expression for disbelief, the woman explained, defensively, "I sleep lightly. Insomnia runs in my family. Besides, they made no effort to keep their voices down."

"I'm sorry, I'm just surprised," Harper said. "They seemed like the perfect couple."

The woman gave her a look. "Not very perfect from what I could hear."

"Was this recently?" Harper asked. "The fighting, I mean?"

"Oh my land. The night he disappeared they had the biggest screaming match you've ever heard. He said he wouldn't move in with her in LA, which *really* upset her. And she accused him of having sex with another girl. Which *really* upset him. She told him she was going back to California and she'd never come here again. She used extremely foul language. And so did he. I meant to talk to them about that but . . . Well, you know." Her words faded.

"Have you talked to the police about this, Mrs. . . . ?" Harper tilted her head. "I'm sorry, I didn't catch your name."

"Masters," the woman said. "Jennifer Masters. And yours? I beg your pardon, I should have asked earlier."

"Harper McClain."

"McClain . . ." The woman's carefully penciled eyebrows drew together. "I know that name."

Harper nudged the conversation back on track. "Did you tell the police?"

"I did. In fact, a detective came by this morning," she said. "She was extremely interested."

She. That had to be Daltrey. Harper hadn't noticed any detectives' cars parked on the street, so she must be gone already. She hoped so, anyway. Either way, she needed to get moving. The last thing she wanted was to run into Daltrey before she could find out what was going on in there.

"I don't blame you at all for going into the city until things calm down out here," she said, taking a step back. "It was nice talking to you."

Taking the hint, the woman got into the car. "I won't feel safe until they catch whoever did this," she said before she closed the door. "You should be careful out here, too."

Harper waited until she drove out of sight before dashing over to number 6. Bypassing the main door in case anyone was watching, she slipped down the path between the two houses. This time, she didn't run into anyone before reaching the arched, wooden gate.

For a second, she feared she wouldn't remember the security code, but as soon as she touched the keypad it came back to her: 0924.

The gate opened without a sound. On the other side, the smooth green expanse of lawn was empty.

She walked across the lawn to the back steps, and up to the veranda, where the white wicker chairs were still arranged as she'd seen them last. A pale pashmina had been abandoned on one, and the wind lifted it, making it flutter like a wounded bird.

Despite the chill, the back door had been left ajar, and Harper stepped tentatively into the grand hallway.

"Hello?" Her voice echoed off the walls as if the house were abandoned. For a moment, she thought nobody would answer. That they'd all gone. Then a voice came from down the hallway.

"We're in here." It was Hunter.

She followed the sound to the living room. With each step, she breathed in the scent that pervaded the place and that, for her, most defined it: the smoky, exotic mixture of patchouli, sandalwood, and tobacco. It was so distinctive she'd have known where she was blindfolded.

When she stepped into the living room, they were all there. Hunter in the same chair he'd sat in the first time she came here. Long, skinny legs sprawled in front of him. On the sofa, Cara, the ice queen, who kept her angry eyes on Hunter. Allegra sat across from her, her face red and blotchy, as if she'd been weeping.

The air sizzled with the tension of an unfinished argument. It felt like walking into the aftermath of a fire.

Harper noticed no charcoal smudges of fingerprint dust on the doors or windows. No missing boards or pieces of furniture. That was puzzling. Surely the forensics team had torn this place apart? And yet it all looked perfect.

"How have you been holding up?" she asked, to break the silence.

"We're getting through it." Hunter's voice was as tight as a wire. Nobody else spoke.

"I understand the police were here for hours last night," she tried again. "That couldn't have been easy."

"It was fucking terrible." Cara fixed Harper with a blue stare of absolute fury. "It was like having our skin ripped off and salt rubbed into the raw wounds by a bunch of knuckle-dragging hicks." She thrust a finger at the spiral binding of the notebook peeking out of Harper's jacket pocket. "Write that down," she ordered. "Go on. That's what you're here for, isn't it? To watch us and then go write it all up for your stupid little paper."

"Cara," Allegra said, sharply. "Stop it. She's trying to help us."

Cara's brittle laugh shattered in the air. "Oh, don't be ridiculous. She doesn't want to help us. She wants to *use us*. Write about us. Make money off us."

"Did I write something that upset you?" Harper asked.

Cara gave her a withering look. "God, I'm so sick of fake Southern politeness. Everyone's so nice and then they rifle through your underwear drawer with their sweaty fingers, looking for anything they can use . . ." Her voice broke, and she turned away.

Hunter picked up the pack of cigarettes, pulled one out, and threw the pack down savagely on the table.

"Why don't you go back to LA if you hate it here so much."

She stared at him, blue eyes shocked.

"Look," Harper interrupted, trying to calm things down. "I know exactly what the cops would have done here yesterday. But they had to do it." Cara flashed her an angry look but she continued, steadily. "I'm so sorry you had to go through it. I know it's awful."

"They went through all of our rooms," Allegra told her. "Every single drawer. They turned over every mattress. Stuart kept threatening to sue them." She drew a breath. "They handcuffed him."

Mindful that the manager would not like this conversation, Harper asked casually, "Where's Stuart now?"

"He went to meet with the record company's lawyers in Atlanta," Hunter said. "Personally, I think he just wanted to get out of here." He drew on the cigarette, his final words coming out in a cloud of smoke. "I wish I could."

"They wouldn't tell us anything," Allegra said. "They treated us like criminals. We don't know what's happening. Or why they did that. We hoped you could help. Do you know what they were looking for?"

"A gun or blood," Harper said, bluntly. "If Xavier was killed here and dragged down to the beach there would be blood evidence left behind. Short of that, bloody clothes. Or the murder weapon."

"That's sickening," Cara said. "How could they suspect us? We loved him. Why would they ever—"

"Harper just told us why," Hunter spoke over her, impatiently.

"Don't talk to me like that." Cara's voice rose.

"Will you please *stop fighting*." Allegra stood abruptly, hands curled in fists. "You're making everything worse."

The other two exchanged a look.

"We're not fighting," Cara said. "We're just upset."

"All you do is fight." Allegra's voice shook. "Ever since Xavier left you've been like that."

Harper noticed she didn't say "died."

"Allegra, come on—" Hunter didn't get to finish. The younger woman stormed from the room.

"Allegra, wait!" Cara followed her out.

Slumping back in his chair, Hunter stubbed his cigarette out. "I'm sorry about that," he said, after a second. "We're exhausted. Do you want something to drink? Tea?"

Harper didn't want anything, but she said, "Sure." He needed to do something and she needed to let him.

Getting up, she followed him down the hall. Like the rest of the house, the kitchen was spotless, the tall cabinets neatly closed. Everything was scrubbed clean and in its place. The air smelled faintly of bleach.

Hunter poured water into an electric kettle and switched it on.

"How bad was it?" she asked.

His shoulders hunching, he said, "They trashed the place. When they were done, it looked like we'd been robbed. We've been cleaning all day. Putting everything back."

Now Harper understood why there was no evidence of the search. They'd done their best to make everything perfect again. She glanced unconsciously at the sparkling white sink, a memory of something Luke said last night surfacing. *"Traces of blood in the kitchen sink."*

"It just feels like they think we're guilty," Hunter said. Stirring himself to action, he pulled a box of tea from the cabinet. "The questions they asked—they were the kind of questions they ask suspects."

"Everyone's a suspect," she said. "Until they get the killer."

"Even you?" Cara had walked in without Harper noticing. She stood in the doorway, her chin tilted up, her eyes damp and the tip of her nose red and raw. "Or is it just us?"

"Not me," Harper admitted. "I have no motive."

"What's my motive?" Cara demanded. "Why would I want to kill the man I loved?"

Harper turned to look at her directly. "Well, if there were problems in your relationship, that could cause tension," she said, meaningfully.

Cara stared at her, her lips parted as if she'd meant to speak but had forgotten the words.

"You argued that last night, didn't you?" Harper said. "About moving to Los Angeles."

Hunter stepped between them, a mug in his hands. "They fought like couples fight. Nothing more than that."

Harper didn't look at him. "Let Cara answer."

Cara held her gaze, those blue eyes wide and stunned.

"I didn't kill Xavier." She drew in a sudden breath. "My God. I can't believe I even have to say that. I loved him."

She was so convincing. But she was also an actress.

Harper said, "Have you spoken to a lawyer?"

The mug slipped from Hunter's fingers and crashed to the floor.

"Shit," he said, looking at the pieces as if he didn't know what they were.

"What was that?" Allegra's voice came from the top of the stairs.

Cara cleared her throat before shouting. "Nothing, Legs. Just a cup."

When no one else moved, Harper stepped carefully back from the sharp shards of porcelain. "Have you got a broom?"

Wordlessly, Hunter pointed at a slim cupboard near the oven. Harper found a broom and dustpan, and quickly swept the broken pieces into a pile. She could sense Cara and Hunter having a silent conversation behind her back.

Cara spoke first. "How did you know Xavier and I argued the night he died?"

Harper dumped the shards into the kitchen bin before answering. "Your neighbor told the police."

A shudder passed through Cara's body.

"So, they were breaking up," Hunter said. "That's all. It doesn't mean anything."

"They were breaking up on the night he died," Harper said. "That's motive."

She kept her focus on Cara, who didn't seem to be breathing.

"I wish we hadn't fought." The woman's voice was barely above a whisper. "I would take every word of it back if I could. I wish I'd never said anything. But I would never *ever* hurt him."

They were both so fragile. So desperate to be believed. They wanted to talk. To be understood. To tell their side.

She had them right where she wanted them.

Harper pulled the notebook from her jacket pocket and set it down on the kitchen island. The granite top felt cold beneath her fingers as she glanced up at them.

"You better tell me everything."

15

Harper was nearly to Savannah when Miles called. "Just heard from the press flacks at the cop shop. There's a press conference at five. I've got two tickets."

"I'm on my way into town." She spoke loudly to be heard above her scanner, which crackled in the dashboard holder. "Any idea what it's about?"

"No one's talking. Maybe they've arrested someone. Maybe they've got the autopsy results and he died of a heart attack."

She could hear his engine racing in the background.

"Where are you now?" she asked.

"Been shooting a wedding in the suburbs," he said. "Stuffed myself on canapés. I'm on my way back in."

Miles worked freelance. Weddings were a lucrative sideline.

"I hope you saved me a crab puff." Harper stopped at a red light, studying the traffic behind her. A dark BMW had been back there for a while. She was keeping an eye on it. Maybe things were heating up with the Xavier Rayne case, but she couldn't lose sight of Martin Dowell. Somehow she had to juggle both cases. "Look, I'm going to stop by the paper first. See you at the police station?"

"I'll be the one with bells on," he said.

The newsroom was Saturday quiet when she walked in. The lifestyle-section writers had already finished and gone. She could hear the sports guys down the hall yelling at some basketball game. No other reporters would be expected in. The Sunday paper was mostly written on Friday, except for crime.

Baxter was sitting at her old desk underneath the three wall-mounted televisions. All the screens were blank, and she was staring at her computer, a silver pen held absently in one hand.

"Did Miles call you?" she asked.

"Press conference at five." Harper perched on top of a nearby desk, feet dangling. Baxter looked up inquiringly.

"I talked to the next-door neighbor," Harper said. "She told me Xavier and Cara 'fought like cats.' And that's a quote."

Baxter's nose wrinkled. "If we use that I'll have the chief of police on my doorstep on Sunday morning screaming at me."

"Yeah, but then I talked to Hunter and Cara." Harper prepared to drop the bombshell. "They verified that Xavier and Cara broke up the night he died. Cara said she broke up with him because he cheated on her. She was going to fly back to LA in the morning and never come back to Savannah again. Except someone murdered him before she got that chance."

Baxter looked astounded. "They told you this on the record?"

"Oh yes."

"My God. Haven't they got any sense at all?" The editor threw the pen down. "You need to talk to your detectives. Tell them what the girlfriend told you. Get a comment. Then we can go with, 'Police are looking into reports of a domestic disturbance at Rayne's house the night he was killed.'"

"You got it," Harper said. "I'll grab someone after the press conference."

The phone in her pocket began to ring. She answered it without getting off the desk.

"McClain."

"Ah, Harper," a male voice drawled. "I've missed the dulcet tone of your gracious hellos."

She knew that sardonic, amused tone, but for a second she couldn't place it.

"That's sweet but I'm busy," she said. "Get to the point."

He chuckled. "There was a time, Harper, when you were more deferential to me."

The second he laughed she knew who she was talking to. "Hang on," she said into the phone. Jumping down, she hurried down the hallway, beyond the break room with its smell of scorched coffee, and out onto the back staircase. Only when the door closed behind her did she speak again.

"Dells?" Her voice echoed off the scuffed white walls. "Is that you?"

"The very same. I've got to say it's nice to hear your voice again, even when you're snarling at me."

Paul Dells had been managing editor until six months ago, when he was fired for refusing to lay off staff. Rumor had it he'd left town—gone up to Charlotte to run a business magazine. Harper had assumed he was out of her life forever.

"Yours too." She found herself smiling. "Are you in town?"

"I am—that's why I'm calling. I have something I'd like to talk with you about. But not on the phone. I have a . . . proposition to make."

His choice of words sent heat to Harper's face. On the night Dells was fired, after a long drinking session, they'd kissed. It hadn't gone any further but that was bad enough.

It was the last time she ever saw him.

"How about we meet for lunch on Monday?" he suggested, before she could think of anything to say. "Do you know The Public?"

"Yes," she said. "I know it."

"Great. Let's meet there at, say, one thirty. I'll explain everything when I see you." He paused before adding, "It's good to talk to you, McClain. It's been too long."

The phone went dead. Harper stayed where she was, thinking.

The two of them had worked well together—too well, some might say. He was driven: a talented editor with an eye for detail. On the last story they'd done together—a complicated murder involving the district attorney's son—they'd taken a lot of chances. He'd pushed her hard, and she'd responded in kind.

It had been a good partnership, and she'd been sorry to see him go.

The kiss had been a fluke—she was certain of that. Ever since, she'd nurtured the faint hope that maybe he'd been too drunk that night to remember it.

I wonder if he's still single. The thought came to her, unbidden. As quickly as it arrived, she batted it away. She wouldn't have even thought it, she told herself, if she hadn't seen Luke the previous night. And if he didn't have a girlfriend.

Besides, it didn't matter whether Dells was single. She wasn't his type. The women he'd brought to the office Christmas parties were always tall, thin, and rich. She didn't match that description.

Turning her wrist, she glanced at her watch and swore under her breath. It was twenty to five. She'd have to run if she was going to make the press conference.

Harper counted nine TV vans in the overflow parking lot as she got out of the Camaro and sprinted through the door of the police head-quarters.

From the front desk, Dwayne Josephs gave her an amused look. "I was wondering when you'd get here," he said. "Got half the reporters in Atlanta here today. Got to have Harper McClain, too."

"Has it started?" she asked, breathless.

"No, they're running late as usual. Should be any second now, though." He pointed to the security door, reaching for the button that would release the lock as she ran across the linoleum floor. "Meeting Room Four," he called after her.

She raced down the hallway, only slowing when she heard the rumble of the crowd and saw a technician struggling to get a tripod through a door. She followed him into the crowded room. She stood at the edge looking for familiar faces. Josh Leonard and Natalie Swanson were in the front row. Miles stood a few feet away, his Canon in one hand.

She waved to get his attention, and he sidestepped over. "Right on time," he teased.

"Any rumors about what's happening?" she asked.

He shook his head. "No one's talking."

Someone waved and she turned to see Jon Graff sitting across the room, watching her with an oily smile. Her lip curled.

A door across the room opened. Blazer walked in first, followed by the deputy chief, then Julie Daltrey and Luke. The lieutenant strode to the microphones. The others arrayed themselves around him. Harper pulled her notepad from her pocket and flipped to a clean page.

"Thank you all for coming today for an update on the investigation into the death of Xavier Rayne." Blazer looked across the room with cold blue eyes. "As most of you know, the body was recovered yesterday evening by a fishing boat, a few miles offshore. It was taken directly to the Chatham County coroner's office. An autopsy is now complete and the initial findings have been made available to us."

Miles crouched in front of him, getting a shot.

Blazer kept his eyes on the back of the room, showing off his sharp jawline at its best angle. "The coroner's investigation found no water in the victim's lungs, indicating that Mr. Rayne died from gunshots or loss of blood before being placed in the ocean."

The crowd murmured.

"The coroner's early estimates are that Mr. Rayne died at some point between midnight and five A.M. on the night he disappeared." He looked straight into the camera for Channel 5 News, which was the closest to him. "At this time, we're appealing to the residents of Tybee Island. If you saw or heard anything on the night in question, please contact the Savannah police or the Tybee Island police immediately. We know there were reports of gunshots that night. Anything you saw or heard could be helpful in catching the killers and bringing them to justice." He shifted his gaze to the audience. "I'll take your questions now."

All the reporters raised their hands at once.

Blazer pointed at Josh Leonard from Channel 5.

Josh held a gray fabric-covered microphone in his hand. "Can you tell us whether you have any suspects at this time?"

Blazer's reply was immediate. "None that I'm willing to talk about." He pointed to an out-of-town reporter nearby. "You in the blue."

"Thank you, Detective. What kind of gun was used in the shooting?"

"We're looking for a twenty-two-caliber handgun," Blazer said.

For ten minutes, he went around the room answering questions, revealing nothing much more than Harper knew already, avoiding every opportunity to identify suspects. She made a few notes—the gun size was new, if nothing else. But she needed to get one of the detectives alone and ask about the fight on the night he'd died.

When the press conference ended, she pushed through the crowd to the door, hoping to grab Blazer or Daltrey before they disappeared in their offices, but Jon Graff stepped in front of her, blocking the way.

"That was interesting, wasn't it?"

Harper gave him an incredulous look. "Why are you talking to me?"

"There's no need to be rude," he chided. "I'm just trying to make pleasant conversation with the locals."

She didn't have time for this. "You know what?" she said. "You need to learn how to write a story without stealing other people's work. Then they might talk to you."

"That's a serious accusation. I hope you can back it up." His smile had a vicious edge.

Her patience snapped. She took an aggressive step toward him, hands balling into fists. "Oh I can back it up, you little piece of—"

"Harper." It was Julie Daltrey's voice. She and Luke walked up together. "You got trouble?"

Before Harper could answer, Luke rounded on Graff, shouldering in front of him. "You need to back off."

"Who is this man?" Daltrey demanded.

Ignoring Luke, Graff turned to her and held out his hand. "I'm Jon Graff from *L.A.B.*"

Daltrey looked at his hand like it was trying to bite her. With a shrug, he dropped it back to his side.

"I do not know what *L.A.B.* is," she told him. "And I don't want to."

Luke towered over him. "You need to be in the meeting room with the rest of the press or out of this building. *Now.*"

Graff didn't budge. He seemed to find the whole scene amusing. "Here you are again, Detective, with Miss McClain. First I see you together in a bar late at night, looking cozy. And now here, where you work. Does your boss approve of all this togetherness?"

Harper shot a sideways glance at Daltrey. The detective's expression didn't flicker. Without a word to Graff, she turned to a uniformed patrol officer who was standing nearby. "Officer, could you escort this member of the press from the building? Please make sure Dwayne knows not to let him in again. His credentials are withdrawn."

"You got it." The tall, heavyset cop stepped next to Luke. The two of them hemmed Graff in.

"Come with me, sir." He made "sir" sound like an insult.

"What are you going to do?" Graff asked Daltrey. "Have me taken to the city limits? You can't stop me reporting."

"You can do whatever you want within the law," Daltrey said. "But come back in this building and I will put you in jail."

Giving in to the inevitable, Graff allowed himself to be guided down the hallway. "This is ridiculous," Harper heard him complain. "I'll want your badge number."

"You can have it outside." The cop pushed open the security door leading to the lobby.

When they were gone, Harper turned to Luke and Daltrey. "Thank you. I'm sorry about that."

"It's not your fault the little creep has a thing for you." Glancing at Daltrey, Luke explained, "He's been harassing Harper since he got to town. I ran him through the system last night. He's got quite a history. Arrests and convictions for trespassing, drunk and disorderly, stalking . . ."

"Let the watch commander know this guy's making a nuisance of himself," Daltrey told him. "Tell him to bring Graff in if he does anything we might construe as illegal." She turned to Harper. "He shows up anywhere he shouldn't be, call my cell."

Harper gave her a grateful look. She didn't like that anyone had to protect her. But it was good having detectives on her side.

Daltrey glanced at her watch. "Well, we better roll. Someone's got to fight all the crime."

"Hey, wait, before you go, I wanted to ask you guys something." Harper followed the two of them as they headed down the hallway. "Do you know anything about Cara and Xavier fighting the night he died? A neighbor told me she heard them."

"Yeah, we know something about that." Daltrey kept it vague, but a slight smile told Harper there was more she wasn't saying.

The other reporters were pouring from the room now, and Harper lowered her voice. "What do you think? I don't think Cara's capable of it. She doesn't seem the type."

Daltrey and Luke exchanged a look. Neither of them replied.

"What?" Harper looked back and forth between them. "What am I missing?"

"The clue's in the bullets," Daltrey explained. "A twenty-two's a woman's gun. Small and light. Easy to shoot."

That's the thing about detectives. They don't care what you do for a living or how pretty you are. They care which gun fits in your hand.

"Doesn't mean she did it," Luke cautioned. "Just means it could have been her. Could have been anyone. A *child* can hold a twenty-two."

"Yeah but, is Cara your main suspect?" Harper pressed. "And if not, who else are you looking at?"

"Now see, this is why I'm always saying you should become a cop," Daltrey told her, amiably. "Because then we could tell you these things. But for now, no comment."

With that, she turned to walk away. Luke followed her a few steps and said something Harper couldn't hear. Daltrey kept going as he turned back.

When he reached Harper, he spoke quietly. "I was going to text you but I thought it would be better to tell you in person."

His expression was serious.

"I made some calls this morning. Martin Dowell got out of prison three weeks ago."

16

Luke's words sent ice through Harper's veins.

"Where is he?" she asked, trying not to panic. "Is he in Atlanta? On parole?"

"I don't know," Luke said. "All they would tell me was he's out. Everyone's tight-lipped about where he's gone." His face was dark. "It doesn't make sense."

"What doesn't make sense?"

"I don't like how secretive everyone's being about this one," he said. "Cops share this stuff with other cops. Always. But nobody will tell me a thing."

Someone called his name from the end of the hall. He lifted his hand in acknowledgment.

Turning back to Harper, he said, "Look, I've got to get going. Hang tight. Let me see if I can find out more. And don't worry too much. The state police will be keeping him close. They know what he's capable of. He'll be monitored."

She mumbled her thanks.

After he'd gone, though, she stood lost in thought. Dowell was out. No one knew where he was. And he wanted to kill her.

Someone jostled her, and she turned to see Josh Leonard from Channel 5 pushing past, a microphone cable draped over his arm.

He shot her a quizzical look. "You just staying here, McClain? Must be nice to have leisurely newspaper deadlines." When she didn't reply, he frowned. "You okay?"

"I'm fine," she told him, curtly, and turned away.

It was nearly six. She didn't have time for any of this. She had work to do.

It took everything Harper had to put her conversation with Luke out of her mind and write the piece on the Xavier Rayne case.

Still, the distraction of knowing Dowell was out there somewhere, of trying to work through everything she didn't know, slowed her down. Baxter grumbled about deadlines and getting her head in the game.

Finally, though, she pulled herself together, and wrote a story that hung Cara Brand out to dry.

Police Investigation Looks at Those Close to Dead Musician
By Harper McClain

Police investigating the murder of Savannah singer-songwriter Xavier Rayne are narrowing their search, focusing on those closest to him, and on his last days alive.

Everyone who lived with Rayne—singer Allegra Hanson, keyboardist Hunter Carlson, and actress Cara Brand—has been questioned.

The large mansion where Rayne lived on Tybee Island was searched by a team of forensics experts late into Friday night. Police declined to state on the record if any evidence was found.

Much attention was clearly focused on Brand, Rayne's girlfriend. Witnesses claimed to hear the two fighting regularly. One described a loud argument on the night Rayne was killed—a fight so loud it woke up neighbors on the quiet lane.

When questioned, Brand admitted the two broke up hours before Rayne's death.

"I was sad to lose him, but it was over," she said. "I was going to leave the next morning but then he disappeared."

Brand swore she never hurt Rayne.

"I would never harm him," she said. "I loved him."

Police confirmed they were aware of these reports, but declined to comment further on the ongoing investigation.

Also Saturday, the coroner issued her autopsy report, which found that Rayne was killed by two gunshots, and was dead before he either fell or was placed in the ocean.

The shots had been fired from a .22 caliber revolver, according to authorities. The gun has not yet been located.

When she'd added more details and polished the article, she sent it to Baxter, who read the first paragraphs with a low admiring whistle. "I guess you're not trying to make friends anymore."

"I guess not." Harper's voice was tense.

She liked Cara. She liked all three of them. And she knew this article would explode in the beautiful, bohemian house like a roadside bomb.

The final spread featured a photo of Xavier and Cara, taken at a party in Los Angeles months before he died. In it, his brown skin and dark hair contrasted strikingly with her pale coloring. His expression was brooding, but she was smiling at the camera, her face so perfect it could have been carved from marble.

The beautiful and the damned.

Harper managed to focus on her work for several hours, but as soon as she was done, Martin Dowell crept back into her mind.

As the hours passed, her mood began to change. By the time she drove back across the marshes to Tybee, her fear had been replaced by a simmering rage.

If she was right, Dowell was responsible for her mother's murder. He might have spent seventeen years in prison for killing someone else, but he hadn't served a single minute for taking her mother's life.

Now, he was out there somewhere. Free.

She'd spent months living in fear. She'd endured years of grief.

Because of *him*.

Her hands tightened on the steering wheel. It was Saturday night and the road to Tybee wasn't quiet, even this late. Several sets of headlights followed her. More came the other way. With so many cars, it was impossible to know if she was being followed.

She almost hoped she was. Right now, if she could get her hands on Dowell she'd tear him to pieces.

When she pulled up in front of the cottage fifteen minutes later, she found lights blazing through the small windows. She stayed in the car long enough to calm herself down. She couldn't unload all of this on Bonnie out of the blue.

When she climbed out of the Camaro, she could hear music. She unlocked the front door and walked in to find the radio blasting. The house smelled so strongly of garlic and oregano it made her stomach growl. She hadn't eaten anything since breakfast.

It was easy enough to locate Bonnie. She was in the kitchen, singing loudly along with Kelly Clarkson.

Her footsteps lost beneath the music, Harper crossed the living room to the kitchen, where Bonnie stood with her back to her, stirring pasta sauce.

"What are you making?" Harper asked.

Bonnie screamed. The wooden spoon she'd been using flew from her hand, leaving a bloodred mark on the ceiling before sailing to the floor by way of the wall. "Jesus Christ on a *unicycle*, Harper." She clutched her chest. "You scared the shit out of me."

Despite everything that had happened in the last twenty-four hours, Harper found herself laughing. "Your face . . ."

"My face?" Bonnie glared at her. "How did you get in so quietly? What are you, a *cat*?"

Wiping tears from her eyes, Harper reached for the radio to turn Clarkson down. "I'm sorry. I didn't mean to scare you." She couldn't remember the last time she'd laughed until she cried. It seemed to loosen something tight in her chest, if only for now. She gestured at the pots on the stove. "What is all this?"

"Dinner." Bonnie beamed. "I'll bet you five dollars you haven't eaten anything since you left the house today."

Bonnie collected the wooden spoon and dropped it in the sink before opening the fridge and pulling out a bottle, which she waggled at Harper enticingly. "Wine, for madam?"

"Oh, yeah, madam will have wine." Harper squeezed past her to get across the tiny kitchen to the cupboard holding glasses. She poured them each a healthy slug and carried it through to the living room.

There was no room for a table in the cottage; they ate with plates resting on their knees.

Harper hadn't realized how hungry she was. She ate steadily and nearly silently, her mind on Martin Dowell. She'd nearly cleared her plate when she remembered she wasn't alone. "God, this is delicious," she said. "Please move in with me."

"I will, if you tell me the truth."

Harper stopped eating. "What?"

Bonnie was holding a glass of wine and watching her. "I want to know what's really going on. I've hardly seen you in weeks and, when I do see you, you're miles away. Something's wrong. Tell me what's up."

Harper didn't want to tell her the truth. She knew she'd take it badly. But she couldn't lie to her. Bonnie knew her better than anyone. She'd see through it.

"It's worse than you can imagine," she said, after a long second.

"I can imagine pretty bad things," Bonnie said.

Harper didn't reply.

Bonnie gathered their empty plates and ferried them to the kitchen. She returned with the wine bottle. "Just tell me," she said, when she'd sat down again.

Harper searched for the right words. "That man," she said, slowly. "The one who called last year. He got in touch again. He told me to look up something called the Southern Mafia. He specifically told me to no- tice who their lawyer was seventeen years ago." Just saying the words made her head throb with tension.

"What the hell is the Southern Mafia?" Bonnie sounded bewildered.

"An organized-crime gang based outside Atlanta." Harper drew a breath. "And their lawyer, as it turns out, was my dad. He forgot to mention this to me for, oh . . . all of my life. The head of this group has killed people—lots of them. And my dad lost a big case for him. Right before my mother was murdered."

Bonnie stared at her, her lips parted in shock.

"And you think . . ." Bonnie's voice trailed off.

"I think he killed my mom," Harper said. "I think my dad knew that from day one and didn't say a word. And now I think that man is com- ing for me."

There was a long silence as Bonnie absorbed this. Then, she leaned forward, resting her forearms on her knees. "You have to get out of here, Harper. Tybee's not far enough. You should leave the state."

"I'm not running again." Harper's rage had returned, in spades. "I'm going to stay right here." She stomped her foot on the wood floor. "And I'm going to kill the man who killed my mother. I'll do it with my bare hands, if I have to."

"You just told me this man killed many people," Bonnie pointed out. "That he's a professional. How would you kill him?"

"I haven't decided yet," Harper said, stubbornly. "He killed my mother with a knife. Maybe I should kill him the same way. That would be poetic justice."

"Yes, it would," Bonnie agreed. "Except he'd shoot you while you were reaching for the blade and then you'd be dead. So maybe not so much justice in the end."

Her cool disapproving tone hit Harper like cold water.

"I understand that you're angry." Bonnie's voice was measured. "And I wish I thought you could kill him. If you're right about him, he deserves to die." She took a breath. "But I don't believe you can. Not if you want to survive."

This only made Harper feel worse. Because if she couldn't kill him, what could she do? After all these years, she finally knew who to blame, and she couldn't do anything about it.

She was going to fail her mother.

She dropped her head into her hands, grief crashing over her like a wave pulling her under.

The sofa shifted. Bonnie moved to sit next to her. "I'm so sorry," she whispered, taking her hand.

"All my life I believed if I just knew the truth about who killed my mother, I'd feel better." Harper lifted her head to look at her. "But I feel so much worse."

"I know." Bonnie smoothed her hair out of her face with cool fingers. "I get it, I really do. But I don't want to lose you. And for the first time, I think I might." Her eyes were bright with tears.

Harper shook her head. "You won't lose me."

"I will," Bonnie said, "if you go out there swinging blind after some gangster. You can't do it, Harper. You're not bulletproof."

"Then tell me what to do," she said, her voice rising. "Because I sure as hell don't know."

Bonnie seemed to be expecting this reaction. Holding Harper's gaze, she said, "You start by calling your dad."

Her words hung in the air between them.

"I never want to talk to him again." Harper leaned away from her. "He lied to me for years."

"I know," Bonnie said. "But he's the one person who knows everything. He knows this mafia guy personally. He knows his weaknesses. He can help you bring him down."

There was logic to this but Harper still wasn't convinced. "My father hates me. Why would he tell me what I need to know?"

"Because you'll give him no choice." An uncharacteristic steely edge entered Bonnie's voice. "I don't know a lot about lawyers, but I know they have rules for corruption. And I have a feeling he's broken all of them. Tell him to talk to you or you'll write every word of this up and put it in the newspaper. He could lose his license." She gave her a fierce look. "I think your dad knows what a good reporter you are. I think you scare him to death. Use that. Get what you need. And then decide how to weaponize that information to bring your mother's murderer to justice."

For a second, Harper was speechless.

"Damn, Bonnie," she said, when she'd found her voice. "I didn't know you could be this ruthless."

She was trying to lighten the mood, but Bonnie didn't smile. Her face was tight with worry. "Whatever happens, don't you dare go after him on your own, Harper McClain. Do you hear me? I will never forgive you if you die."

"I'm not going anywhere," Harper promised, pulling her into a hug.

Even as she said it, though, she wondered if it was true.

Because it suddenly occurred to her that her father might know where she could find Martin Dowell.

17

Just after eight o'clock the next morning, Harper's phone buzzed on the bedside table. She sat up, pushing her hair out of her eyes groggily. Watery light spilled through the slats of her blinds onto Bonnie, asleep on a pallet on the floor, with Zuzu curled up by her feet in a silver-gray circle.

Grabbing the phone before it could wake her, Harper slipped out of bed and padded barefoot down the hall before answering. "McClain."

"You fucking bitch." The voice was furious and had a New York accent.

"Good morning to you, too, whoever you are," she said, yawning.

"Don't you good-morning me, you piece of garbage. I'm going to sue you and that rag you work for until you can't afford to eat. Do you hear me? You are *done*. Your career is *ova*."

The accent, the spitting rage. Suddenly Harper knew who she was talking to.

"Stuart," she said, pleasantly. "I guess you've seen the paper."

"Seen it? I've already sent it to our lawyers. How dare you imply that Cara or any of them had anything to do with Xavier's death?" he demanded. "That's unfounded slander. I'm going to sue you for libel so fast your head'll spin."

"You'll be wasting your money. Nothing in that article is untrue." Her lack of panic seemed to make him angrier.

"Bullshit. You know what you implied," he snarled. "You're all the same. Bunch of vipers. I told them not to talk to you. But they trusted you. And you threw it back in their faces."

There was truth in that, and it stung, but she kept her voice even. "I simply wrote what I was told by the police and the coroner. You have no case."

"Well, your boss will be hearing from my lawyer *today*." He hung up.

With a sigh, Harper headed to the kitchen. There was no way she was getting back to sleep now.

Morning light poured softly through the window above the sink, making all the surfaces gleam. Bonnie had insisted on scrubbing everything before going to bed. Even the mark on the ceiling where the spoon hit it was barely visible.

Before she made a pot of coffee, Harper texted a warning to Baxter.

> Screaming call from Xavier's manager. Says he's going to
> sue us.

She was pouring her first cup when the editor's reply came through.

> Tell him I said bring it.

Yawning, Harper carried her mug out onto the small porch, brushing the leaves off the seat of the whitewashed chair. It was cool but not cold. The breeze helped clear her head.

She and Bonnie had stayed up until after three, talking. By the time she'd gone to bed, Harper knew just what she was going to say to her father when she called him.

As she took a sip of coffee, it occurred to her that she might as well do it now, and get it over with.

Taking her phone from the arm of the chair, she scrolled slowly to his number. Her thumb hovered over his name for a long time.

Gritting her teeth, she pressed the call button.

His phone rang four times before voice mail kicked in. When she heard his familiar voice say, "Hello, this is Peter McClain . . ." her heart twisted.

She cleared her throat, waiting for the beep. When the time came, the words came out too fast and too nervous. "Hey . . . Dad. It's Harper. I need to talk to you about something important. Could you give me a call back as soon as possible? Thanks."

Hanging up with a palpable sense of relief, she dropped the phone on the arm of the chair.

There'd never really been a time when she and her father were close. He had been away working a lot when she was young. His absence had made her relationship with her mother more important. And her death even more wrenching.

In the immediate aftermath of the murder, he'd tried to be a parent to her. He'd rented a house in the suburbs and moved her into it from her grandmother's house outside the city. But it had backfired. The house was miles from Bonnie. Far from her grandmother. At twelve, bereaved and lonely, she'd found herself isolated.

When he tried to introduce her to the paralegal he'd been having an affair with before her mother died, Harper withdrew further. One night when he was working late, she'd called a taxi. She used the money he'd left for a pizza to pay the fare to her grandmother's house.

"I'm never going back," she'd announced, when her grandmother opened the door to find her standing on the porch with a suitcase.

She never lived with her father again. Within months, he'd taken a job in Connecticut, married the paralegal, and moved away. Leaving her an orphan of sorts at thirteen.

After that she was raised by her grandmother, Bonnie's mother, and about half the Savannah police force.

At the time she'd felt sorry for herself that she hadn't had a "normal" family. But, then, other kids didn't get picked up from camp in a patrol car, blue lights flashing. They didn't get to ride on the traffic cops' motorcycles on the way home from school.

The thought made her smile, and she pulled her feet up onto the chair. Her eyes drifted shut. She must have drifted off, because when she opened her eyes, Bonnie was walking out on the porch barefoot with a cup of coffee.

"Christ," Bonnie said, hoarsely, "how late did we stay up?"

Neither of them felt much like cooking, so they walked twenty minutes down the beach to a local joint called The Breakfast Club.

For some reason, the churning ocean didn't feel like Harper's enemy today. She didn't mind the hiss of the waves, or the mournful cries of the seabirds overhead. In fact, looking out at the container ships plowing determinedly through the rough seas was oddly comforting.

The restaurant was packed and they had to wait twenty minutes for a table. They didn't talk much until they were ensconced in a booth and had placed their orders. Even then they avoided serious subjects, focusing instead on Bonnie's work—she had been painting a new collection, and she was excited about it.

"It's mostly little kids dressed as royalty, holding stuffed birds and wearing crowns I make myself," she explained. Seeing Harper's blank face, she pulled out her phone to show her. In the painting, a rosy-cheeked girl stared into the distance, her face expressionless. On her head was a crown of willow branches painted gold. On her arm, she held a small, hooded hawk.

"Where did you find the kids?" Harper asked, scrolling through several photos of similar paintings.

"Friends." Bonnie leaned over to see which one she was looking at. "I just take their pictures holding a stuffed animal and make up the rest."

"These are so striking," Harper marveled. "I like these even more than the angels you did last year."

"They're sure selling better. I've only finished four and I've already sold them. I'm raising my prices. I should have painted kids before. People are throwing money at me. If this keeps up I can stop bartending." Bonnie's eyes were bright with excitement.

Some part of Harper didn't want her to leave the Library. She loved going there after work for a drink and decompression. But it was Bonnie's dream to live off her art and the classes she taught at the art college. And yet, ever since Bonnie had left Savannah when they were teenagers to go to Boston to study, Harper had been secretly afraid that her work would take her away someday.

The thought was melancholy, and she was relieved when a waitress appeared at the table, bearing plates of food, and providing a natural end to that conversation.

An hour later they were walking back down the beach, full of food and talking about where Harper could live if she moved back to the city.

"Is your old place rented out right now?" Bonnie asked, bending over to pick up a pale clamshell.

"Must be." Even as she said it, though, Harper hoped she was wrong. Ever since Myra had reminded her she'd have to move out soon, she'd let herself dream that she could go back to East Jones Street.

She knew it was a fantasy. The place had to be rented out. The comfort she'd taken from the walk faded, replaced by a churning anxiety that made her regret that last cup of coffee.

The two of them were largely alone on the vast expanse of windswept beach. The gloomy day hadn't enticed many people out. The only other person she could see was a man on a wooden footbridge over the dunes. There was something familiar about him, but she couldn't place it. He was tall, his spine as straight and true as a gun barrel. He had short, graying hair.

She squinted at him, trying to make out his features. It bugged her that she couldn't remember how she knew him. She'd seen him before . . .

Her breath caught in her throat.

Forgetting about Bonnie, she began to run toward him.

"Harper, what the hell?" Bonnie shouted, but she didn't look back.

For a brief moment—fleeting but real—the man caught her eye, and then he turned and walked away, his long stride carrying him quickly across the bridge.

Harper tried to speed up, but her feet sank into the soft sand. It was like running in a dream. "Wait!" she called, but the man kept moving.

Behind her, she could hear Bonnie's labored breathing and occasional curses as she struggled to follow her. The sand grew deeper as they neared the dunes. With every step they sank to the ankle. By the time Harper reached the footbridge she was sweating and breathless.

The man was nowhere to be seen. On the other side, a row of grand houses with tall corner columns and wide, wraparound balconies stood imperiously. It was Admiral's Row.

They must have walked right by it earlier but she hadn't looked up.

A sandy footpath angled past the tall hedges. It was empty as far as Harper could see.

"Harper, what is going *on*?" Bonnie had reached the steps, red-faced and panting.

"It's nothing. I saw someone I have to talk to." Harper was already in motion, hurrying down the ramp on the other side. "I have to find him. Stay here."

The path from the beach to Admiral's Row sloped gently upward. At first it was packed sand, but as it neared the street, it was roughly paved. She passed the curved gate into number 6 without slowing.

Her lungs were burning. Her hair clung to the sweat on her cheeks as she followed the narrow sidewalk between the houses until she emerged into the lane.

There, she stopped so abruptly Bonnie nearly ran into her.

More TV vans had parked at the grassy edge of the short lane. Several had their engines running. One satellite dish was raised, and Harper saw an unfamiliar reporter talking to the camera, holding a microphone to his mouth as he gestured at the white house behind him. Other reporters were standing in a cluster between the vans, talking and looking at their phones.

There was no sign at all of the gray-haired man.

"Who are we looking for?" Bonnie asked, breathlessly.

Harper gave the gathered faces one last, searching look and gave up, turning to her.

"It was him," she said. "The man who called me."

Bonnie's eyebrows drew together. "Which man?"

"The *man*." Harper's voice sharpened with frustration. "The one who told me about Martin Dowell."

Bonnie looked baffled. "How do you even know what he looks like? You've only talked on the phone."

She'd never told Bonnie about that moment outside her apartment last year. She'd never told anyone except Luke.

"I saw him once," she said. "Just for a second. Standing outside my place on Jones Street the day he called me."

Bonnie stared. "Why didn't you tell me this before?"

"I was never certain it was really him. But I just saw the same man again and it can't be a coincidence. He's looking for me." Again she scoured the lane for any sign of him. "He was standing on the footbridge, watching us walk down the beach. We have to find him."

"Okay. . . ." Bonnie still didn't sound entirely convinced, but she was going with it. "What does he look like?"

"He's tall, over six feet. Maybe fifty-five years old. Gray hair. He was wearing a leather jacket." Harper gestured at her shoulders. "He had a mustache . . ." Her voice faded as she tried to recall whether the man she'd just seen really had any facial hair. He'd been too far away, and her view of him too fleeting. Her mind might already be filling in the gaps.

There was no time for this. "Come on," she said, motioning impatiently for Bonnie to follow.

The two of them half ran down the narrow lane. It was nearly midday, but thick clouds held back the February sun, casting the street in gloom.

There was no sign of him as they ran by the nursing home and followed the street around a bend. Here the houses were smaller, with neat gravel driveways beneath huge trees with branches that touched across the road.

Finally, the road ended, intersecting with another winding street lined with bungalows.

Harper turned left and right, uncertain which way to go now. Everything looked perfectly normal. A woman in a long cardigan was walking a Boston terrier. A guy in his twenties jogged past in skintight shorts, eyes hidden behind wraparound sunglasses.

There was no point in going farther. They'd just be randomly searching the island for a man who didn't want to be found.

She'd lost him.

18

Harper stared down the road. "I can't believe I let him get away."

The two of them stood on the sidewalk, as the woman with the dog walked by without giving them a glance.

"Maybe it wasn't him," Bonnie suggested.

Harper thought about what she'd seen—the way the man paused to look at her, the recognition on his face. His smooth, controlled retreat.

"It was him." Swearing under her breath, she kicked the root of an oak tree hard enough to make her foot ache. "I'm sorry to drag you here for nothing."

The two of them turned and trudged back the way they'd come.

"What happened the first time you saw him?" Bonnie gave her a puzzled look.

Slowly at first, and then faster, Harper told her about that day. A killer had come to her door and she'd knocked him unconscious with a baseball bat. Only the police arriving and taking the bat from her had kept him alive.

She'd been standing on the porch, still in shock when she saw the man across the street, eyes as steady as the horizon. Unfazed by what he'd just seen her do.

A tour bus rattled by, blocking him from her sight. When it passed, he'd disappeared. Just like today.

"So much was going on back then, I was never completely certain I hadn't imagined him," she confessed. "Besides, there was no way to make sure it was him—I just felt it. Like I did today."

Bonnie nodded, as if that made perfect sense. "Who do you think he is?"

Harper answered without hesitation. "Someone involved in the case. State police, maybe. Or FBI."

They were passing the nursing home now. She could see the TV vans ahead.

"You'll find him." Bonnie looked thoughtful. "Maybe he didn't want to talk to you today because you weren't alone."

It was a good point. He wasn't exactly an extrovert.

At least now Harper knew he was still alive. Still out there. And closer than she'd realized.

For the first time, Bonnie noticed the TV vans. As she took in the satellite dishes, and the station emblems, she took in a breath. "Oh my God, is this where Xavier Rayne lived?"

Harper tilted her head at number 6. "The one at the end." As she did, she noticed there were three cars parked outside: The old-model Jeep and the convertible sports car had been there every time she'd visited. The third car was a black Toyota Prius. That one she hadn't seen before. Thinking she'd make note of its license number, she felt in her pockets for her notepad, but she'd forgotten to pick one up when she left the house. The absence made her feel naked.

"I need paper," she muttered, mostly to herself.

"You can borrow some of mine." The voice came from behind them.

Jon Graff walked up and held out a battered notebook. She stepped back, instinctively.

"Loved your story this morning," he said. "Couldn't have written it better myself."

Harper fixed him with a look. "Did you steal it line for line again?"

"Only the best parts. You're a little wordy." His smile widened, revealing nicotine-stained teeth. "So, you finally saw through Cara's act."

His approval made her skin crawl.

"I just wrote what I was told by the police and the coroner." Motioning for Bonnie to follow, she shoved past him, trying to get away, but he trotted beside them.

"Stuart must have blown a gasket when he read the front page," he said.

Harper wheeled on him. "None of this is any of your business. Why don't you just go back to LA and leave us in peace?"

Bonnie looked back and forth between them, a puzzled frown creasing her forehead as Graff stepped closer. His worn gray jacket looked rumpled, and he didn't smell all that clean. "You think you're so pure," he said, a jagged edge of malice in his voice. "You think you're a real journalist and I'm a hack. But you're wrong. We're the same. We're both reporters. It's just that you're old journalism. I'm the new wave."

Harper glared at him. "God help us, then."

He didn't back down. "I've been doing my research. Your newspaper's in trouble. Been laying people off. Newspapers like yours don't stand a chance. The world is changing." He snapped his fingers in front of her face. "People want their news fast and they want it exciting. Paper's what they read in school. They want news on their phone. And they want it updated all the time. You can't do that. Not with your big office building downtown. Your bloated staff. Advertising department. Sports department. You look down on me but someday you'll be coming to me for a job," he told her, with satisfaction. "I guarantee it."

"Not as long as any other job in the world exists." Harper said it through gritted teeth.

He wasn't convinced. "You'll wipe tables for a living when you could write?"

"I won't ever work with con artists like you." Motioning for Bonnie to follow, she turned on her heel and strode away. She could hear him laughing but she didn't look back.

"Who was that guy?" Bonnie sputtered. "He's repellent."

"Some tabloid reporter," Harper said, contemptuously. "Nobody."

But Graff's words stung more than she cared to admit. He wasn't wrong about the piece she'd written. It was completely legal but it wasn't fair. There wasn't any real evidence that Cara had anything to do with a murder. She'd written it because she had the information, and because Baxter needed a compelling front page to keep the newspaper's owner happy.

She didn't like what this case was doing to her. Why didn't the police just solve the damn thing?

Then she could focus on finding the man who killed her mother.

Bonnie went home a short while later to prepare for the classes she would teach the next day. Harper had the day off, and spent most of it looking for more information about Martin Dowell. Still, she could find nothing in any newspaper about him being released from prison. And little that she didn't know already about his long list of crimes.

Late that afternoon, Luke texted:

SP tell me they're monitoring Dowell. Ankle bracelet; limited freedom.

Harper knew "SP" would be the state police. This information should have made her feel better, but for some reason, the worried feeling in her chest didn't lift.

After a second, she texted back:

Is he in Atlanta?

His response was instant:

Don't know. No one's talking.

She frowned, turning the phone over in her hand. There were very few circumstances in which police would protect an ex-con in that way. None of them made sense in this case, except one.

She typed:

Is he cooperating with them? Is he a witness?

There was a long pause before he replied:

Can't be. He's too dirty. He's tainted.

Normally, she'd have agreed with him. But she'd been thinking about this all day and nothing else made sense.

I hope you're right,

she wrote back.

I've got a bad feeling about this.

His reply came shortly:

Yeah. I don't feel too good about it either.

She wanted to ask more. To find out what he thought, based on his old days working undercover. For a brief moment she considered calling him, but then put the phone down again. After all, he hadn't called her. That might mean he was with his girlfriend right now.

The thought was a needle jab to her chest.

She didn't have any right to be jealous. After all, she was the one who'd told him she didn't want to try a relationship again.

So why did she feel left behind?

In an attempt to distract herself, she made food she couldn't eat. Poured a glass of wine and didn't drink it. Through it all, her mind kept going back to Martin Dowell, and wondering what he'd offered the police in return for his freedom.

Just after eleven o'clock, her phone finally rang, but it wasn't Luke, calling to throw ideas around.

It was her father.

"I got your message." His voice was clipped, distant. "That was a surprise."

"Yeah, well." Harper lowered herself onto the sofa and made her tone as cold as his. "Sorry to bother you. I won't keep you long. There's just something I need to ask you."

"This rarely goes well," he said dryly.

"I want to ask you about a man named Martin Dowell."

Her father was two thousand miles away but Harper could swear she felt him stop breathing.

All he said, though, was, "I'm not sure I know that name."

How could she have reached this age without knowing what a good liar her father was?

"That's funny, because you were his lawyer for years." Her voice dripped sarcasm. "I would have thought you'd remember. You look so cozy in the pictures."

After an infinitesimal pause, he said, "Harper, what is this about? Get to the point. My family needs me."

Harper flinched. When she spoke again, her voice was ablaze with fury. "This is about whether or not you lied to the police when they interviewed you after Mom died. This is about whether or not you are complicit in her murder. There is no statute of limitations on conspiracy to commit murder in the state of Georgia, as I imagine you know. Or on obstruction of justice in a homicide case. That's what this is about. Now tell me about Martin Dowell. Did he kill my mother?"

"Don't go down this rabbit hole, Harper," her father began, but she cut him off.

"Don't you dare give me advice. You give me answers, or there'll be police knocking on your door with a warrant within forty-eight hours— and you know I can make that happen. Worse, I can make sure everyone knows it happened. So, I suggest you answer my questions right now. After all, your *family* needs you."

In the silence that followed, she could hear his uneven breathing.

"What do you want to know?" His tone had changed. He sounded tired now. Tired and scared.

Harper opened her notebook. "Several months before Mom was murdered, you lost a murder case. It was the first case of his you ever lost. Until then, you were his golden boy. You fought like hell to keep him out of jail, and then you let him get a twenty-year sentence. Did you lose that case on purpose?"

"Your faith in me is heartwarming," he said. "But sometimes even the best lawyers lose."

"Stop lying," she snapped, before he'd even finished speaking. "I read up on the case. There was a witness who was going to provide Dowell with an alibi. The witness didn't show up in court and Dowell was finished. The victim was a known member of his operation. They'd had a falling-out and Dowell had left him a threatening message, saying he'd blow his head off. Then he blew his head off. He didn't know the man had been cooperating with the FBI and his calls were being recorded. Dowell's only hope was an alibi, and for some reason that didn't happen."

"I'm not the one who decides whether or not witnesses show up," her father growled.

"Like hell you're not." Harper said. "Don't underestimate me, Dad. This is what I do. That man, the one who didn't show up, he was never seen again. His family never reported him missing. In fact, his wife and kids are also MIA, which undoubtedly means he's in the federal Witness Protection Program. Now why would that be?"

There was a long silence.

"You just don't give up, do you?" The way her father said it, it didn't sound like a compliment.

"No, I don't," she replied. "So you might as well cooperate."

There was a long silence before he exhaled, audibly.

"You're mostly there, anyway. Dowell was a killer. He'd killed far more people than I ever knew. During the trial, an FBI agent laid it all out for me—everything they had on him. I knew Dowell would come after me if I didn't get him off but I did the right thing. I told the FBI who the witness was, where they could find him. I told them what they'd need to offer him so he wouldn't perjure himself."

Harper wasn't buying his hero act. "It would be nice to think you did it for the right reasons but I'd imagine it had more to do with the FBI laying out all the laws you'd broken. And telling you what their next steps would be if you didn't cooperate."

"Is that everything now, Harper?" Her father's voice had a razor's edge. A warning that he'd hang up and walk away.

"Oh, no. We're nowhere near done yet." She propped her elbows on her knees. "Tell me about Dowell and my mother. Tell me everything you know."

"You were always a stubborn child," he said. "It didn't suit you. As a grown-up it suits you even less. It's made you sour."

Anger flared hot in Harper's chest. "Tell me. Or I swear to God I will ruin you."

"Promises, promises." He sounded almost amused. "Look, it's obvious, isn't it? Martin figured out what had happened. I told the FBI he would. I said there would be consequences. They told me they'd keep me safe. What a joke. They just wanted him in jail."

"Dowell threatened her," Harper guessed.

"He didn't have to." He gave a ragged laugh. "I knew there would be blowback. I assumed it would be me he went for. I waited every day for the bomb to blow when I started the car. For the motorcycle to pull up alongside me and fire through the window. For the truck to come up behind me and push me off the road. I knew I'd die. But Martin knew me better than I thought."

Harper frowned. "What do you mean? Why was killing Mom worse than killing you? You were cheating on her. You didn't love her."

"Come on, Harper," he scoffed. "You're supposed to be the reporter. Figure it out. He set me up. He wanted me to go to prison, just like him. That was his revenge. I'd lose my family, my reputation, my freedom, and I'd end up in a cell next to his. Then he could torture me forever."

Harper froze, as the pieces all fell into place.

"He knew you'd be with your girlfriend that afternoon," she breathed. "She was your only alibi. And he knew the police would suspect you. They always suspect the husband."

"Exactly. That's why he used a knife," he said. "The knife is the weapon of a domestic homicide. A gangster uses a gun." He paused. "Did you know he used one of our kitchen knives? Another clue that it was me."

Harper *had* known that, but she didn't say anything. She waited for the rest.

"When I was arrested, Martin had a basket of flowers sent to my . . . girlfriend." He'd nearly said wife. "The note said, 'Our condolences on Peter's impending life sentence.' It was unsigned, but I knew who it was from. That was Martin's style." His tone was bitter. "He liked a colorful flourish."

Harper cut in. "So, you knew it was him, but you never told the police. You never told the FBI. You never told *me*. You let me spend my life trying to figure this out alone."

"You're alone because you want to be alone." He said it almost casually.

Harper swallowed hard. How could this man be her father? He was so cruel.

She didn't want to talk to him anymore. But she had one piece left to play in this game.

"Did you know Martin Dowell got out of prison three weeks ago?" she asked.

There was a long silence. And then her father began to laugh.

"Oh hell," he said, and it sounded like a sob. "We really are screwed."

"I need to know if you know what he's likely to do now," Harper said.

Instead of an answer, she heard the distinctive sound of liquid pouring into a glass. Her father swallowed before speaking.

"If Martin's out," he said finally, his voice thick, "then he'll come to kill me. Or maybe you. He may want to wipe out the whole family." He took another drink. "He never did like to leave a job unfinished."

It was chilling to hear her father say that in such hopeless tones.

Harper ordered herself to stay focused. She needed to know everything he knew.

"Who will he go after first?" she demanded. "Will he come for me?"

"I don't know," he said wearily. "If Martin's out, it doesn't matter who he goes for first. He'll come for both of us. Either way, my sons are about to lose their father. So, take everything you know to *The New York Times* if you want to. I don't think it matters anymore."

It was clear he was done sharing information. She'd gotten all she could out of him.

"Tell your sons they have all my sympathy," she said. "I know what it feels like to lose a dad."

19

The next day, Harper pulled into Savannah just after noon, driving fast.

She hadn't slept at all last night. As she idled at a long red light, she finished her coffee and threw the empty cup in the back seat. Caffeine was the only thing keeping her going right now.

She wished she didn't have this lunch scheduled with Paul Dells. She was in no mood to talk to her old boss. There was too much happening. Only curiosity stopped her from canceling. She needed to know why he'd been in touch after so many months of silence.

After finding a parking spot not far from the restaurant, she fed the meter all her change, and headed down Liberty Street on foot. But she didn't go straight to the restaurant. Instead, she stopped in front of a grimy building where thick metal bars secured the doors and windows. A sign out front promised cash for gold.

When she opened the door, an alarm gave a shrill warning. In a seat near the register, a burly man with buzz-cut hair glanced up from his newspaper.

The room had a stale scent of sweat and dust. A long counter traced the edges of the small room. Behind it, the walls were covered in guitars, long guns, and tools—anything that could be sold and resold. Under the glass-topped counter were more guns—mostly semiautomatic handguns—and jewelry.

Gold and guns—the merchandise of pawnshops.

"What can I do you for?" the man asked with a smile that didn't reach his eyes.

"I need a gun." It felt strange to say it aloud. But in the long sleepless night, she'd made a few decisions, and this was one of them.

His expression didn't change. "Hunting gun?" he asked.

"Handgun," she said. "Something small, light, and accurate."

He didn't move. "You got a Georgia carry license?"

She shook her head. "It's for home protection."

He nodded as if that simple, four-word sentence answered every reasonable question, and rose to his feet. "We keep our ladies' guns in this cabinet over here." He motioned to his left.

Pulling a jangle of keys from his pocket, he unlocked the back of the display case. Harper approached cautiously.

Fifteen guns were set out in the long cabinet against a grubby suede base. They came in all shapes and sizes, from long, sleek automatics to short, rounded revolvers, and tiny, snub-nosed pistols no bigger than the palm of her hand. One was garish pink. The rest were silver or coal black, oiled to a glossy sheen.

He stood back, letting her look. "Which one takes your fancy?"

Harper didn't like any of them. For as long as she could remember, the cops had been after her to get a gun. She'd always refused. "I'd shoot my foot off," she explained whenever the subject came up.

The truth was, she didn't like guns. She spent her nights walking through the aftermath of people underestimating the power of a bullet, trying not to get the residue of their mistakes on her shoes.

She'd never wanted one because she knew all too well what a pistol could do. Which was precisely why she needed one now.

"What's most accurate—a nine-millimeter?" she asked, bending over the cabinet, the astringent smell of gun oil cutting the dust that tickled her nose.

"They're all fine at close range." He pointed at a revolver. "Nothing wrong with a snub-nose, but they're heavy as a brick and hard little suckers to aim." Holding up his fist with his index finger extended, he explained, "You move when you breathe. With a short little barrel like that a fraction of an inch is enough to screw up your shot if the guy ain't right in your face. You end up blowing a branch off a tree, instead of whatever you were aimin' for." Warming to the topic, he gestured at the longer-barreled automatics. "Nine-millimeter's lighter and the aim's good, but there's more to remember before you shoot and they're bulky as hell. Some people don't think they stop a shooter as well as a revolver, although I'm not in that camp." He stepped back, hands behind his back. "Depends on what you need it for."

This was not Harper's area of expertise. All the guns looked equally deadly to her.

She glanced up at him. "If someone was threatening your girlfriend— someone well armed, who'd killed before—which one would you choose for her?"

He gave her such a long assessing look that for a second, she thought he'd refuse to answer. But then he leaned over and slid the back of the cabinet open. He pulled out a black weapon with a squared-off muzzle, tilting his hand so she could see it better. "I'd get her this Glock, no question."

He twisted and turned it in the light as if it were a diamond necklace. "Lighter to hold, got a small grip. Great accuracy. Soft trigger." He flipped it over with the practiced ease of a gunslinger and held it out to her. "Take it for a spin."

Tentatively, she lifted it from his hand. It was not as heavy as she'd expected but it had a nice solidity. It fit in her hand as if it were made for her: her fingers fell comfortably into the grooves on the grip. Turning sideways, she pointed it at the wall on the far side of the room, and stared down the sights.

She dropped the gun to her side and handed it back, grip first. "How much?"

His eyes narrowed. "You got cash?"

She nodded. She'd emptied her bank account on her way in this morning.

He turned the gun, studying it as if it would provide him with the figure. Finally, he glanced up at her. "I'd take four hundred for it."

It was a good price.

"You'll throw in some bullets?" she asked.

He gave a somber nod. "I reckon I could spare a few."

Harper pulled out her wallet. "A few is all I need."

Setting the gun down, he picked up a stack of forms and slid them across to her.

"Just got to do the paperwork first. Uncle Sam's got his rules."

Twenty minutes later, Harper walked out of the pawnshop with the gun tucked at the bottom of her shoulder bag, along with a small box of bullets and a shoulder holster similar to the ones detectives wore under their suit jackets. While they waited for her background check to go through, they'd both abandoned the myth that she wouldn't be carrying the weapon illegally. He didn't seem to mind. But when she'd packed everything up and was heading for the door, he'd stopped her.

"You asked what I would tell my girlfriend if someone was coming for her." He gave her a measured look. "I'd tell her to go for the head or the heart. It's the only way to know for sure you'll stop him. Don't pick up that Glock unless you're ready to kill."

It was nothing she hadn't thought of already. Still, his words were sobering, and as she walked through the lunchtime crowds, she was overly aware of the gun in her purse. She felt convinced everyone must know it was there. It was so heavy and obvious. By the time she walked into the restaurant a few minutes later, nervous sweat beaded her brow.

The Public was a trendy lunch spot for local office workers, and the main dining room was packed. Harper couldn't see Dells anywhere. When she gave his name to the guy at the door, he immediately directed her up the stairs.

The building was sleekly furnished with spare, dark wood tables and slim chairs. She spotted Dells at the far end of the room. His head was bent over his phone, his high forehead creased. The navy suit he wore looked like it would be soft to the touch. His crisp white shirt set off the tan he sure hadn't gotten around Savannah lately.

"Sorry I'm late," she said, when she reached the table.

"You're forgiven." He stood up, a smile spreading across his face. He looked as good as she remembered—all high cheekbones and sharp, knowing eyes. He took off his frameless glasses before holding out his hand to shake hers. "Sit down. Let's have some food."

"Good, I'm starving." Harper sat across from him and dropped the bag to the floor. It hit with a heavy thud and she froze, her stomach flipping. But no bang followed.

Dells didn't seem to notice. "I've got to admit, I did wonder if you'd show up." As he spoke, he motioned for the waiter, who appeared at her shoulder seconds later to pour water into one glass and wine into another. "I hope white wine's okay?"

She never drank wine during the day, but she nodded. "I had to come," she said. "I need to know what happened. You disappeared for months." She cocked her head, looking at him. "Wherever you been, it worked. You look good."

It was true. He looked rested. She didn't know exactly how old he was, but she guessed early forties. He had good bone structure—a clean jaw and narrow nose. With the suit, and styled hair, the whole picture was that of a successful business executive.

In other words, not her type at all. And yet she'd never forgotten that kiss.

"You look great, too." He leaned forward, looking at her critically. "You also look tired. What's been happening at the paper?"

"Why do I think you already know?"

He smiled. "Well, I gather MaryAnne Charlton hasn't backed down about funding cuts. Emma's working unpaid overtime, as are you. Everyone's exhausted by the pace, and three people have quit in the last few months. Only one of them was replaced."

"You make it sound like so much fun," she said.

Laughing, he motioned for the waiter. "Let's order," he suggested. "Then we can talk."

The menu was all wedge salads and sandwiches with cranberries on them. Wrinkling her nose, she looked up at him. "Cranberry sandwiches?"

"Have the shrimp and grits," he told her. "It's a crowd-pleaser."

"Fine." She handed the menu to the waiter.

"I'll have the same." Dells handed his menu to him. "Bring us some olives to start, and a green salad."

With a nod, the waiter disappeared.

"So." Harper took a sip of wine. "What's this all about?"

"I'd like to offer you a job."

Harper choked. "Wait . . ." she said, coughing. "What? Where?"

"At Channel Five."

Her coughing attack subsiding, she stared at him. "You can't be serious."

"I am very serious. I've taken over as head of news. That's why I'm back in town. I want you to leave the paper and come work for me." He seemed to be enjoying this.

"But *how*?" She was bewildered. "I don't know anything about TV. I'm a newspaper reporter."

He waved that away. "A reporter is a reporter. I could list twenty famous television journalists who started out in print."

It was true but Harper had never imagined herself in that group. "What would I cover?"

"Exactly what you're covering now. Cops on the late shift—four to midnight. The only difference would be, instead of doing it for the paper you'd do it for Channel Five."

"Isn't that Josh Leonard's beat?" she asked. "What would he do?"

"Oh, don't worry about Josh. He'd sacrifice a testicle to move to the anchor desk. He'll be thrilled if someone takes over crime." He angled forward, holding her gaze. "Look, Harper, you're the best crime reporter I've ever worked with. We make a great team. I want you with me." He paused before delivering the kicker. "I will increase your salary by twenty-five percent."

She opened her mouth to reply and then closed it again. Twenty-five percent. That was a huge amount of money.

Money for a deposit on a new apartment. To replenish the savings she'd just drained to buy a handgun.

She was tempted. Dells was right: They did work well together. He was a ruthless editor, very certain of what he wanted from each reporter. His instructions were clear and inviolable. But he also listened. When they'd worked together on the story about the district attorney's son last year, he'd had faith in her theories, and fought to publish a story the owner wanted to quash. In the end, he'd been fired because he refused to let the owner lay off more workers. He was loyal.

The waiter appeared with a dish of olives, and his presence gave her an excuse to stay silent as she thought through her options. In truth, she'd never considered doing anything other than working for a newspaper. It was the job she'd wanted from the moment she first discovered journalism at Savannah State. From the very beginning, she'd fallen in love with the work. The pressure of a deadline that made it hard to think about anything except getting the story, the rush from knowing things nobody else knew.

But standing in front of a camera. Could she do that? She got along well with the TV reporters in town, but she didn't always feel like they were doing the same job. She worked sources at the police station, got down and gritty at homicide scenes. She never thought about how she looked.

Natalie Swanson, Channel 12's reporter, wore an inch of makeup all the time and her hair was styled and sprayed into an immobile helmet. She'd told Harper once that although she ran around crime scenes nightly, "I think half the viewers only watch to see if I've gained five pounds. I won't give them the satisfaction."

And Josh, who wore nearly as much makeup as Natalie, was a good reporter. But all anyone thought about was his tie, his hair. His miraculously white teeth.

The camera was a distraction. It made appearance the most important thing. The story came second. The *news* came second.

"I don't know what to say," she said, when the waiter was gone again and her silence was becoming awkward. "I never thought about working in television."

"You could do it," he said confidently. "You've got the voice and the looks." He gestured at her head. "That red hair would be a knockout if we styled you up a bit."

There was a pause.

"That's the thing," she said quietly. "I don't want to be styled up."

He leaned back in his chair. "Come on, Harper. It's not an insult. TV reporters have a certain look. Everyone gets a makeover when they first start. It's part of the deal. It takes a couple of hours. You get a budget for some clothes we help you pick out, and that's it."

Harper thought of Natalie's bright yellow suit and her fake eyelashes, and her dreams of a twenty-five percent raise began to evaporate.

"Paul." She used his first name and saw him clock it. "Thank you for this offer. I'm honored that you thought of me. And I would love to work with you again. I just don't think I'm cut out for TV."

Seeing that he was formulating more arguments, she held up one hand to stop him.

"I know what you're going to say and you're right. Technically, I could do it. I could learn how to stand and what to wear. I could go to crime scenes and try to keep my hair perfect and my weight perfect and smile so my cheekbones looked higher, all while a body lies on the sidewalk behind me. But I don't want to. Can you understand that?" She searched his face. "I'm not that kind of a reporter and I never will be. I don't want to be recognized, or sign autographs, or get hate mail because someone doesn't like my face. I just want to go out every night and write what I see. That's all I ever wanted to do."

For a long second he held her gaze. A faint smile lifted the corners of his lips. "That's what I thought you'd say." He picked up the wine bottle and poured more in their glasses. "Josh is going to be disappointed. He's sick to death of covering cops."

"At least he gets to keep his testicles." Harper reached for her glass.

Dells snorted a laugh. "Look, I want to work with you," he said, growing serious again. "I meant every word I said. But I understand."

"No hard feelings?"

His smile was genuine. "None."

The waiter approached with a tray of food, and they fell silent again as he worked. Harper looked around, surprised to note that the other tables in the dining room had emptied while they'd been talking.

Dells waited impatiently for the waiter to leave.

"I think it's the right decision but I'm disappointed—I'm not going to pretend I'm not." He speared a shrimp. "Harper, the newspaper is in real trouble."

"I know," she said, trying the grits. The garlic smell of the shrimp was making her mouth water.

"No, you don't." A warning note entered his voice. "It's worse than you know. She's nearly bankrupt."

"Who, Charlton?" Her fork hovering in midair, Harper stared at him. "She can't be bankrupt. You told me she bought a villa in the Caribbean."

"She did," he said. "And an apartment in Manhattan, and several businesses in Atlanta, and a house on St. Simons Island. Along with half of Chanel's winter line. Money runs through her hands like water, and the board has been too weak to stop her. That's why she keeps laying people off." He paused. "There's a rumor going around that she's putting the paper on the market."

Harper set her fork down with a clatter. "I don't believe you. It's been in her family for decades. Her great-grandfather started it."

"And MaryAnne destroyed it," Dells said.

Harper stared at him as her mind ran through a series of possibilities. "Who buys newspaper companies these days?" she asked finally.

He paused before replying. "Nobody good."

They exchanged a gloomy look. Then Dells gestured at her plate. "Eat your food," he ordered. "Now that I've ruined your appetite."

"No kidding."

She popped a shrimp in her mouth. It was delicious—rich and buttery—but he was right. Her appetite was shot. Still, she made herself eat. She'd managed about half her plate when he smiled at her as if she'd done something funny.

"What?" she said, touching her chin in case there was food on it.

"Nothing," he said, but he kept smiling.

"Really, *what*?"

"I was just wondering," he said, "whatever happened with that guy you were waiting for."

She didn't need to ask what guy he was talking about. She'd told him about Luke. That it wasn't working out, but that it didn't feel right kissing someone else yet.

"Last time I checked he was dating someone." She kept her tone light.

Dells took a deliberate sip of wine, setting the glass down carefully. "Well, he's an idiot."

The two of them exchanged a smile.

He straightened his neatly folded napkin. "What about you? Are you still waiting for him?"

Harper thought about how nice it had felt being with Luke at the bar the other night—the way he'd wanted to defend her—and looked down to where the tines of her fork made straight lines through the snowy grits on her plate.

"Not anymore," she said, hoping it was true.

"Well, since you refuse to work for me, is there any chance you'd go out with me?"

Her head jerked up. He was watching her with a curious mixture of tension and amusement.

"What, like a *date*?" she asked, surprised out of any subtlety.

"Exactly like a date, actually. I'd like to go for a drink with you."

It was so ridiculous. A killer was hunting her. She'd just learned that her father was at least partly responsible for her mother's murder. There was a nine-millimeter semiautomatic handgun in her bag. And Paul Dells was asking her out on a date.

She fought back a sudden delirious desire to laugh. None of it was funny.

"I'm not your type," she insisted, and his eyebrows rose.

"How do you know what my type is?"

"Oh, come on." Setting her fork down, she folded her arms. "I saw the women you brought to office parties when you were at the paper. They were all very pretty and very . . ."

". . . shallow?" he finished for her.

She lifted one shoulder in response.

"Look, Harper," he said, "I've lived in this town for ten years and never dated anyone seriously." He was watching her so steadily it was making her nervous. "I enjoy spending time with you. You're smart. You're funny. You don't put up with any bullshit. I need that in my life. If you're not going to work for me, and you have no objection, I'd like to take you out for a drink."

Harper searched his face for deception, but he seemed to really mean it. She thought about all the things she could say. Then she thought about Luke, going home to someone every night while she went back to her empty house. To her cat. And she heard herself say, "Sure. Why not?"

His face brightened just enough that she could see he hadn't been certain of her answer. "How about tomorrow night?"

"I can't. I'm working."

"I know," he said patiently. "I meant after you get off. We could go back to that bar around the corner from the paper." He tilted his head. "You remember the one I'm talking about?"

The way he looked at her made her insides soften.

"I remember it," she said. "But you know what my job's like. I might get tied up."

"I don't mind waiting."

He smiled then, and she found herself smiling back. She didn't know what was wrong with her. Why was this happening now, when her life was spinning out of control?

But there wasn't any point in asking questions like that. It was time to move on from Luke. That was the past. The man sitting in front of her was good-looking, successful, charming, and interested.

If she was still alive tomorrow, she'd have a drink with Paul Dells after work.

That was all she could say for certain.

20

After Harper left the restaurant, she barely made it back to the car before Baxter called.

"Where are you?" the editor demanded.

Harper wondered with a flash of panic if Baxter somehow knew she'd been meeting with her ex-boss.

"In the city," she said, vaguely.

"I need you to come in to work. Nobody can get anywhere with the Rayne case and it's dying on us. We need something today."

Mondays were Harper's day off but she'd been expecting this.

"No problem. I'll run by the cop shop and see what I can find out." Harper pulled her scanner out of her bag and set it in the dashboard holder. Glancing in her rearview mirror, she saw one of Savannah's infamous parking-enforcement officers working his way down the street toward her. Hurriedly, she started the engine and pulled out into Bull Street traffic.

The sun was bright overhead, the day was warm for February. In its holder, the scanner crackled. If it weren't for absolutely everything else, this could be a normal day. But there was a gun in the bag on the seat beside her and nothing was normal.

Five minutes later, she pulled open the heavy, bulletproof door at the Savannah police headquarters. At the front desk, Darlene shook her finger at her. "Girl, go home. It's your day off."

"Tell me about it." Harper grimaced. "Boss says work."

The room, which had been freezing last week, was stifling.

"They finally fixed the heater?" she guessed.

"Soon as the weather got warm again." Darlene's tone was condemning. "You couldn't make this stuff up." She leaned her elbows on the counter. "What do you need?"

"Is Luke Walker in? I've got some questions about that Tybee floater."

"I saw him earlier. You want me to check?"

"Yes. Oh, and if he's there, would you ask him to come down?" Harper couldn't face a roomful of detectives right now.

"Sure thing." Darlene picked up the phone and dialed quickly. As she waited for someone to answer, she confided, "Sometimes detectives don't pick up. They think they're too impor—Oh hello, Detective." Her tone grew abruptly sweeter and she gave Harper a comic look. "Is Luke Walker around? Would you tell him he's got a visitor in the lobby? Thank you."

Harper waited by the door. She knew if she was purely doing what she'd promised Baxter, she would have gone upstairs looking for Daltrey. But there was more going on in her world right now than Xavier Rayne, and that was why she'd sought out Luke instead, right after her lunch with Dells.

That, at least, was what she was telling herself when the security door opened a few minutes later and Luke strode through it.

"I thought it might be you," he said, when he reached her, his voice low. "What do you need?"

"Do you have a second to talk?" Harper shot a meaningful glance at Darlene, who was hanging on every word. "Somewhere quiet?"

"My car's outside," he said. He led the way, guiding her across the lot to a small two-door sports car.

Luke started the engine and shifted into gear, motioning for her to talk.

"First I have to ask about Rayne or my editor will kill me," she said.

"There's nothing new," he said, steering into city traffic. "Off the record, we're still looking at the people in that house. But we've got no murder weapon, and they are sticking to their story that he walked out alive, and that's all they know. We've widened our investigation to take in the manager, a couple of enthusiastic fans. But everything points at the people he lived with. Particularly, the girlfriend."

"But you're no closer to an arrest?" she guessed.

He shook his head.

The traffic slowed to a crawl, and he glanced at her, his eyes hidden behind sunglasses. "So, tell me. Why are we really here?"

"I talked to my dad," she told him. "It's worse than we thought."

"How much worse?"

"It's all true. He worked for Martin Dowell. He thinks he's going to try to kill us both. But he's mostly worried about himself." She tried to strip all the emotion from her voice the way a cop would, but a slight tremor betrayed her at the end.

Luke gave a disgusted headshake, and signaled a right turn. "How close was he to Dowell?"

"He said Dowell owned him."

Silently, Luke swung the car into an anonymous parking lot behind a downtown office building, and backed into a shady corner. He killed the engine and removed his sunglasses. His dark blue eyes held hers.

"You better tell me everything."

Quickly, she described the phone call. Saying it all aloud made it clear how bad the situation really was. At the end, she told him the one thing she hadn't admitted to anyone else, "Luke, I'm scared I'm going to die like my mom. Today I bought a gun."

He swore softly. Reaching across the central console, he found her hand and pressed her fingers. "You're not going to die. We'll figure something out."

He'd always been able to convince her of almost anything. This time, though, she wasn't sure she believed him.

"I saw the man—the one who called me," she told him. "Out at Tybee. Near my house."

He looked stunned. "How the hell did he find you?"

"I don't know, but I'm guessing he thinks Dowell's going to find me, and he wants to be close when it happens. Either to save me or kill him.

I don't know which, anymore." A headache had begun to throb behind her eyes, and she rubbed her forehead. "I keep dreaming . . ."

She looked out across the long rows of cars. There were no people around. Just rows of cars glittering black and red and silver in the winter sunlight like jewels.

"I keep dreaming I'm being chased. Every night I dream it. Every time I die."

He studied her face, his hands resting on the wheel. "I think we need to take this to the lieutenant."

"Blazer?" She didn't hide her surprise. "Why?"

"I had a talk with him after I found out Dowell got out of prison. I hinted that he might have had something to do with your mother's murder. At the time, he said he'd need more proof before he could do anything. But if your father's basically admitted he's always known it was Dowell . . ."

Harper swallowed hard. "You think he's really coming for me."

His face had taken on the look it got when things were going badly wrong—his brow creasing, his dark eyes focused on some undefined point in the distance.

"I think it's possible," he said, starting the car. "And if he is, we're going to need help."

Lieutenant Blazer listened in silence as Harper and Luke filled him in.

When they finished, he fixed Harper with an icy look. "We should contact the Connecticut State Police right now and request a warrant for your father's arrest—you know that, right?"

"I know." Her voice was measured. "But I'd appreciate it if you didn't do that. He's not the one trying to kill me."

The three of them were alone in Blazer's office. Harper and Luke sat in the chairs facing the lieutenant's desk as Blazer turned his attention to Luke. "You say you were undercover with what's left of Dowell's group?"

Luke nodded.

"You still got contacts there?"

"It's been nearly three years," Luke said. "Two of the guys I worked with are still in prison. There's one, though." He rubbed his jaw, think-ing. "I'll make some calls."

"Do that," Blazer ordered. "See if you can get anyone to tell you where Dowell is. I'll reach out to some contacts in the Atlanta office. Let them know what we're dealing with here."

He turned his glacial eyes on Harper. "No one from Martin Dowell's group has contacted you directly? You've received no threats?"

"None," she said. "Just this guy, whoever he is."

"We need to find out who your anonymous advisor is," he decided. "I've had just about enough of playing hide-and-seek with him."

"I've always wondered if he was a cop," Harper said. "Ex-cop, maybe."

"Same here." Luke looked at Blazer. "His methods remind me of the feds."

Blazer didn't disagree. "The FBI might have an idea who he is, given Dowell's been on their books for so long. Either way, we've got to put an end to this situation. I don't like having this on my beat." He pointed at Harper. "You need to be careful. How are you protecting yourself?"

"She's bought a gun," Luke said before Harper could reply.

Blazer didn't look surprised. "Is it on you?" he asked Harper.

She nodded. "I just got it today."

He held out his hand. "Let me see it."

Reaching into her bag, Harper retrieved the Glock. Turning it so the barrel pointed down, she held it out to him gingerly.

He took it, angling his body away from them as he pulled back the bolt and peered into the chamber. "Where'd you get it?"

"Pawnshop on Liberty."

He nodded as if this was what he'd expected. "You got a clip?"

Harper fumbled in her bag for the metal bullet clip, nearly dropping it as she handed it over.

He snapped it into place, and pulled the bolt, peering inside. Then he flipped the gun over and held it out to her. "Keep it locked and loaded from now on," the lieutenant ordered. "If you're going to have one keep it close." He gestured at her bag with disapproval. "Purses are a terrible place for a gun. By the time you dig it out of there you're dead."

Harper reached inside and pulled out the mesh strap. "I got this shoulder holster," she said.

"Use it." Assuming the lesson was over, Harper went to tuck the gun back in her bag.

Blazer gave her a withering look. "Use it *now,* McClain."

"Oh." Harper studied the holster doubtfully. There were no instructions.

The two men watched as she took off her jacket, and stuck her arms through the straps.

"That's backwards," Luke told her quietly.

Harper's face flamed. She shrugged the holster off without a word and flipped it over, shoved her arms back through the straps, and snapped it together across her chest. It felt uncomfortable under her arm, but she set her jaw and picked up the gun, carefully inserting it into the holder.

Blazer watched all of this impassively. "How's it feel?"

She glared at him. "Like I've got an explosive rock under my arm."

"You do." He didn't look happy. "And you need to practice with it. Practice pulling it out. Practice shooting." He turned to Luke. "Talk to Darlene. Arrange for her to have a session at the firing range. Today, if possible. Tell them it's on my authority."

"You got it," Luke said.

Blazer turned back to Harper. "I'll pull some strings—get you a permit. I want you ready in case you need to use it." He gave her a hard look. "And do me a favor, McClain. Don't get yourself killed."

21

Harper left the police station with the gun strapped in place. She was halfway to the newspaper before she realized with a sudden sense of horror that everyone in the newsroom would see it as soon as she took her jacket off.

Whatever Blazer thought, however dangerous things were, she couldn't wear a gun at work.

On impulse, she parked the car in Chippewa Square and ran into the Pangaea coffee shop, dashing straight into the small, one-seater bathroom at the back. In the harsh fluorescent light, she slipped off her jacket and looked at herself in the chipped mirror. The black straps holding the gun made her look like a character in a TV crime drama.

Carefully, she unsnapped the strap that held the pistol in place and pulled it out. She held it for a second, feeling the grip, before stuffing it into her bag. The she stopped and rested her hands on the cool porcelain sink, letting her head drop.

Blazer's reaction had scared her. Nothing ever got to him. But he'd seemed genuinely disturbed about Martin Dowell.

How was she going to fight someone like Dowell? She didn't even know how to shoot. Taking a deep breath, she straightened.

"You'll figure it out," she told herself.

But even as she said it, she didn't believe it.

DJ arrived at the paper at the same time she did, and the two of them walked in the building's back door together, Harper clutching an extra-large, black coffee.

"This is good timing. I've just been down to Forsyth Park to talk to some people organizing a vigil for Xavier Rayne," he told her.

Harper glanced at him as they turned in to the stairs. "What are they like?"

"Really earnest art students." He paused. "Actually, a couple of them are super hot. I'm going back later to hold a candle and look as sad as possible."

Despite everything, Harper laughed. "That is disgusting."

He gave a rakish grin. "Hey, I liked Xavier Rayne, too. It's not all fake."

When they reached the newsroom, he paused in the doorway, glancing at her face. "You okay? You look tired."

"I'm fine," she insisted. "Just feeling a bit like a hamster on a wheel, you know?"

"I'm pretty sure that's the first line of my job description," he said.

As soon as they walked into the busy room, Baxter appeared in the doorway of her glass office and motioned for them to join her. "About time you got here, McClain," she said. "What have you got?"

"Basically nothing," Harper admitted. "The cops aren't talking but I don't think they're getting anywhere with the case."

"Well, great," Baxter grumbled. "We'll just change the front page to 'Nothing New Today, Folks!'" She turned to DJ. "Tell me you've got something."

"Rayne's fans are unified in believing the evil girlfriend is a jealous murderess who should be hanged," he reported.

Baxter gave Harper a look. "We should try to get a comment from her. See if she wants to say more."

Talking to Cara was the last thing Harper wanted to do right now, but she didn't argue.

"I'll call her," she said. "But, I don't think she'll talk. Not now."

"I don't want you to think. I want you to call her and humiliate yourself if that's what it takes to get the best quote." Baxter looked at her watch. "I need as much as you can get me by seven for the website."

Standing, DJ headed for his desk. When Harper didn't move, he glanced back at her. "You coming?"

"Two minutes," she told him.

Harper had already decided not to tell Baxter what was going on with Martin Dowell. It would muddy the water at work, and she had enough problems right now. But there was something else she had to confess.

After DJ closed the glass door, Harper turned to Baxter.

"I had lunch with Paul Dells today."

"Oh, really." Baxter's expression grew guarded. "I heard he was back in town."

"He's going to be head of news at Channel Five." Harper paused. "He offered me a job."

Baxter dropped the silver Cross pen she was holding. "I suppose he offered you more money?"

"Twenty-five percent."

"And?" Baxter's tone was frosty.

Harper held up her hands. "And . . . I'm thinking about it."

"Are you now." The editor's tone was dry, but her eyes searched Harper's face with real worry.

"It's a lot of money," Harper pointed out. "I've got to move in three weeks. I'll have to come up with a deposit. And I haven't had a raise in three years."

"No one has," Baxter snapped.

"Look," Harper said. "I don't want to be on TV. But I've got to live. And life isn't cheap."

They held each other's eyes. Baxter looked away first. "I know you're overdue for a raise," she conceded, an edge of frustration in her voice. "It's Charlton that stops anybody making a living here. She squeezes every damn penny to try and get a little more for herself." She picked up her pen again. "I'll do what I can. I've got a little space in the budget to work with. It won't be twenty-five percent. But it'll be something."

Harper shifted in her seat. "You know I hate to ask, right?"

Baxter pointed the pen at her, fiercely. "Don't apologize. A man wouldn't apologize. And you deserve more. This paper lives or dies by your work." She waved her hand. "Now, go write that story."

Harper headed for her desk.

As she left the glass-walled office, Baxter called after her, "And you should get some sleep. You look terrible."

Harper delayed the call to Cara for as long as she could, finding other things to do to fill the time. By six o'clock, though, Baxter was getting impatient.

When she couldn't put it off any longer, she finally picked up her phone. She didn't have Cara's direct number—she was the only person in the house who had never called her. So, after turning on the app that would record the conversation, she dialed Hunter's number.

It rang for so long, she was expecting voice mail by the time he finally answered.

"I can't believe you're calling me." He sounded livid.

"I'm sorry to—" she began, but he didn't let her finish.

"You fucking destroyed us, Harper. Do you know that? That article was the vilest piece of attack journalism I've ever read. You must have balls the size of your head to call me now."

Harper knew better than to defend herself. Instead, she said, "You're right. I went too far."

"Damn straight you did." She could hear his ragged breathing. "Do you understand the damage you caused? You destroyed Cara's *life*. She's been harassed for the last twenty-four hours by the tabloid dickheads. Her career's in the toilet—she's been suspended from the TV series she was supposed to start shooting next month. I mean, my God, Harper. What is wrong with you?"

Harper's throat tightened. She'd secretly hoped a story in the Savannah paper wouldn't reach Cara's bosses in California.

"I am truly sorry if she's suffered because of what I wrote," she said, honestly. "I didn't intend to hurt her."

A moment of frozen silence passed before he asked, "What do you want? Absolution? Because you won't find it here."

She hesitated, bracing herself. "I need to talk to Cara."

He gave a harsh laugh. "You've got to be kidding."

"I'd understand completely if she refused." She kept her voice even. "I'm working on a follow-up story and I wanted to give her the chance to comment. She can say my last story was all lies. She can tell the world I'm the worst writer she's ever known. And I'll put it in the paper."

"Why on earth would she trust you after everything you've done?" His tone was dubious.

"I wouldn't blame her if she told me to go to hell and hung up," Harper said, frankly. "But I am giving her the chance to say whatever she wants." When he didn't respond, she pleaded, "Please, Hunter. Just let her know I'm calling."

"I'll tell her," he said, finally. "But she won't like it."

She heard the sound of movement, and imagined him going down the wide hallway, with its faint smell of spice. Past the elegant dining room. His feet scuffing on the steps as he ran up the sweeping staircase to the airy second floor. Faintly she heard him knocking on a door. The muffled sound of voices. Finally, more footsteps. A door shutting.

And then nothing, for so long she thought he'd hung up. In the silence, she thought she heard the faint sound of breathing.

"Hello?" she asked, tentatively.

"Harper." It was Cara's voice.

Unlike Hunter, she didn't sound angry. She sounded sad.

"Cara, I know I'm the last person on the planet you want to talk to right now."

"Well, you're definitely not who I was hoping to hear from." Harper heard her let out a breath before she continued. "If you think I killed Xavier, you're wrong. Yes, we had problems. Yes, we argued. But my God, I loved him." Her voice quavered. "It's funny, I can't even describe how much I miss him. I sleep with one of his shirts in bed with me just so I can smell him." She paused. "I think I miss his smell most of all. He smelled amazing. Like cinnamon and sandalwood and fresh air. I've never met anyone whose scent alone was enough to . . ." Her voice trailed off. A moment passed before she spoke again. This time, her voice was stronger. "I wanted to marry him. I wanted to spend the rest of my life with him. Someone took that away from me. And to be blamed for it . . . It's the most exquisite pain I can think of. Because it takes away my right to mourn. I don't know if you can understand that. But I hope you can."

Harper rested her head on her hand. "I can," she said, quietly. "I understand completely. And I am truly sorry I hurt you."

There was a pause, and then Cara spoke again.

"Good." She sounded satisfied. "I want you to be sorry. That means there's still hope for you. You can go out there and find the real killer. Because all I'm living for now is seeing that person pay." Steel entered her carefully calibrated voice. "You find that person, Harper. You're a good reporter and I think you can do it. You were wrong about me, but I think you're right about one thing. I think it was somebody close to him. Close to us."

"You do?" Harper couldn't keep the surprise out of her voice.

"It makes sense." Cara talked with steady determination, her voice low. "And if it was someone in this house, then I'm in danger, too. So, you have to figure it out. As fast as you can. I need you to."

This was absolutely not what she'd expected from this call. "Do you think it was Hunter?" she asked.

"I don't know," Cara admitted. "Three days ago I would have called you crazy. But now anything's possible. The police haven't found a single threat from fans. They can't find anyone with a motive. That's why they think it must be me. Because it's always the girlfriend. If it wasn't me . . ."

". . . it had to be one of the others," Harper finished the sentence for her.

"How could it be them, though?" Cara stifled a sob. "Oh God. I'm so scared."

"Is there somewhere else you could go?" Harper asked.

Cara drew a shaky breath. "The police say I can't leave town. I found a place I could rent in Savannah, but Allegra saw me looking at it and she asked a lot of questions. I panicked and made up an excuse—I told her my mom was coming to see me. I'm trapped. I think they're watching me."

There was so much fear in her voice, Harper believed her. This wasn't acting.

Luke had said he was convinced someone in the house was the killer.

If he was right, and Cara was telling the truth, then she really was in danger.

"Listen," she said. "Sit tight. Keep playing along. I'll talk to the detectives, see what I can find out. Do you have their number?"

"Yes," Cara whispered, tearfully.

"If anyone threatens you, call them," Harper ordered. "They will help."

"Okay." Her response was muffled, she was crying in earnest now.

"Text me your number," Harper told her. "I don't want to have to call Hunter if I need to reach you. I'll work as fast as I can."

"Thanks," Cara whispered.

Harper hesitated before saying, "Cara? I'm really sorry about that article."

"I know," the actress said.

22

That evening, Harper paid Cara back. She kept her article short and clean. But she fixed what she'd broken.

Cara Brand Tells Her Side
By Harper McClain and DJ Gonzales

As detectives continue their investigation into the murder of local musician Xavier Rayne, his girlfriend, Cara Brand, spoke of her pain at being included on the list of suspects.

"I wanted to marry Xavier. I wanted to spend the rest of my life with him. Someone took that away from me. And to be blamed for it is the most exquisite pain I can think of. Because it takes away my right to mourn."

Detectives this weekend again verified that their investigation has focused mainly on those who were drinking with Rayne the night he died. That includes

Brand, and the musician's housemates Hunter Carlson, a keyboardist in Rayne's band, and Allegra Hanson, a singer.

All three deny involvement in the shooting death of the charismatic singer/songwriter.

She was filing the story when Luke called. "I got us booked in at the firing range," he told her.

"Oh good." Harper's voice held no enthusiasm. She was starting to regret ever buying that gun.

He didn't seem to notice. "Can you be there at ten tonight?"

She didn't want to go. But he and Blazer were right—she needed to be ready. And being ready meant doing whatever it took to stay alive.

"I'll be there," she told him.

The police firing range was a dingy warehouse-like building at the edge of downtown, in the industrial area near the river. When Harper pulled in, just before ten, the small parking lot was largely empty. A dark sports car she recognized as Luke's was parked near the door. The only other vehicle was a pickup truck in a spot designated for staff.

The door was unlocked. Inside, the front lobby was small and scruffy, with scuffed wood-paneled walls and a few battered chairs. The air held the faint, metallic tang of gunpowder and oil. The rudimentary reception desk, with its myriad notices demanding that officers "BE SAFE—BE AWARE" and warning that "GUNS MUST BE SECURED AT ALL TIMES ON THIS PREMISES," was unmanned.

A single door led from the lobby back into the firing area, and she pushed it open cautiously. The room on the other side was dimly lit.

"Hello?" she called. Her voice echoed back at her.

"Over here, Harper." Luke's voice came from a shadowed corner.

The long, narrow room was barely more than a barn with a concrete floor and metal walls. The acrid smell of recent gunfire was much heavier here. She could taste it on her tongue.

Ahead, she could see two men standing in front of a low counter beyond which lay five separate firing lanes. One was Luke, in jeans and a button-down shirt. The other was a burly man with short, dark hair and a graying beard.

As Harper walked up, Luke gestured at him. "Harper McClain, meet Jerry Lester. He's in charge of things around here."

"Welcome." Jerry held out a meaty hand that all but consumed Harper's. He examined her with piercing eyes. "Trying out a new weapon, I hear?"

"Yes." Her tone was apologetic. "It's just a used Glock."

"Mind if I take a look?"

Setting her bag down on the counter, she wrestled the gun from the depths and held it out to him, with the barrel pointed down.

If Luke noticed she wasn't wearing the gun as Blazer had dictated, he didn't show it. He watched as Jerry checked the pistol with the quick movements of an expert, snapping back the bolt to peer inside, listening as it slid into place. He popped the clip out and then slid it back in before staring down the sights at the targets at the far end of the room.

When he was satisfied, he handed it back. "It's in good shape," he told her. "Someone took care of it."

"You're happy for us to try it out here?" Luke asked.

"Fine with me. Just don't shoot out the lights."

"I'll do my best," Harper promised.

He gave her an approving look and then glanced at Luke. "Well, I better git. You're okay to close up?"

"No problem," Luke said. "I'll bring the keys back in the morning."

There was an easiness between the two men that made Harper think they might be old friends.

Jerry held out a scrap of paper with a number scribbled on it. "Here's the alarm code. Eat it when you're done."

"You got it." Luke folded the paper and tucked it in the pocket of his jeans. "Thanks again for fitting us in."

Jerry grinned. "What Larry Blazer wants, Larry Blazer gets. I abide by that rule and it has kept me gainfully employed for years now." He aimed a warm smile at Harper. "Good luck with that weapon, Miss Mc-Clain. Just do whatever young Walker here tells you to, and you'll be perfectly safe." He turned away and headed for the door, his last words floating back behind him. "Y'all have a good one."

His footsteps faded until, a few seconds later, the clang of the door closing echoed hollowly.

Harper glanced at Luke, who was gathering ear protectors and goggles from a locker.

"I didn't realize the place would be closed."

"Yeah, it was the only way to get it done today. Hold this." Luke handed her a stack of targets, the shape of a man's head and torso at the center.

"Thanks for doing this," she said. "I'm sure you have better places you could be."

He closed the locker. "This is important. You need to be ready."

She followed him to the middle lane, where he set the supplies down on the counter.

"I like Jerry," she said.

A smile flickered across Luke's face. "Yeah. Jerry's good people." He pushed a button, and a used target rattled noisily to them from the end of the lane. He removed the old target from the clip that held it in place, talking as he worked. "I went to school with his kid brother. Jerry's ex-Marine. Served in Iraq. Left the military with distinction."

He held the target up so she could see how the holes were clustered in the center of the head and chest. She wondered if he was the one who'd put those holes there.

"He taught me to shoot. Now I'm teaching you." He replaced the used target with a clean one, then pushed the button and sent the pulley rattling again as it swept the target to the far end of the lane. Once there, it seemed impossibly small.

Harper stared at it doubtfully. "There's no way I'm ever hitting that."

"You might surprise yourself." Luke pointed at the gun, which lay on the metal counter. "Pick up your weapon."

After a momentary hesitation, Harper lifted it, without enthusiasm. He showed her how to do all the things Jerry had just done—remove the bullet clip, check the chamber, ensure it was empty. He made her do it over and over until she could go through the motions with quick assurance.

"Now"—he motioned for her to face the target—"let's look at your stance."

Squaring her shoulders, she lifted the gun, using her left hand to brace her right wrist as she stared down the sights at the tiny target.

"Lower your shoulders—they're up by your ears," Luke advised, pressing down lightly on her upper arms. "Spread your feet wider to give you stability."

He walked around her, looking at her critically. She was conscious of him behind her, looking over her shoulder. He placed his hands on either side of her waist, fingers firm against her body. "Straighten your hips or you'll aim crooked."

He was so close.

Swallowing hard, she did as he instructed.

"Now move your left hand from your wrist and cup it around the bottom of your right hand," he instructed. "It'll give you more support."

Harper tried, awkwardly holding one hand with the other.

"No," he said, "you need to cup it like . . ."

Standing behind her, he slid his hands down her extended arms, until his hands covered her own. His body was pressed against her back. She could feel the warmth of him against her. She had to fight the urge to sink back into his arms. Instead, she stood stiffly, as he lifted her left hand and arranged it around the hand holding the gun.

"The Glock has a powerful kick." His breath stirred her hair. "This will brace you so you don't lose the shot."

When he let go and stepped back, she felt colder.

"Let's try this for real," he said, and for a second she didn't know what he meant. But then he picked up the ear protectors and handed them to her.

Hoping her confusion didn't show in her face, Harper hurriedly set the gun down and slid the headset on.

The ear protectors filtered out most sounds, but she could hear Luke's voice, muffled but clear. "Line yourself up."

Forcing herself to focus, she went through the steps he'd shown her, aligning her hips, spreading her feet, lowering her shoulders, raising her hands with the gun clasped firmly, finger light on the trigger guard.

Slipping on his own ear guards, Luke stepped behind her again.

"I'm going to help you get started." He put his arms around her, holding her hands in his. "Finger on the trigger. Be ready for the kick. Fire when you're ready."

Lining up the sights on the target's chest—because it was bigger than the target's head—Harper peered down the barrel. She could feel Luke's chest moving as he breathed in and out, and she found herself syncing her breath with his.

Goose bumps rose on her arms.

Exhaling slowly, she squeezed the trigger.

A huge bang split the silence. The gun seemed to leap in her hands, but Luke held her steady, barely flinching from the recoil.

"Again," he said, his lips close to her ear.

Harper aimed at the target. Waited until she felt Luke breathe.

She fired.

This time she was ready for the kick. The gun moved, but only a little.

"Again," he ordered.

She aimed and fired.

Dropping his arms, he stepped back. "On your own now."

Harper kept her eyes on the black silhouette. When she pulled the trigger this time, the kick didn't feel as bad. On her own, without Luke's hands covering hers, she was holding the Glock steady.

She fired again and again. Until she heard his voice. "Stop."

Harper lifted her finger from the trigger and looked at him questioningly. The air smelled of hot metal.

"Drop the clip, check the chamber, set down the gun," he instructed. "Go through the steps."

She did as he ordered. The gun was very warm now. When the empty weapon lay on the counter, he recalled the target. Removing it from the holder, he held it up to the light.

About half of her shots had missed the silhouette completely, but the rest hadn't. A few holes were right in the middle of the chest.

"Not bad," Luke said approvingly.

Harper stepped closer to see, her shoulder brushing his. "I can't believe I did that."

"Let's do it again and see if you can get a bit more accuracy," he said. "But this is damn good for a first try. You're a natural."

Warmth spread through her. She was surprised by how much his opinion mattered, and caught off guard by how much she enjoyed shooting. The skill required—keeping her hands steady and her eyes focused—was strangely relaxing.

They went through the same process for another half hour until Luke decided they'd done enough. By then her aim was better. Most of her shots hit the silhouette.

"We can come back in a few days if you want," he told her, as they stacked the gear back in the storage locker. "Get in a bit more practice."

She lifted her head to smile at him. "I'd like that."

Luke's expression grew dark and serious. "I hate that you're going through this. I feel so helpless."

Harper looked for the right words to say but couldn't find them. For a second, neither of them spoke. Moving slowly, as if unable to stop himself, he reached out and caught an errant strand of her hair and let it run between his fingers.

Every part of her felt that touch.

"I'm sorry we blew it," he said quietly, out of nowhere. "I don't think I ever said it before. But you knew, right?"

His unexpected honesty took the air from her lungs.

"I'm sorry, too," she said.

"I always thought we'd find a way to make it work." His voice simmered with suppressed emotion. "It seemed like it *had* to work. We just fit, you and me."

He was so beautiful, she had to clench her hands into fists to stop herself from cupping his face and pulling his lips to hers. She knew exactly where that could go: amazing sex and wishful thinking. Followed by weeks of loneliness.

She couldn't keep making the same mistake.

"But it didn't work," she reminded him. "Every single time we tried, it didn't work. And we both got hurt."

A flash of surprise and hurt in his face. "I know. I wish it wasn't like that."

"It *is* like that, though," Harper said. "It will always be like that as long as you've got your job and I've got mine. The second we even think about getting together everyone figures it out, you take heat at work, and it all falls apart." Her throat tightened. "It hurts too much to go through that."

He looked at her then, with those regretful eyes, and she had to tear her gaze away or she knew she'd ignore everything she'd just said and pull him to her.

"Besides," she said, staring at the targets in the distance, "don't you have a girlfriend now?"

Her words echoed in the long silence that followed before he finally responded. "Yeah."

Hearing him confirm it caught her short. It took her a second to summon enough false enthusiasm to respond, "Well, that's great. Is it someone I know?"

He watched her guardedly. "It's Sarah Blake."

"Oh." It was the only thing she could think of to say.

Sarah was a patrol officer. Young and blond, with a heart-shaped face, a quick wit, and deep dimples. She was smaller than Harper, with the muscular build of a gymnast. All the cops had a thing for her.

Somehow that made it worse.

With effort, she asked, "Is it serious?"

He looked uncomfortable. "Maybe. I don't know." His jaw tightened. "I'm sorry. I don't want to talk about this." He closed the locker hard. The metallic clang echoed in the long room. "We better get out of here."

"Sure." Heat rose to Harper's cheeks.

She shoved the gun into her bag and got her keys out.

Luke's brow furrowed. "Aren't you supposed to be wearing the shoulder holster?"

"I carry it how I want," Harper snapped.

She'd had enough of the gun range. Enough of pretending that she was fine. And that she didn't have endless regrets. She turned and walked quickly across the shadowy shooting room to the dingy lobby. She heard the sound of Luke's footsteps as he followed.

Neither of them spoke as he pulled the piece of paper Jerry had given to him from his pocket and set the alarm and locked the door.

Outside, Harper took a deep breath and stared up at the cloudy night sky. A hazy golden halo encircled the moon.

Ring around the moon—rain tomorrow, she thought, distantly.

When she glanced back, Luke was watching her with a strange, unreadable expression.

"Thanks for the lesson," she said.

"No problem." His tone was as clipped and cool as hers.

There was no point sticking around. No reason to drag this out. Every word between them was salt on their wounds. The best place they could be was away from each other.

She unlocked the Camaro and climbed in, her shoulders stiff. When she put her hands on the wheel, they felt numb.

She didn't know why she was so upset. She'd known—or suspected, at least. And they were through.

It seemed she had let him go with her mind, but not with her heart. Because, this felt like breaking up all over again.

Shifting the car into gear, she drove away without saying good-bye.

Before she pulled out of the parking lot, she allowed herself one glance at the rearview mirror. Luke hadn't moved.

He was standing right where she'd left him, watching her go.

23

After leaving the gun range, Harper couldn't bear to go home. She didn't want to drive through the marshes alone. She didn't want to be in that cottage by herself, thinking about Luke and pretty blond Sarah Blake. She kept hearing the same words over and over.

"Is it serious?"

"Maybe."

Instead of going to Tybee, she drove across town to a little duplex with a sweet front yard, where roses grew over the metal fence.

When she knocked, Bonnie cracked the door, peering out cautiously. She wore pink pajamas and fluffy white slippers that looked like she'd killed two rabbits and stepped into their corpses.

Seeing Harper, she flung the door open.

"Hey!" But her smile faded as she clocked Harper's expression. "Shit. Something happened. You better come in."

Inside it was warm, and all the lights were on. She'd obviously been painting—the room smelled pleasantly of oil paints, and a wet canvas leaned against a wall in the small living room. The painting was of a redheaded child who looked a lot like Harper, dressed in midnight-blue velvet, wearing a crown made of daisies and holding an owl on her arm. It was disturbing and beautiful.

"I like that," Harper said.

"It's going to make me rich," Bonnie predicted.

Her house was a tiny Victorian two-story. Two little bedrooms upstairs, a small living room and kitchen downstairs, with a bathroom at the back. The living room was crowded with furniture draped in bright throws and cushions. A fire had been burning earlier in the hearth: now, glowing embers were all that was left. It looked as though she'd been heading to bed.

"I'm keeping you up," she said, embarrassed. "I should go."

"Don't you dare." Bonnie shoved her gently onto the sofa and headed for the kitchen. "Stay right there. I'm getting wine."

From the kitchen, Harper heard her open the refrigerator and pull out a bottle. "Isn't this your night off?"

"Something like that," Harper said.

Bonnie returned from the kitchen holding two glasses. She handed one to Harper. "I was meaning to call you anyway." Bonnie dropped onto the other end of the sofa. "That gig on Wednesday night at the Library with Allegra Hanson—she didn't cancel. It's going to happen. I double-checked today."

This was a surprise. The last time Harper saw her, Allegra seemed shattered.

"I'll come along," she decided. "Might learn something useful."

"I thought you'd want to." Bonnie studied her face. "Now—what about tonight?"

Harper blinked hard. "Luke's dating a cop named Sarah Blake. She's younger than me. And really cute."

"Oh, hell." Bonnie reached across to squeeze her hand. "He's such an asshole. He really, really is."

"I know." Harper sank into the pink cushions. "At least now I don't have to wonder if Luke found someone else. There is no if."

"Well, it's his loss," Bonnie told her loyally. "That cop, cute or not, she's no Harper McClain."

"Yeah," Harper said, thinking of the way it had felt when he'd put his arms around her. How she'd let herself wish again for the things she couldn't have.

Bonnie was watching her with a worried crinkle between her blue eyes. Harper forced a weak smile. "Now might be a good time to tell you I'm going on a date with my ex-boss."

Bonnie's face lit up. "That's my girl," she said, picking up wine. "Tell Aunt Bonnie everything."

Harper woke just after nine the next morning in Bonnie's rose-colored spare bedroom, with a vague memory of terrible dreams.

The two of them had talked until the bottle of wine was empty. Bonnie had made her eat a sandwich while she told her about Paul Dells. Even though the evening with Luke had made the whole idea of dating Dells seem faintly absurd, it still felt good talking about something that wasn't murder and danger.

Maybe that was why she felt a bit lighter as she showered, helping herself lavishly to Bonnie's floral-scented shampoo, and wrapping up in warm towels. Talking about something so normal made the craziness of her world recede, just for a little while.

"Make coffee," Bonnie called hoarsely from her bedroom as Harper padded downstairs, barefoot. "I've got a class to teach in an hour."

As the coffee brewed and Bonnie showered, Harper dug through her closet, finding a few things to wear that didn't make her look like an artist.

There was only a small mirror in the cottage at Tybee, and when Harper stopped in front of the full-length mirror on the back of Bonnie's bedroom door, she was arrested by her own image.

For as long as she could remember, Bonnie had been one size smaller than she was, but these clothes fit comfortably.

She studied the new angles and edges to her body, running her fingers across the bones of her clavicle—they pushed against her skin in a way they hadn't before. She was paler than she used to be—her freckles stood out against the milky pallor. Her eyes appeared hollow, as if the last few months had drawn some of the life from her.

She tore herself away, hurrying back to the spare room to finish getting ready.

There was little time to chat as Bonnie downed a cup of coffee and ran out without even drying her hair, calling back for Harper to stay as long as she wanted. Deciding to take her up on that, Harper settled on the sofa with a mug and some toast. She texted Myra and asked her to feed Zuzu and let her out.

Once that was done, she began thinking through her situation. Her most immediate problem was finding somewhere to live.

She didn't think she could wait three weeks. Not with everything going on. She wanted out of Tybee. She needed to be back in the city as soon as possible. But where could she go?

She knew coming here last night was a mistake. She'd taken a long route and made sure she wasn't followed, but still. Now, more than ever, she didn't want to involve her best friend in her messed-up life. And she certainly wouldn't move in with her and expose her to danger. She needed somewhere on her own, not too far from the police.

There was one person who might be able to help.

Billy Dupre had been her landlord in Savannah. He knew everyone who owned property in Chatham County. When she called him, he sounded delighted to hear from her.

"How're you doing, Billy?" she asked, holding her coffee in one hand and balancing a notepad on her knee.

"Can't complain, can't complain," he said jovially. "How about yourself? How's your situation?"

"I'm good," she lied. "Things are looking better. It's just . . . Myra's throwing me out."

"Yep." He didn't sound surprised. "Summer starts before Easter for Myra. Got to get that money while she can. You got someplace to go?"

"Actually, I thought I'd check with you. See if you had anything."

A self-made man from a dirt-poor background, Dupre had gotten into the property market in the city more than twenty years ago. He'd started with a duplex—living in one apartment, renting out the other. Gradually, he'd added to his rental portfolio. Now, he owned about ten buildings in Savannah, most in the historic district.

He was a great landlord. And a trusted friend. She didn't want to live anywhere except in one of his places if she could help it. But the news wasn't good.

"I've got nothing right now, *chère*. I got a couple coming up in a few months, though, if you can find a place to see you through until then."

Biting her lip, Harper moved the mug across the coffee table with one finger. "Is Jones Street one of them?"

"I wish it was," he said, gently. "I got a family in your old place right now. A mother and two little babies. She works downtown so it's a good location for them. They've got six months left on their lease. Seem pretty happy there, though, so maybe they'll want to stay longer."

Harper felt gut-punched. She'd known it was crazy to think it might be empty. It was a great apartment in a perfect location. But for some reason she'd thought it would be waiting for her.

"Of course," she made herself say. "But you have other places maybe coming up?"

"I got a gorgeous place on Huntingdon Street coming up in May." Instantly he was enthusiastic again. "Big old building. The apartment's twice the size of Jones Street. Two bedrooms. Lots of light. It's even got a fireplace. It's a little more than your rent was, but it reminds me of Jones Street. Got the same feel. Nice neighbors. You come take a look at it whenever you want."

"Thanks, Billy, I'll do that." She forced a smile into her voice. "It sounds great."

"You'd love it," he assured her. "It'd be a fresh start."

A fresh start. But in two months. What would she do until then?

She knew Bonnie would let her stay if she needed to, but she couldn't. Her presence here could put her best friend in danger. She needed someplace else. Small and hidden.

When she hung up the phone, she sat for a moment, lost in thought. Then she grabbed her jacket and bag, heading for the door. As soon as she was in the car, she called Miles. "I need to pick your brain. Can I come over?"

All he said was, "Bring coffee."

Twenty minutes later, she stood in front of the warehouse apartment building next to the river holding two cardboard coffee cups. She pushed the button for number 12 and looked up at the little camera above the door, holding the cardboard coffee cups high.

The door lock released with a click.

Harper's footsteps echoed as she walked into the cavernous lobby of the converted warehouse, with its angular leather sofas and metal coffee tables. She'd always described its cold, modern décor as "serial-killer chic."

The subtle lighting didn't disguise the security cameras in every corner. There was no reception desk, but the place was remotely monitored and Miles said the security firm was good. Nobody in the building had ever had a break-in. The elevator opened the second she touched the button.

Maybe she could live here for a while, Harper thought, as the elevator rose. Rent a place.

Miles had left his front door ajar and she pushed it open, calling, "It's me."

"In here."

She followed his voice to the kitchen—a masculine space with tall cabinets painted dark gray—and found him sitting at the dining table, a Nikon camera disemboweled on a sheet of white paper in front of him. A police scanner sat on the kitchen countertop next to the toaster, burbling a steady stream of misdemeanors.

Setting the cup of coffee at his elbow, Harper took the chair across from him, observing the tiny metal pieces with interest. "Is this new?"

"I've had it awhile, finally getting to it." He picked up the body and held it up to the light, peering inside with the same air of professional interest Jerry had shown when studying the Glock the night before. "It has a bit of internal damage. But nothing I can't work with."

Buying broken cameras being sold for parts and fixing them was Miles's hobby. Harper had never known a time when he wasn't working on one. He found the work meditative. "It's why my blood pressure's so low," he'd told her long ago. "Some people do yoga. I fix things."

Setting the camera down, he picked up the cup. "What's going on?"

"I need a place to stay in the city," she said. "And soon."

He already knew her history. He listened quietly as she told him the latest in the Martin Dowell case. "Luke and Blazer say the state police refuse to give out his location, or explain why they're refusing," she said, when she'd told him everything.

Miles looked at her over the wire-framed glasses he wore for close work. "Why do they think they're hiding him? It can't be witness protection, can it?"

"It's the only thing we can think of," she said. "If he's cooperating with the police on bringing down his own organization they'd keep his location a secret. But I don't know." She pushed the cup a few inches away. "I just feel like I can't stay out at Tybee anymore. Not with this happening."

He gestured at the living room behind them—it wasn't big, but it had high ceilings and a wide view of the river through the loft windows. "My couch is your bed if you need it for a few nights."

Harper gave him a grateful look. But his apartment wasn't meant for friends to share—the only thing separating the living room from the bedroom was the bookcase where he kept his LP collection. To get to the bathroom, you had to walk through his bedroom. He'd have no privacy.

"You're the best for offering, but I can't crowd you like that. Actually, I was wondering if maybe you could find out if there was a studio apartment for rent in the building. Something small."

"I'll ask around for you. Last time I checked, though, it was fully occupied." He thought for a second. "Could you stay with Bonnie?"

She shook her head. "I don't want her getting caught up in this." Standing, she walked to the window and stood looking out at the muddy water of the river below. "I honestly don't know what to do. I'm trapped."

"Now hang on." He frowned. "You're assuming he's going to get to you, but there's no sign of that. Seems to me, if he could find you he'd have shown up by now. Maybe you should find another place out at Tybee. Lay low until this works itself out."

"But if he does find me out there, I'm miles from a police department that can take him on." The thought of Tom Southby trying to take on Dowell was chilling. "I'd be all alone."

"If Martin Dowell finds you, it doesn't matter where you live." He gave her a level look. "Harper, you can't fight someone like him and expect to win. All you can do is stay the hell out of his way and Tybee's a good place to do that." He picked up the broken camera. "I think you're safer out there. Stay as long as you can."

His words stayed with her long after she'd left to go to work. He had a point. She'd been safe out on the island all these months, but for all she knew that was because Dowell had still been in prison. He was out now.

And there were too many ways to track her down.

Baxter felt the Xavier Rayne story was done for now, and wanted Harper to find new crimes to investigate until someone was arrested. But she kept thinking about that phone call with Cara the night before. It was difficult to know if she was telling the truth, but she'd sounded genuinely scared.

When work fell quiet, and Baxter was away from her desk, Harper dialed Cara's number.

The phone rang six times before her voice mail came on. Harper hung up quickly, leaving no message.

It didn't make sense. If Cara really was afraid to leave the house, why didn't she answer?

A few minutes later, though, her phone rang. Cara's name was on the screen.

Harper snatched it from the desk. "McClain."

"I'm sorry. I couldn't answer when you called. The others were in the room." Her voice was just above a whisper. "They can't know I'm talking to you."

"I just wanted to make sure everything was okay out there," Harper said. "Did you see the article?"

"I did. And thank you." Cara said it with apparently genuine warmth. "It meant a lot to me that you listened."

"Are things any better? This isn't for the paper, by the way," Harper added hastily. "I'm just asking."

"I wish they were," Cara said. "It's just weird out here. I want to leave."

"What's so weird?"

Cara lowered her voice to a whisper. "Hunter doesn't sleep. He just sits in the living room smoking all night. I think he's going crazy. His temper is so quick. He's angry all the time."

Harper could imagine this. He'd been furious last night on the phone.

"What about Allegra?" she asked. "Is she still in denial?"

"I don't know. It's hard to tell what's real with her," Cara said. "She doesn't talk about the investigation at all. She acts like everything is normal. It's so weird. I just want *out*."

Her voice cracked, and she fell silent.

Harper gave her a second to recover and then said, "Do you really think one of them could have killed Xavier?"

There was a long pause before the actress spoke. "No. I can't believe it. They loved him. But who else could it have been?"

Harper turned the newspaper on her desk over, looking at Xavier's fine-boned face.

"Grief makes people act strangely," she said. "Everyone reacts differently to a loss like this."

"I know." Cara exhaled. "And I know I sound paranoid. But they're always watching me. Asking where I'm going. It's not normal—"

Through the phone, Harper heard the sound of knocking.

"Cara? Are you okay?" It was Allegra's high-pitched voice.

Harper heard Cara whisper, "I've got to go."

The line went dead.

After she'd hung up, Harper thought for a second and then, on an impulse, checked the Library Bar's website. Allegra was still listed as performing the next night.

She needed to be there. Someone in that house was lying.

She just didn't know who.

24

Harper was late for her date with Dells.

The bar where they'd agreed to meet was in one of those pricey, anonymous hotels with cold, blue lighting and Sinatra playing through invisible speakers. The kind of place where the staff are discreet, and nobody cares how much you drink as long as you can pay the bill when you're done.

The man at the reception desk nodded politely when she walked in and then looked back at his computer as she made her way to the bar. It was quiet this late on a Tuesday. Most of the tables were empty. Dells was at a table in a corner, looking at something on a tablet.

As if sensing her arrival, he looked up. Instantly, Harper didn't know what to do with her face. Smiling felt weird. Not smiling felt wrong.

His navy suit was perfectly tailored, making the most of his narrow build. His white shirt was crisp. He'd taken off his tie and without it, he looked younger.

But he was still *Dells*.

It was so strange to be on a date with him. For so long he'd been her boss. And she'd been in love with Luke.

Arranging her face into something like a smile, she walked over to join him.

"You did make it," he said. The hint of relief in his tone told her he hadn't been sure she would.

"It was close." She dropped down in the chair next to his without ceremony, hoping to avoid the "do we hug or shake hands" awkwardness. "Triple shooting at eleven thirty."

"Fatalities?"

"If there were I wouldn't be here."

With a smile, he slid a glass of neat Jameson to her and raised his glass of Scotch. "To Savannah's survivors."

"I'll drink to that." She clinked her glass against his.

The sweet, smooth sip of whiskey was just what the doctor ordered. The warmth of it burned the nerves away.

There was a brief silence as they each considered which way to take the conversation. Harper decided to stick with work. It was the safest bet while she was still deciding what she wanted from this night.

"How's Channel Five treating you?"

He arched one eyebrow before replying. "I'm knocking it into shape. It'll be fine."

Before she could ask more work questions, he leaned back in his chair, shifting a little to see her better.

"You look good," he said. "Still too tired. But good."

She didn't think it was true. She was still in Bonnie's clothes, although she had at least brushed her hair and dabbed on a little lipstick. She was conscious that she lacked the gloss of his usual type and, whatever he said, she couldn't really believe that he found her attractive.

"Thanks." She took another sip of courage. "It's been a long couple of weeks."

"You said something like that yesterday." He tilted his head. "What's been going on? It can't just be work. You could cover this Xavier Rayne story with one hand tied behind your back."

"It's nothing," she said, waving her glass. "Just life. You know?"

The thing that had always made Dells a good editor was that he could spot a story a mile away. He had a nose for it. And he always knew when someone was bullshitting him.

He studied her intently then emptied his glass, ice cubes rattling.

"Drink up," he said. "I'll get us another."

He walked to the bar. She watched as he spoke to the bartender and wondered how much to tell him. She trusted his instincts. Editors give better advice than they take. He was someone who might know what she should do.

When he returned he slid a fresh glass in front of her, and took his seat.

"Now," he said, "tell me what's going on."

Still, she hesitated. "It's a long story. Are you sure you want to hear it?"

Instead of replying, he lifted his glass and motioned for her to talk.

She took a deep breath. "You know what happened to my mother, right?"

His eyes darted up to hers, a crease forming above them. "She was murdered when you were a child."

Harper nodded. "And all this time I've been looking for her killer. Now I think I've found him. Which would be great. Except I think he's coming to kill me."

Dells had gone still. His intelligent eyes searched hers. "You're going to need to start at the beginning."

She told him everything. As she talked, Dells listened seriously, never interrupting. When she'd finished, he sat in silence for a moment, and then emptied his drink, setting the glass down with careful deliberation.

"Okay," he said, calmly. "You have to get out of that house. You have to get back in the city. And you have to get somewhere safe."

This was precisely the opposite of what Miles had said earlier that day. Harper couldn't hide her frustration.

"Miles thinks I should stay where I am. You think I should move. The cops don't know what I should do." She set her glass down hard. "Nobody knows anything."

Dells wasn't backing down. "I did a piece on the Southern Mafia years ago when I was based in Atlanta. They are ruthless. If what you're telling me is true—if your father really betrayed Dowell—he will take revenge. And you would do nicely. These guys are psychopaths."

"*I know that.*" Her anger flared suddenly. "You think I'm not scared? I don't sleep. I don't eat. I bought a gun. You think I should be afraid? Well, congratulations. I'm fucking terrified." She stopped for a moment, shocked at her own admission, before repeating it more quietly. "I'm terrified. And I don't know what to do."

To her surprise, Dells didn't argue. Instead, he picked up her hand. "I'm sorry," he said. "I don't mean to make things worse."

He had long, artistic fingers. His skin was warm against hers.

Suddenly, Harper was glad she'd come tonight. Glad that she wasn't alone, trying to deal with this by herself.

"Look," she said, "I agree with you. I think I should get out of there as soon as I can. I just don't know where to go."

"Let me help." Releasing her fingers, he reached for his phone and made a note to himself. "I know people. Maybe someone has an apartment free right now. I'll ask around. And you can always stay with me." He looked up at her. "In fact, why don't you stay with me tonight? Don't go back to Tybee."

Harper held his gaze. Electricity flared between them.

It was tempting. The idea of not having to go all the way back out to the island. To sleep someplace where no one would ever think to look for her.

On the other hand, she knew what would happen if she spent the night in his apartment, and she wasn't ready for that yet. She was still trying to figure out what she wanted.

"Actually," she said, softly, "I think I'll go home tonight. But . . . thank you."

"Well, the offer stays open. I don't like the idea of you out there alone."

There was a protective note in his voice.

This wasn't at all what she'd expected from tonight. Dells wasn't her type. But then, what was her type? Before Luke, she'd gone out with grad students and artists—mostly guys Bonnie set her up with. None of them had worked out.

Besides, she liked the way Dells listened. The way he trusted her judgment. She felt comfortable with him. Maybe the suit didn't matter. Maybe it was just clothes.

On impulse, she leaned forward, took him gently by the collar.

"Thank you," she whispered, and pressed her lips lightly against his.

She felt his quick, surprised breath, and then his hands slid across her shoulders, pulling her to him, as he deepened the kiss, parting her lips with his tongue.

After a second, he pulled back, and looked down into her eyes.

"Where did that come from?" He was breathless, his face flushed.

"Does it matter?" Harper leaned back in her chair, enjoying how flustered she'd made him.

"I'll tell you one thing, Harper McClain," he said. "You never stop surprising me."

They talked for more than an hour. Harper switched to soft drinks while Dells nursed another Scotch.

By the end, they'd agreed that, one way or another, she had to be out of the house by Friday at the latest.

"If you won't come stay with me, stay in a hotel." He'd gestured at the building around them. "This place would do. I'll bet they have space."

When she tried to explain that she'd just spent most of her savings on a gun, and this place probably cost two hundred dollars a night, he'd waved that away. "I'll pay for it. If money's the problem you haven't got a problem."

She'd argued but he was adamant, and by the time they left the bar, she felt better. Things were in motion. As they headed to where she'd left her car, in the lot behind the newspaper building a few blocks away, they walked side by side not touching, but almost.

It was after two in the morning; there were no cars on the street. A cool, damp breeze blew in off the river, but Harper didn't really notice. She was noticing the way his lips curved up just a little when he caught her eye.

When they reached her car, she pulled him to her without hesitation, sliding her hands inside the warmth of his jacket. Raising her lips to his.

Kissing him wasn't like kissing Luke. It was less urgent. Less familiar. But she had to put Luke out of her mind. After all, he was kissing someone else now, too.

The heat of him against her, the feel of his body against hers—she needed it. She needed to be wanted. To be desired.

When Dells lifted his lips from hers and gazed down into her eyes, they were both breathless.

"You're one hundred percent positive there's no way I can talk you into spending the night at my place?" He pressed his forehead lightly against hers. She could smell the smoky scent of Scotch on his breath. "Because I would give almost anything for you to come home with me right now."

She smiled, and shook her head.

She liked Dells, but she needed time. Everything was happening so fast.

Whether she liked it or not, Luke was a constant presence in her mind. Somehow, she needed to let him go before she could really be with someone else.

"I've got a lot to think about," she told him.

She could see in his eyes that he knew this wasn't the whole story. But he didn't pressure her.

"I can wait. I don't want to. But I will."

"Where are you parked?" She pulled out her keys. "I could give you a lift."

He pointed to the far corner of the lot, where an Audi sports car was tucked away in the shadows. "No need. I figured the least MaryAnne Charlton owed me was a free parking space for the night."

Laughing, Harper climbed into the Camaro, rolling down the window before starting the engine.

"I'm going to ask around about an apartment for you. I'll call you tomorrow." He raised his voice to be heard above the sound. "And probably the day after that."

"I'd like that." She put the car in gear.

He stepped back, arms spread. "And my guest room is always waiting."

She was smiling as she drove away.

All the way across the marshes, she tried to imagine being in a relationship with him. Dells had a way of fixing things. He saw a problem and envisioned a solution almost simultaneously.

There was something wonderful about that.

But she also wondered if she would ever stop thinking of him as the guy who used to sign her paychecks.

She was almost to Tybee when a pair of headlights appeared in her rearview mirror.

Her mouth went dry.

She kept her eyes on the lights as she curved through the last stretch of highway, waiting for it to get closer. But then the bridge appeared ahead, the headlights dropped back, and she was safely through.

A few minutes later, she pulled into the driveway of the little cottage, parking under the tree in her usual spot. Overhead, a waning moon cast a pale blue light as she made her way to the front steps.

Zuzu was sitting on the porch, watching her with judgmental green eyes.

"Did Myra feed you?" Harper asked, pausing to stroke her soft back. "Don't worry. I'll never do it again."

She straightened and raised her key to the first of the three locks. That was when he stepped out of the shadows beside the house.

His military posture, broad shoulders, and gray hair were instantly recognizable.

The keys slipped from Harper's nerveless fingers, landing on the front porch with a clatter of metal. Zuzu leapt from the porch and melted into the darkness behind the house.

"You," Harper whispered.

"I thought it was time we met." His voice was deep and authoritative, with no hint of Southern accent. "There are some things we need to talk about."

25

For a moment that seemed to last forever, Harper stood frozen. Around them, the island was sound asleep. Nothing stirred. They were completely alone.

There was a gun in the bag on her shoulder, but she knew if she made a move for it, everything would be over.

Blazer had been right about that holster.

The man stepped into the light. "I think you have some questions for me. Can we go inside?" He held up his hands the way you might try to calm a frightened animal. "I promise I'm not here to hurt you."

His words spurred her to action. Bending swiftly, she swiped the keys from the porch and held them like a weapon. "How do I know that's true?"

"Frankly, Miss McClain, if I wanted to hurt you, I wouldn't be standing here talking," he said, bluntly. "I'd be hurting you." He took another small step. "All I ask is that you give me a chance to explain. Don't notify anyone that I'm here. If you do that I'll have to leave and I will never come back. And you will never have the answers you're looking for."

He spoke calmly and with confidence. Like a cop.

Harper wavered. She desperately needed to hear what he had to say. But she knew nothing about him. Nobody knew this was happening.

In the end, though, there was no question what she would do.

She fumbled with the keys, hoping he couldn't see her hands shaking. "You have to tell me everything this time," she warned. "Or you can just leave now."

"That's what I'm here for," he said.

He kept his distance until the door was open. Only then did he slowly walk up to join her, keeping space between them as Harper turned on the lights and motioned wordlessly for him to sit. Slowly, he lowered himself onto the chair she indicated and sat still, as if trying not to startle her.

He was a tall man—the small living room seemed smaller with him in it. Harper perched stiffly on the sofa across from him. She placed the bag holding the Glock at her feet.

He had a long, angular face with a square, solid jaw. Beneath steel-gray hair, his eyes were steady but gave absolutely nothing away. He didn't take off his dark jacket as he sat there, his long hands folded on top of his thighs.

"Ask your questions," he said.

She cleared her throat nervously before asking, "What do I call you? Can I know your name?"

"You can call me Lee."

"Lee what?" she challenged. "Mr. Lee?"

"Just Lee." His firm tone told her not to push it.

His resistance to revealing his name after all this time made her angry. And anger gave her strength.

"Fine then. Lee," she said, coolly, "do you know why the government is protecting Martin Dowell?"

His answer came without hesitation. "As you've no doubt suspected, he's agreed to cooperate with them on their investigation of the group known as the Southern Mafia. He's given them enough information to convince them he's got more to share. And they are foolish enough to trust him." His tone was contemptuous.

"Why would they believe him?" she asked, bewildered. "He just got out of prison for murder."

"In my experience, everyone underestimates Martin Dowell. They want to believe he's another redneck drug dealer. They all went to West Point or the University of Georgia, and got shiny criminal-justice degrees. No shitkicker's going to play them. And then he plays them." He flexed his hands against his knees. "I've seen it over and over again."

He spoke easily, as if he'd anticipated every question she would ask, but the venom in his voice when he talked about Dowell made her tend to believe him. It's hard to fake hate.

"You know where he is, don't you?"

"I do," he said. "And no, I will not tell you." He looked at her, eyes steady. "My goal is to keep you alive."

She searched his face. "How do you know all of this? Are you a cop?"

For the first time he hesitated, as if deciding how much to tell her. "My interest in Martin Dowell's case goes back as far as yours."

This was the opening she'd been waiting for. She leaned forward. "How did you know my parents? Will you tell me that much, at least?"

He paused. "I'll tell you what I can. But could I trouble you first for a cup of coffee? It's been a hell of a long day."

She wondered if this was some sort of ploy and the minute her back was turned he'd kill her. But as he'd said earlier, if he wanted to hurt her, he'd had his chance. And there was a weariness in the set of his shoulders that suggested he wasn't lying.

"No problem." She stood and headed for the kitchen.

"I take it black," he said.

She glanced over her shoulder. "So do I."

In the tiny kitchen she quickly filled the machine, twisting around periodically to look at him through the open doorway and make sure he wasn't following her. But he never moved.

She was just finishing when he began talking.

"I first met your father when I was a law officer in Atlanta," he said, his deep voice carrying easily across the small house. "I was assigned to investigate organized crime."

Harper turned the machine on and stepped back into the living room, where she stood leaning against the wall as he talked.

"For more than a year I worked to build a case against the Southern Mafia. My primary target was Martin Dowell. I was sure I could prove he'd murdered at least three men, ordered the murders of more, and violated the law in more ways than I could count."

"What happened to your case?" she asked.

"Your father happened to my case." His voice cooled. "Your father's an arrogant man, Miss McClain, but I'd imagine you know that."

"I know that better than most."

"Well, back then, as an up-and-coming criminal defense lawyer, he was worse," he assured her. "He'd won a high-profile case defending a business executive who'd got himself in deep water when a hooker turned up dead. After that, every criminal wanted him on their side. He was good, I'll give him that." He shook his head. "The state attorney hated to come up against him. Law enforcement hated him, too. You'd work half a year putting a case together, and then along would come Peter McClain to rip you to shreds in front of a judge. Make you look like a fool."

"Then he went to work for Martin Dowell," Harper said.

"Dowell sought him out," Lee told her. "He knew how to win anyone over and he had a lot of money. He was smart enough to understand that your father was the one person who might keep him out of jail. We were getting close by then. I imagine he could feel our breath on his back every time he moved. And your dad? Well, he saved him from justice many times."

The frustration of those old cases gave an edge to his voice. It still stung after all these years.

"I don't like my father," Harper told him. "I'm sorry he's like that."

"I know," he said. "That's why I'm here."

Before Harper could reply, the coffeemaker beeped. Tearing herself away, she poured two cups and brought the steaming mugs into the living room, handing one to him. He took it, his dark brown eyes watching her with a look she couldn't fathom.

"Thank you," he said.

He had an oddly formal politeness Harper had encountered before, usually from federal agents.

"You were with the FBI back then, weren't you?"

After a brief pause, he gave a curt nod.

She settled back down across from him. "What happened with your case against Martin Dowell?"

"On that last case, we had a wire in his office. A member of his group was working for us—someone very close to him. But Dowell was too sharp. Too clever. He never talked to anybody except in code. And he constantly had his guys checking on each other. There was no trust in his organization, only suspicion. I don't know why anyone would want to be part of that world, but those men were loyal. Except for our guy. He was the only one we could get to." He took a long sip from his mug. "Dowell had good instincts—the best I've ever seen. He figured out we knew too much. And that meant someone close to him must be betraying him. Eventually, he tricked our guy: gave him false information. When we showed up ready to make the bust, Dowell was innocently watching TV. And now he knew what was going on." His shoulders sagged at the memory. "They beat him to death, our guy," he said softly. "Stuffed his body in a barrel, and threw it in a chemical-waste dump." He gave a slow headshake before continuing, "He went too far that time. With the wire evidence, we had motive, and that was enough to charge him."

"That was the murder where my dad defended him," Harper guessed.

Lee nodded. "That trial was something else. Your father fought like a tiger. Dowell had invented an ironclad alibi with the help of someone who wasn't even part of his organization but who was willing to perjure himself. We were done. We had no physical evidence. No DNA. No prints. All we had was one hell of a motive and Dowell and three of his lieutenants at the scene. Only with this false witness, suddenly we didn't have Dowell there. Instead, he was in a house in the suburbs, having dinner with a friend. The case was over."

He drained his coffee and set the mug down neatly on the coaster. "We'd given up, to be honest. We were going through the paces, knowing we'd lose. Then, out of nowhere, the witness showed up at an FBI field office asking for protection. Said Dowell threatened his family if he didn't lie in court. He told us your father convinced him to tell the truth." He studied her from beneath lowered brows. "With that, Dowell's entire alibi went out the window."

Harper looked down at her coffee cup. It all fit with what her father had told her. For once in his life, he'd done something that wasn't self-serving and venal.

"Why would my dad do that?" she asked, as much of herself as Lee.

"That is a question I'd like to know the answer to. A crisis of conscience?" He made a dismissive gesture. "Your father never struck me as the type."

"But this is where it started, isn't it?" she said. "This is why Dowell killed my mother."

"That is my belief," he said. "On the day he was convicted, Dowell told your father that he would kill his family and then he'd kill him. So, there was a threat. But your father must have believed he was safe, knowing Dowell would be locked in a federal penitentiary for twenty years."

"But Dowell didn't do it himself," Harper guessed. "He got someone else to do it."

Lee nodded. "I believe Martin Dowell orchestrated every step of that murder. Where it should happen. How it should happen. That your father should be implicated." He paused. "Dowell always knew everything about the people who worked closely with him. That's how he kept them cowed. He knew about your father's mistress. He knew what days he visited her apartment. That was another one of his twisted decisions. Another way to punish Peter McClain. In one move he could destroy his family, his reputation, and his career. And he knew if he did it right, the police would look at your father as the killer. Being with his mistress wouldn't save him—a lover is a terrible alibi. We lie for people we love." He drew a breath. "Dowell planned it all."

Harper sagged back in the chair. She could see it all the way Dowell must have seen it—a clean, vicious payback. Except for one thing.

"You say he threatened my dad's whole family," she said. "Why not kill me, too? He's had years."

Lee regarded her somberly. "After your mother's death, you were very close to that homicide detective—Robert Smith. He was a good cop. If you were murdered, he was going to put the pieces together. And Dowell knew if that happened it would get him the death penalty. He didn't dare touch you."

So that was why Dowell never came after her at the paper, even though she was easy to find. Smith had kept her alive just by caring about her.

She blinked hard. "And now?"

"Now your protector is in prison," he said simply, "and your enemy isn't. That's why I called you. I knew this day was coming as soon as I saw he was up for parole. I knew he'd come for you."

"But *why*?" Her voice rose. "How can he still want to do this? Hasn't he had his revenge? Wasn't killing my mother enough?"

"Martin Dowell is a psychopath, with an obsessive personality disorder," Lee told her, calmly. "All this time he's been biding time until he could finish the job. He *has* to finish it. In his mind, you need to die. Then your father needs to die. Then he can pick up the pieces of his drug-dealing empire and get back to work." He paused. "As crazy as it sounds, that is what he's thinking right now."

It was all so damned pointless, Harper thought, numbly. So much loss and pain. All because of two men and an old feud.

Lee rubbed his forehead wearily. He'd finished his coffee. The two of them, forced close together by the nature of the cottage sat in a pool of light. Everything around them was darkness.

Harper was aware that it was after three in the morning. She needed to ask her questions quickly. "What about you?" she said. "Why are you still on this case?"

He looked down at the hands folded loosely on his knees. "I owe your mother." His voice grew softer; filled with self-incrimination. "I knew she was in danger, and I didn't move fast enough. It was a mistake that cost her life." He met her eyes again. "Maybe I'm as obsessive as Martin Dowell, but I need to finish this case. For her."

"You knew my mom?" Harper searched his impassive face. "Outside of work, I mean?"

There was a long silence. Lee looked past her to where an oil painting of a field of daisies in the sunshine leaned against a wall near the kitchen. It was the only one of her mother's paintings she'd brought to Tybee. He studied it with a kind of recognition that inspired a thousand more questions in her mind.

"I guess you could say, I sought her out," he said, finally. "She was innocent in all of this. Maybe the only truly innocent person, aside from you. She trusted your father to do the right thing." He paused, looking down at his hands. "I arranged to meet her several times. First, to get to know her and find out what she knew. And, eventually, to ask for her help."

Harper frowned. "Her help? Doing what?"

He lifted his head. "I asked her to watch your father for me. I told her he was in trouble and that your family was in danger. And I asked her to find out what he was doing."

"You asked her to *spy*?" Her voice went up. "She would never do that."

"No, she wouldn't." He gave a wry smile. "She told me it would be a betrayal. She wasn't wrong about that but I believed at the time—and still believe now—that betraying him in that way, given how he was betraying her, would have been justified." He straightened. "But she couldn't see it. I got angry. Told her she deserved whatever happened to her." His voice faded. "I am still sorry about that."

His words sent a stab of pain into Harper's chest. She could imagine her mother facing this man, being told things she'd never imagined about her husband. Having to refuse to help. Lee had obviously cared about her—there must have been something between them. Attraction, maybe? Or more.

She couldn't imagine her mother ever cheating on her father. But she'd been alone so much, with her father constantly away for work. Who knew what went on? She must have been so lost in those last months. And yet she'd never shown any sign of that to Harper. Her mother had protected her from the chaos her father was creating in their lives until the very end.

I'm so sorry, Mom, she thought, fighting back tears.

Lee gave a quick look at his watch. "I'm afraid I can't stay much longer. But before I leave, I need to be sure you understand what's going to happen now. Whatever the state police believe, whatever lies he's spun for them, it doesn't matter." A new intensity entered his voice. "Martin Dowell is coming for you, Miss McClain. He has a plan. And he's closer than you think."

Harper swallowed hard. "What do you mean by that?"

There was a long pause before he said, "My understanding is he's in Savannah."

"But *how*?" She w..s stunned. Dowell should have been monitored constantly and kept close to where his family lived. That was normal procedure for high-profile parolees.

Why would the police let him choose to wander the state—and worse, provide cover for him?

"It makes little sense to me." The lines on his face were carved deep. "I think the state police have lost their minds. He's convinced them he needs to be in Savannah to see his son. And they've allowed it."

"Why are they listening to him?" She held up her hands. "I don't understand."

"It doesn't matter why." He cut her off, curtly. "All that matters is that he intends to kill you. He will get away from them, and he will track you down." He glanced around the little cottage, eyes narrow. "This is a good place to hide. Using an assumed name to rent it was smart. But the simple truth is, if I can find you, so can he."

"What am I supposed to do?" she asked, helplessly. "Stay here and hide? Go somewhere else and hide? Run across the country and hide?"

She was scared and angry, but Lee didn't flinch.

"My advice is, stay on the move. Find somewhere new to stay every few nights—hotels, rented apartments. Be very careful walking in and out of the office—it's the one place he knows to look for you." He angled his body forward, his eyes holding hers intently. "Whatever you do, don't try to go after him. I am tracking him. I have contacts in the state police who are helping me. I will find him. And I promise you, I will put an end to this."

His voice was stiff with resolve. "I've lived with this guilt for seventeen years. Martin Dowell is not the only one with a score to settle."

26

After Lee left that night, Harper found sleep impossible. All her questions had been answered at last, but the truth was far worse than she'd imagined. She paced the house, going over and over it all in her head. More than anything she wished she could call Lieutenant Smith and ask him what to do. But he was gone. She had to face this on her own.

When she was too tired to keep walking, she pulled out the Glock and set it on the table next to Lee's empty mug. Then she curled up on the sofa with Zuzu beside her and waited for the sun to rise.

When it finally came, the morning was bright and sunny, but the weather reports carried dire predictions of another late-winter storm looming.

"Get those coats back out of the attic," a TV weather reporter warned, perfect teeth flashing white. "Old Man Winter isn't done with us yet."

It was hard to believe, the day was so warm and springlike. When she walked into the Savannah police headquarters late that morning, the sky was a clear, crystalline blue.

At the reception desk, Darlene was flirting with a tall, wiry patrol officer. He gave Harper a curious look as she approached, her scanner held loosely in one hand.

"Your watch must be broken," Darlene decided, surveying her with a smile. "Because this is *too* early."

But Harper was in no mood for banter. "I need five minutes with Blazer," she said. "Is he in?"

Noticing her tone, Darlene grew serious. "Go straight back," she told her. "He's in his office. I'll let him know you're coming."

Harper hurried across the room as the desk officer released the lock on the security door. On the other side, she threaded her way through the morning throng, looking neither left nor right. Blazer was setting down his phone as she walked in.

Harper didn't mince words. "The man—he came to my house last night."

The lieutenant's eyes widened. He motioned for her to sit. "What happened?"

"He wouldn't tell me his full name, but he called himself Lee. He's ex-FBI." She spoke rapidly, rushing to get it all out. "He said Dowell's under state police protection. They think he's giving up his organization but it's a ruse to get at me. Lieutenant, he says he's already in Savannah."

Blazer's brow furrowed. "That can't be true. They wouldn't bring Martin Dowell into my jurisdiction without notifying me."

But she could hear the doubt in his voice. He knew it was possible. If Dowell was under some sort of modified witness protection, they wouldn't tell anyone where he was.

"Lee said Dowell convinced them he needed to see his son," she said.

Blazer picked up a pen and turned it over in his hand. "I spoke to my FBI contacts yesterday, and they verified state is working with Dowell—they don't approve, but state is off-roading here." His face hardened. "If they brought that thug into my town without due notification, they're crazy."

The air conditioner blew cold air against Harper's neck, making her shiver.

"They think he's going to crack the Southern Mafia for them," she said. "Lee thinks Dowell's going to get away from them and find me."

There was a brief silence as the two of them exchanged a look.

Blazer broke it first. "You've got the gun?"

She nodded.

"Good." His tone was grim. "I'll increase patrols at the newspaper. Let the security guards at the paper know. I'll alert the Tybee PD to have more patrols at your house." He paused to think, studying her like a problem. "Actually, I'll see if I can get the sheriff to station a county deputy there overnight. I think it's time to get them involved, too. If Dowell really is in town, we'll need every resource we can spare."

"Thanks," she said. "Lee thinks I should stay on the move. Find new places every few nights."

He considered this. "Stay there for the next couple of nights at least. I'll make sure you've got security. I can't protect you if you're constantly moving."

She nodded uncertainly. Everyone was giving her conflicting advice. Who was right?

"Let me know if this Lee person reappears," Blazer continued. "I'd like to have a word with him."

The meeting was over. Harper stood to go, but the lieutenant stopped her.

"By the way, you haven't heard from your friends out at Tybee, have you?"

When she gave him a puzzled look, he clarified, "Rayne's housemates."

With everything that had been going on, she'd pushed the case to the back of her mind. Suddenly, the conversation she'd had with Cara flooded back. Had that only been last night?

"Why?" she asked. "Is something going on?"

"No, and that's the problem. Daltrey and Walker, they're working the case well but without physical evidence, and with those three backing each other up, we can't pin it down. I was hoping they'd let something slip with you."

"I talked to Cara last night," she told him. "She told me she was afraid of the other two. She suggested she's starting to wonder if one of them was the killer. But she said she didn't know for sure."

Blazer looked interested. "Did you believe her?"

Harper thought of Cara whispering on the phone, the tense timbre of fear in her voice.

"There's definitely something going on. They're not a cozy group anymore." A thought occurred to her. "Actually, Allegra's playing a gig tonight at the Library Bar. I'll try and talk to her. I think she trusts me. Maybe I can get something out of her."

"I can send Daltrey and Walker," Blazer offered. "You shouldn't go in there alone."

But Harper shook her head. "If detectives are there nobody will talk," she said. "Let me give it a shot on my own. I'll be careful. If they're starting to turn on each other, maybe I can make them turn faster. Besides, it'll take my mind off everything else for a while."

Blazer studied her. "You know, Smith used to tell me you'd make a great cop. I'm starting to think he was right."

Heat rose to Harper's face. The lieutenant was not one to hand out praise.

He waved one hand. "Go. See what you can find out. Just don't arrest anybody. Leave that to us."

"I'll do my best," she said, opening the door. The sounds of the busy hallway poured in.

"When you get home tonight expect a deputy on your doorstep," he told her, gruffly, as he wrote something on a sheet of paper. "If you don't find one there, don't go inside. Turn yourself around and call me on my cell. Here's my number. Do we have a deal?"

She crossed back to his desk took the paper. Their eyes met and she gave him a grateful look.

The strangest thing to come out of this situation was that she was actually starting to like Larry Blazer.

But all she said was, "You've got a deal."

27

When Harper arrived back at the newspaper a short while later, there was a patrol car parked in front of the building. The lieutenant hadn't wasted any time. Unfortunately, this meant there was no way to hide the situation from Baxter any longer.

She'd dreaded this moment, convinced the editor would make her pull back from daily reporting. To her surprise, though, Baxter took the news calmly.

"This is why you look like you haven't slept in three weeks, I gather."

"Sleep isn't something I'm getting much of lately," Harper conceded.

They were in Baxter's glass-walled office. Bright sun slanted in through the blinds, striping the room with light and shadow.

"Is it safe for you to be here right now?" the editor asked.

"Aside from the police station, this is the safest place I go," Harper told her. "There's an off-duty cop downstairs with a gun, and a cop car sitting outside the door."

The editor considered her in silence for so long, Harper was sure she'd send her home. But then she sighed and said, "Well, then. Get your ass to work." But Harper had seen the worried look cross her face.

"I'll be fine," she promised.

"Make sure you are," Baxter told her, sternly.

"Oh, one more thing," Harper said. "Allegra Hanson is playing a gig at a bar in town tonight. I'd like to go to it. I want to see if I can get her talk."

Baxter didn't look thrilled. "There's no story there. Unless she shoots someone onstage, no one's going to care."

Harper didn't back down. "They'll care if she tells me who killed Xavier Rayne. Allegra's fragile. She's young. She loved Xavier—he gave her a career in music. If I can get her alone, I'm sure I can get her to talk."

Baxter still wasn't convinced. "Even if you get a story out of her it's page three at this stage," she pointed out. "And, who's going to monitor the police scanner while you're sitting in a bar?"

Turning, Harper pointed across the newsroom to where DJ was sitting at his desk typing furiously.

Baxter gave her a look. "You treat him like he's your assistant."

"He loves it. His beat is boring."

"It is boring," Baxter agreed, making a note on the spreadsheet in front of her. "Actually, I was thinking I might move him to courts."

That didn't make any sense. "Ed Lasterson does courts. Is he leaving?"

"Oh, didn't I tell you?" Baxter stopped writing. "MaryAnne Charlton called this morning. She'd like to have her layoffs now."

Harper's stomach dropped. With everything that was going on, she'd forgotten what Dells had told her about the newspaper's owner.

"Oh, come on. She can't be serious."

"Charlton doesn't do humor." Baxter sighed. "I hate that woman more than cancer."

"You can't do it," Harper told her. "We have half the staff we did seven years ago. And Ed's good. He's got contacts no one else has. Judges call him personally. Nobody else gets that. You can't let him go."

"He's been here twenty years," Baxter said, pointedly. "He's the highest-paid reporter on staff. DJ's the lowest-paid. As far as MaryAnne is concerned, it's that simple. Ed goes. DJ stays."

Harper knew she shouldn't be surprised by anything at this point—she'd seen numerous layoffs over the years—but she was shocked nonetheless. It was so callous. So heartless. And Baxter showed no sign of fighting it.

"Ed's on the highest salary because he's the best at what he does," she reminded her. "DJ is great. But he'll be starting from square one. And where will Ed go?"

Baxter didn't even try to argue. "I don't have the answer to that. I can't think about it. I just have to do what I'm told to do by the woman who owns this newspaper. If I don't, she'll fire me and get someone else to do it. She's done it before."

Harper was so angry it was hard for her to speak. "Dells was right. She's going to sell this place, isn't she? First she's going to hollow it out, then she'll sell what's left to some banker."

"Probably. And then you and I will be following Ed to the unemployment office." As she set her silver pen down, Baxter looked defeated. "In newspaper, you take what you get."

"I hate this." Harper stood up so abruptly her chair scratched against the floor. "It's a messed-up, shitty thing that one woman can ruin so many lives."

"You're preaching to the choir." The editor's tone was bitter. "I can honestly say this is the best job and the worst job I've ever had."

The revelation about upcoming layoffs threw Harper off her game. She couldn't bring herself to even look at Ed. It was a relief when the day reporters went home at six o'clock, leaving only her and DJ.

She didn't want to stay in the newsroom—every time she saw Baxter looking at her computer, she imagined her crossing people's jobs off a list.

"Come on, DJ," she said, just after seven o'clock. "Let's go get something to eat."

All the way to Eddie's 24-Hour Diner she thought about telling him the news about layoffs, but she couldn't. DJ was chattering happily about how he'd joined a gym and was going to start lifting weights. "Finally getting in shape." He patted his stomach. "Got to get washboard abs by summer."

Eddie's had retro 1950s décor, and a short while later they were seated in a vivid red booth, blinded by chrome, listening to the Beach Boys as Harper picked at some fries.

"You know, if I got overtime pay," DJ said, spinning the scanner on the tabletop between them, "I'd be loaded."

"Same," she said, barely looking up.

"Unpaid work . . ." he mused. "Isn't there a word for that? When you're forced to work without money. What is that word?"

"It's called modern life. Eat your burger," Harper said shortly. "Anyway, you're lucky you have a job."

The edge to her voice was unmistakable. He gave her a puzzled look but, when she didn't say more, let it go, demolishing the remains of his meal with quick efficiency. Harper, her thoughts veering between Martin Dowell and layoffs, hadn't made much of a dent in hers. After he pushed his plate away, DJ watched her not eat for a while in silence before saying, "Hey. Is something going on with you?"

Harper folded a napkin, primly. "Not really."

"Come on. You look terrible. Are you sick? Addicted to meth?" He gestured at her plate. "Giving up food for Lent?"

Harper cut him off. "Too much work. Not enough sleep."

But he wasn't about to take that as an answer. "Why aren't you sleeping? Is it this case?"

Harper hesitated. She liked DJ. And she knew he'd want to know what was going on. But she couldn't bring herself to go into it again. Not today. Luckily, before she had to summon an excuse, the scanner crackled to life.

DJ, one foot propped up on the chair next to him, looked at it with only mild interest.

Harper shot him a glare and, remembering it was his job for the night, he jumped, grabbed it, and held it to his ear.

Harper reached for the bill. The least she could do was buy him dinner.

"What's a code four?" he asked.

Harper's hand stopped in midair, hovering over the slip of paper. "It's a dead body. Are you sure they said code four?"

He nodded, listening. "They're sending more officers."

Harper motioned impatiently for the scanner.

When he handed it over, a patrol officer was talking. "This is unit three-nine-eight, out at the code four on Veterans. I'm going to need some extra units out here for crowd control. Also, alert forensics for me."

It sounded like a juicy story, but it was nearly time for Allegra's show. Reluctantly, she handed the scanner back to him.

"You better get out there," she said. "It's probably natural causes but it's hard to tell from what they're saying. I'll drive you to your car." She pulled cash from her wallet and set it down on the table and got up, grabbing her bag, feeling the reassuring weight of the Glock inside.

He followed her out to the Camaro and climbed into the low-slung passenger seat. "You don't want to come along?"

"I've seen enough dead bodies, thanks," she said, although really she did want to go. "There's someplace I need to be tonight."

"Come on. What's going on that's so important?" he cajoled, as she backed out. "Normally you'd never let me handle something like this on my own."

"The Xavier Rayne case." She merged into Drayton Street traffic. "One of the housemates is playing a gig. I'm going to see if anyone will confess to murder."

As she turned left and headed back to Bay Street, he stared at her. "You get the best stories every single time."

28

Just before nine o'clock, Harper walked into the Library Bar to find an empty stage. The crowd—good-sized for a Wednesday—talked loudly at tables that had been arranged in front of the performance space. A gloomy acoustic song whispered unhappily from the jukebox.

Bonnie waved from behind the bar as she walked up.

"This is cheerful," Harper said, sitting on an empty barstool.

"We tried to choose appropriate music for the event." Bonnie made a face. "I think we went too far." She gestured at the beer fridge, but Harper shook her head.

"I'm working." She glanced around the room. "Is she here?"

"She's in the back. Came in with a guitarist. Said she needed a minute. That was over an hour ago."

Harper's eyes swept the room falling on a familiar figure. Cara had her back to her, but her honey-blond hair and slim profile were unmistakable. She was alone.

A few rows behind her, she noticed the unpleasantly familiar profile of Jon Graff. He was staring at his phone, but had positioned himself near enough Cara to watch her openly.

It made Harper's skin crawl. She knew how it felt to be stalked. The suffocating, creeping threat of it.

Leaving Bonnie at the bar, she weaved through the crowd to Cara and sat down in the empty chair at her table.

The actress gave her a startled look. "What are you doing here?"

"I came to talk to Allegra," Harper told her. "I'm surprised to see you. After our conversation, I didn't think you'd come."

Cara's hands fluttered nervously. The drink in front of her was untouched. "I didn't have a huge amount of choice," she said, her gaze skittering around the room. "They wouldn't give up until I agreed."

Harper wondered what that meant, but Cara was as nervous as a frog in a kitchen. She didn't want to push her too hard.

"Don't look now," she said, "but Jon Graff is sitting a few rows back."

Cara shuddered. "That man is disgusting."

"I can't argue with that." Harper glanced behind them. Graff was staring at her with open dislike. His presence made her plans for the evening much more difficult. But now that she was here, she had to try.

"I was going to call you," she told Cara, quietly. "I talked to the detective overseeing the investigation today."

Cara leaned toward her, lowering her voice to a whisper. "What did he say?"

"He thinks you're right—someone in that house killed Xavier." Harper searched her face. "Has anything changed? Are you still suspicious of Hunter and Allegra?"

At that moment, though, the lights in the room went dark, save for a few spotlights pointed at the stage. The audience gave a smattering of applause.

"About time!" someone shouted.

Cara looked at Harper, her eyes unreadable and gleaming in the shadows, but turned away without answering. She held her head stiffly, staring at the stage, unblinking as Allegra walked out with Hunter at her side, holding a guitar. She waved at the crowd briefly before flitting straight to the microphone and adjusting it down to her low height with quick, practiced moves.

"Sorry to make y'all wait," she said in that rich, husky voice. "They say some things are worth waiting for. I hope you think this is one of them."

She was dressed in a short black skirt and a fitted dark top. With heavy eyeliner and her hair back-combed, she looked older. Professional. She was confident on stage in a way that diverged completely from her soft-spoken off-stage persona. It was as if she was another person.

As the crowd shifted, settling down for the show, Hunter strapped the guitar across his chest. His glasses sparkled in the spotlight's glow as he counted off the first song. "One, two, three . . ."

He began playing the guitar with skilled ease, summoning a delicate melody from the strings. In Xavier's band, he'd played keyboards, but clearly his musical skills transcended one instrument.

The first song was a melancholy, elegant interpretation of "La Vie en Rose"—Hunter's guitar giving it a modern twist and Allegra's voice lifting the lyrics into something beautiful and rare.

Harper, who had meant to get up and go back to the bar, found herself transfixed. It was easy to understand what Xavier had seen in her as a performer. She was tiny and yet she held attention. It was hard to take your eyes off her.

The audience fell silent—absorbed in the music. When the song ended, the applause was rapturous.

Cara didn't clap. Her gaze remained fixed on the stage as Allegra sang one beautiful song after another. Watching the light play across her features, Harper wondered what she was thinking.

It was near the end of the show when Allegra, flushed and glowing from the attention, spoke into the microphone. "This next song means everything to me. I want to dedicate this one to the love of my life. I miss you, Xavier."

Even through the crowd's applause Harper could hear Cara's sharp intake of breath. Her fingers gripped the edge of the table as Hunter broke into the first notes of "Revolver Road."

"I love you more than I ever thought I could," Allegra sang in an ominous minor key. "I did things I never thought I would. Now the night grows long and the hour grows cold. Meet me on Revolver Road."

Cara made a broken sound and jumped to her feet. Harper looked at her, confused, but the woman didn't look at her. Covering her lips with one hand, she fled the room. Harper saw Jon Graff turn to watch with interest as she hurried blindly across the floor.

On the stage, Hunter fumbled a note as his eyes followed Cara. Allegra, though, didn't miss a beat. Her perfect voice slid over the notes of Xavier's song as if he'd written them for her.

Harper lost sight of Cara. She stood and made her way to the bar. Bonnie, who was drying glasses, lifted one eyebrow as she approached. "What the hell was that about?"

"I'm not sure," Harper admitted, looking around. "Where'd she go?"

"Ladies' room," Bonnie said. "At a hundred miles per hour."

Harper glanced back at the stage. Allegra was singing the last notes of the song. When she finished, the crowd roared. Ignoring their enthusiasm, Hunter stepped quickly to Allegra's side and whispered in her ear.

She shook her head and said something in reply, quick and angry. Whatever it was, it wasn't what he wanted to hear.

His face darkening, he resumed his place.

Beaming, Allegra grabbed the microphone. "Just one more song," she said. "You've been the best audience. I'm so thankful for you being here."

Hunter began to play again, thin shoulders hunched. Harper could sense him watching as she crossed to the ladies' room. When the door closed behind her, the music faded into the background.

The room appeared empty, the row of graffitied cubicle doors all closed. The room smelled strongly of some aggressive air freshener.

"Cara?" Harper asked cautiously. "Are you okay?"

There was a long silence and then, after a second, movement—a shuffling of feet. Cara walked out of the stall at the end, a tissue in one hand, her eyes red.

"That bitch. How could she do that?"

"Do what? You mean the song?" Harper prompted, trying to piece it together.

"That song . . ." Cara's voice broke and she sagged against the sink, covering her face. "Out of everything she could have chosen. She picked that song." She was crying again. "I could see it on her face. I could see everything."

Harper wasn't sure what was happening. Cara looked absolutely shattered. "I'm sorry," she said, "I don't mean to be insensitive but why shouldn't she sing it?"

Cara gave her a look of disbelief. "Harper. Can't you see? It's so obvious what was going on. The two of them . . ."

Harper's brow furrowed. "What are you talking about? Something between Hunter and Allegra?"

"Not Hunter." A bitter laugh tore from Cara's throat and she dropped her head to her hand. "God, I'm so stupid."

"Cara. I don't understand." Harper stepped toward her. "Tell me what's going on."

A burst of applause poured in from the other room. The song must have ended.

"I'm such an idiot." Lifting her head, Cara gave her a haunted look. "I was wrong about everything."

Behind them the door flew open. A group of young women in short skirts and jeans walked in chattering loudly. Abruptly, Cara turned and ran, shoving past them to the door.

"Rude," one of them commented. The others giggled.

"Cara, wait!" Harper ran after her, but she had to pause to let the women pass. When she got through, she raced into the main barroom. The stage was empty, the spotlights illuminating the two abandoned microphones. Music poured from the jukebox speakers again.

There was no sign of Cara.

The audience had moved from the tables and were now thronging around the bar.

Harper threaded her way through the crowd, toward the stage. It was quieter on that side of the room and she could clearly hear raised voices coming from the back room. When she reached it she paused, pressing her ear to the door. Hunter was shouting something.

Harper turned the handle, opening the door just wide enough to peer in.

Allegra, Hunter, and Cara stood in the harsh glare of a bare bulb surrounded by boxes of beer and wine in vivid green, red, and blue stacks. The room was cold, and smelled of dust and cardboard. Hunter and Allegra were side by side, facing Cara.

"Did you invite her?" Hunter was asking heatedly. "Are you trying to destroy everything?"

"You can't be serious." Giving them an incredulous look, Cara stepped toward them. "*I'm* trying to destroy everything? You're out of your mind. There's nothing left to destroy. It's already gone." She rounded on Allegra. "And you. How dare you sing his song? How dare you even touch his words? You disgust me."

Whip-fast, Allegra slapped Cara's face. The crack of the blow was so loud and violent, Harper gasped. The sound echoed in the sudden silence. Allegra and Hunter spun around to look at her. Cara didn't move. She stood stock-still, one hand raised to her cheek, which bore the red imprint of Allegra's hand.

"Harper." Allegra cocked her head, dark eyes suddenly alert. "What are you doing here?" She seemed curiously unashamed, given what Harper had just witnessed.

Hunter, on the other hand, looked anxious. "It's just an argument," he explained. "Allegra didn't mean . . ."

With a muffled sob, Cara turned on her heel and ran for the door. Harper stepped aside to let her pass, holding the door wide. When she was gone, she hesitated long enough to see Hunter and Allegra exchange a weighted look before heading off in search of Cara.

She wasn't sure what she was witnessing here: whether this was three guilty people who'd done something awful bowing to the pressure, or a group of friends crumbling beneath the unbearable weight of grief and public attention. Or something else entirely. Something involving Xavier Rayne and Allegra.

Cara's pale top fluttered around her frail frame as she sped through the crowd. She was fast, and Harper was running by the time she reached the door. Junior, the bouncer, gave her a questioning look as she hurried by, but she shook her head. There was nothing he could do to help.

On the dark street she turned left and right, finally spotting Cara getting into the convertible she'd seen parked in front of Admiral's Row the other day.

"Cara!" Harper ran up to the car, where Cara had already started the engine and was strapping on her seat belt. "Can you just tell me what's going on? Maybe I can help."

Through her tears, Cara gave a bitter laugh. "It's so funny," she said. "I always thought reporters were smart. But they fooled you like they fooled everyone. How can you help when you can't even see?"

"Just tell me," Harper pleaded. "What happened that night? Who killed Xavier? You know, don't you?"

Cara looked for a moment as if she wanted to tell her. But then the door of the bar opened and Jon Graff walked out. He stood watching them with interest.

Cara gave Harper a long, tormented look. "It doesn't matter, anymore. Nothing will bring Xavier back. He's gone forever. And I don't know if I can live with that."

"Wait—" Harper began, but Cara slammed the car into drive and floored it, shooting out of the parking place.

She stood on the curb as the car's brake lights blinked red at the corner, and then disappeared into the night.

"What was that all about?" Graff asked. "Looks like a guilty conscience."

Harper turned and hurried back inside, ignoring him.

Cara had not behaved like a murderer looking to cover up her crime. She'd seemed much more like a bereaved girlfriend, betrayed by her friends.

Betrayed how, though? Had something been going on between Allegra and Xavier? What had she said before she sang his song? "I dedicate this to the love of my life." Was that any way to talk about someone else's dead boyfriend?

And hadn't the neighbor heard Cara accuse him of having an affair? What if that affair had actually happened inside his own house?

Pieces were beginning to fall into place. But the picture was still not clear. She needed to talk to the others.

In the bar, Allegra was perched on a stool holding a drink as if nothing had happened. Hunter leaned on the bar next to her. They were talking to a small group of admirers. They both looked relaxed—not at all like they'd just been in a knockdown fight in a back room.

Bonnie wiped the already-clean bar. "What happened?" she asked, sotto voce. "I saw the blonde fly out of here like someone was chasing her with a sword."

Harper leaned over to whisper. "A fight. Very intense."

"Over what?"

"Still trying to figure that out," Harper said.

Bonnie shot a dark look at Hunter and Allegra, surrounded by adoring fans. "Well, I don't like them."

As if he'd heard her, Hunter looked up. She thought for a second she saw a flash of contempt in his eyes, but then he lifted a hand and there was nothing there but melancholy. He leaned over and whispered something to Allegra, who glanced at Harper and said, "I see someone we need to talk to. It's been great meeting you."

She slid off the stool and the two of them walked over to where Harper waited, their faces somber.

"Can we go somewhere?" Hunter asked.

"Give me a second," Harper said.

Jon Graff was walking back into the bar. She leaned over and motioned for Bonnie. Gesturing at Graff she said, "Make sure he doesn't follow us, okay?"

Bonnie didn't ask any questions. "I'll put Junior on him," she promised.

Straightening, Harper looked around for a quiet space. She led Allegra and Hunter to the side room known as "Poetry," where lines from famous poems had been painted on the dark walls in white paint.

"What was that about?" she asked, as soon as they were alone.

"Cara's still dealing with everything that happened." Allegra said it in that soft, timid voice, quite different from the one she'd used onstage. "I can't blame her for being upset. She won't get over it. No one could."

"Get over what?" Harper gave her a direct look. "Xavier being murdered? Or Xavier being murdered by someone she knows?"

"Oh, come on," Hunter interjected. "You can't be serious. You've been hanging out with us for days. Do we look like killers?"

His innocent act grated on Harper's nerves. Suddenly she could see the manipulation—the way his eyes searched hers to gauge whether she was buying it.

She was tired of wasting time on these people, when somewhere out there tonight a man was hunting her.

"Do you really want to ask that question?" She squared up to him. "Are you sure you want to know what I think? Because I don't think you do. Why don't you just tell the truth?"

"But it *is* the truth," Allegra insisted. "Cara is upset. Her boyfriend is dead and the police haven't found the killer. How would you feel if that was you?"

"Terrible." Harper rounded on her. "Worse, perhaps, if my friend dedicated a song to my dead boyfriend and called him the love of her life." She paused, then added, "Especially if I thought she was sleeping with him."

Allegra didn't react. She just watched her with those huge, enigmatic eyes.

"Were you sleeping with him?" Harper prodded. "Is that what Xavier and Cara fought about that last night? Was it all about you?"

Hunter stepped between them. "You know half of everything and you think you're a genius," he said, angrily. "Now you're throwing allegations around like a tabloid hack. I thought you were better than this."

Ignoring him, Harper kept her focus on Allegra.

"Here's what I think happened," she said. "Xavier and Cara had a fight that night. A big one. About you. Cara was angry. She followed him down to the beach to finish it. She was planning on leaving the next morning. But she brought a gun. Maybe to kill herself. Maybe to kill him. It doesn't matter. Xavier tried to take it from her. It went off in the scuffle. It was an accident. You two helped her drag the body out to the water and got rid of the gun. You were all involved. Now you're rubbing it in her face, and it's falling apart."

Allegra watched her with something more like fascination than fear.

"Tell me I'm wrong," Harper demanded.

"You're wrong." Allegra said, flatly.

"Then what *did* happen?" Harper demanded. "I'm sure Xavier didn't die alone on that beach. You were there. You were with him. You all were. That's why none of you will turn each other in. You're all guilty in some way."

For a long second Allegra stood still, barely breathing, her eyes fixed on Harper. The music and voices from the next room seemed to fade. Harper could sense how much the other girl wanted to tell her—could smell it in the air like electricity. And she might have. Except Hunter broke the spell.

"You're out of your mind," he told her dismissively. Turning to Allegra, he said, "Get your stuff. We're leaving."

For a second she didn't react. She gave him a look Harper couldn't read.

He shook his head in answer to some unspoken question. "Go." His voice softened. "I'll take care of this."

Allegra bolted from the room, her small shoulders high around her neck as if braced for a blow.

When she was gone, Hunter turned back to Harper and gave a small, understanding sigh. "Look, I know why you think we were involved but I promise you we had nothing to do with it. Yeah, he and Cara had a screaming fight, but that was what they did. They loved each other and they fought. That was them. That's why Cara's such a wreck." He bit his lip, hunching his thin shoulders in that boyish way Harper had once thought charming and vulnerable, but now saw as purely manipulative. "Maybe we shouldn't have done 'Revolver Road' tonight with Cara out there, but that's all that upset her," he continued. "Hearing that song— it was too much. I'll apologize to her and things will be fine."

"Are you saying Allegra and Xavier weren't having an affair?" Harper challenged.

"Of course not." He looked horrified, as if the suggestion were ridiculous. "They were like brother and sister."

Harper didn't hide her doubt, but if he noticed he didn't show it. Instead, he moved closer to her.

"The last couple of weeks have been the worst thing any of us has been through. And I just want to thank you for helping us." He reached for her hand before she realized what he was doing. "I'm sorry I got angry earlier. It's just so stressful. But you have really helped—"

Startled, she yanked her hand free and took a hasty step away from him. "Don't."

If he was embarrassed by her reaction she saw no sign of it in his unconcerned shrug. "Hey, it's cool. I didn't mean anything by it."

"All I want to know is what really happened that night," she said, evenly. "Nothing more."

"You know everything there is to know." He held her gaze, his eyes as flat as coins.

Across the bar, Allegra emerged from the back room, carrying a guitar case and shoulder bag.

"I've got to go," Hunter said. "Thanks for coming tonight. We'll see you around."

He sloped off to join Allegra, lifting the guitar case from her hand.

As Harper walked back to the bar, she spotted Jon Graff in a corner being talked to by Junior, who towered over him. Graff's face was red with rage.

That, at least, was satisfying.

She joined Bonnie, who was watching Allegra and Hunter leave.

"It's so weird to think they were Xavier Rayne's friends," Bonnie said. "He was so spiritual. They're just thirsty for fame." She paused as the door closed behind them. "That girl can sure sing, though."

Harper didn't reply. Everything was starting to make sense.

At last, she thought she understood who killed Xavier Rayne.

29

Fifteen minutes later, she parked the Camaro on Bay Street, directly in front of the newspaper building. The road was nearly deserted. There was no patrol car waiting for her.

Overhead, clouds scuttled across the dark sky, obscuring the moon. A cool wind blew her hair into her eyes and she shoved it back, hurrying across the sidewalk to the front door and grabbing the handle. It didn't turn.

She shook it harder. The door stayed stubbornly locked.

Cupping her face with her hands, she peered through the glass at the desk where the guard should be. It was empty.

In fact, she could see no one at all through the smeared pane. She knocked hard on the glass, twisting her head to peer down the corridor, but no one emerged from the shadows.

Suddenly feeling exposed, she pounded harder on the door. "Hello?" she called, raising her voice. "Is anyone there?"

When no one replied, she turned around, surveying the dark street. She shouldn't be out here alone. She remembered Lee's warning about the newspaper building. *"It's the one place he knows to look for you."*

Her throat went dry. She should go back to her car, she decided. Drive away. Call Blazer, maybe.

The city seemed dangerously quiet. The only people she could see were two men a block away on the otherwise lonely street, walking toward her.

As she took a step toward the car, Harper found herself watching them, nervously.

They were probably tourists, she told herself. Or friends out for a drink.

But there was something about the way they moved. They weren't talking. They weren't even looking at each other.

They were looking at her.

They stuck to the shadows—she couldn't get a good look at their faces. One was short and stocky, with thick hair that gleamed white in the darkness. The other was tall and walked about two steps behind the first.

Her heart began to beat faster. Keeping her eyes on the two men, she dug into her bag, fingers sliding off the cold metal of the Glock, and she hesitated.

Could she do it? Could she shoot two men on the steps of the newspaper?

The men were crossing the street, now, moving faster. There was no question in her mind that she was their target. She could sense it, feel it in her bones the same way a rabbit could sense a coyote.

Dropping the gun, she turned back and beat her fists against the door.

"Come on," she whispered, her lips growing numb. "*Come on.*"

As if he'd heard her, the gray-haired man smiled.

A metallic *click* broke the quiet and the door behind her gave way. She stumbled backward into the reception space.

The guard held the door open with one hand, a fresh cup of coffee in the other.

"Is everything . . ." he began.

Harper slammed the door hard and jumped back from it. "Lock it," she told him, her voice trembling.

He looked confused. "What?"

"*Lock it,*" she demanded, frantic.

"It locks automatically." He set the coffee down on the desk and stepped closer to the door, looking out before glancing back at her. "What happened?"

"Two men." Harper stared at the glass door, waiting for them to appear.

"Following you?" He was surprisingly calm, moving to the side of the door, pushing her gently out of the way so he could look.

"I think so," she said. "I parked. I got out of the car. All of a sudden they were coming at me on foot. Fast."

He crossed to the other side of the door in one long step and peered in the opposite direction, talking as he searched the street. "They didn't address you? Threaten you?"

She shook her head. Suddenly she felt foolish. Maybe she'd over-reacted. She was paranoid.

"It was nothing, probably." But even as she said it, she thought back to that moment on the street. And the steady, focused energy of the two men. The shorter man could have been Martin Dowell. Seventeen years older than the most recent picture she'd seen. White haired. Smaller than she'd expected. But she wasn't certain.

The guard kept his eyes on the street outside. He was the youngest guard at the paper: African American, maybe early thirties, with short hair and a lean build. She knew little about him except that he was an off-duty Savannah cop who worked security for extra pay.

"Nobody's out there now." He turned to look at her, his expression hard to read. "The street's empty."

The men had been less than a block away when Harper ran inside.

"They must have turned around," she said, momentarily bewildered. "Why would they turn around?"

They exchanged a long look as the implications of this became clear to each of them.

Ice settled in the pit of Harper's stomach. It was him. It had to be.

"Describe them," the guard ordered.

Harper told him about the stocky, gray-haired man and the taller man walking beside him. "I think it was Martin Dowell and his son," she said. "But he's supposed to be in police custody. So it can't be him."

The guard didn't ask anything else. He pulled out his phone with one hand and punched the door-release button with the other. "Stay here," he barked.

Harper watched through the smudged glass as he spoke on the phone while scanning the street in both directions then disappeared, heading toward where she'd last seen the men.

After no more than three minutes, a patrol car prowled past, moving slow. It stopped in front of the building. The guard leaned forward to speak to the cop through an open window, gesturing down the sidewalk. Moments later, the patrol car took off in the direction indicated.

Harper's breath fogged the glass. The guard looked both ways one last time before letting himself back into the lobby. "The PD are searching the area. If those guys have any sense, they won't come back this way. If it was Martin Dowell—and I do mean if—they'll find him." His face grave, he pointed at the desk. "Nine times out of ten when you walk through that door I'll be right there, but after dark, you should call the desk before you get out of your car. Tonight I was just getting a cup of coffee and you could have been hurt. I don't want anything to happen to you if I step away for two minutes."

Harper nodded, her stomach in knots. Was this really how she was going to live?

He gave her a reassuring look. "I don't think they'll come back tonight. Not with the PD hunting for them."

As she climbed the stairs to the newsroom, Harper kept remembering the way the gray-haired man smiled. Had she just seen the man who ordered her mother's murder?

Pulling her phone from her pocket, she typed a quick message to Lee:

I think Martin Dowell was outside the newspaper tonight.
He saw me.

But had she, really? She needed to see a picture of him again to be sure.

When she reached the newsroom, she crossed straight to her desk and logged into her computer before she even sat down, bending over the keyboard, fingers flying.

DJ swung around in his chair. "How'd it go?"

"Badly," she said, typing Martin Dowell's name into the system. "I haven't got a story."

"Baxter won't mind. It wasn't going on the front page anyway." He rolled closer, excitement lighting up his warm brown eyes. "That dead body earlier—it turned out to be a homicide."

Harper was only half listening. Her computer had opened up dozens of pictures of Dowell, and she stared at the images of a stocky man with a pugnacious face, short hair the color of steel, and cold, small eyes. It could be the man she'd seen outside. But she wasn't certain. If it was him, age had done its work. His face had been deeply lined. His build bulkier.

"Was he shot?" she asked, without looking up. "Some sort of robbery?"

He shook his head. "Stabbed. Nothing stolen. They found the body at this no-tell motel on Veterans. I'm still waiting on the police information guy to call me back. But I overheard some of the detectives talking. Said he had a card in his wallet identifying him as retired FBI. They were running him through the database to see—"

"DJ." Harper went cold. He must have heard the shock in her voice, because he gave her an odd look. "The dead man. What was his name?"

"I think it's Howard. Let me check." He picked up his notebook as she waited, unable to breathe. It couldn't be him. It couldn't.

"Yeah, here it is." DJ turned around. "Lee Howard."

He said something else but Harper didn't hear it.

Last night Lee had promised to get to Dowell before Dowell got to her. And now Lee was dead.

"Harper?" DJ's frown deepened. "What's wrong? Do you know him?"

She nodded, her lips tight, and picked up her cell phone, dialing with shaking hands.

Behind his glasses, DJ's eyes were filled with worry. "Was he your friend?"

She couldn't find the words to explain and she didn't trust herself to speak. She walked away, her steps wooden and stiff. She was in the hallway by the time Luke answered. "Harper? Everything okay?"

"Your homicide victim. Lee Howard." Her voice trembled. "He's the guy who told me about Dowell. I talked to him last night." She took a shuddering breath. "He's six-three, about one-ninety, late fifties, gray hair, recently shaved mustache . . ."

He interrupted her. "Wait. Hang on, hang on. . . . You saw him last night? What time?"

"He left my house at three thirty in the morning. I told Blazer." She leaned against the wall, her forehead hot against the cool plaster. "Luke, it was Martin Dowell, wasn't it? He got away from the police. And I think I saw him on Bay Street five minutes ago."

"My God." Luke sounded stunned. "How the hell could the state lose someone like Dowell?"

Harper didn't have to answer. They both knew how. Dowell was good. He'd been planning this for years.

"*Everyone underestimates Martin Dowell,*" Lee had said.

"Check the hotel room for anything that could be Dowell's," she told him, pressing her fingers against her eyes. "Anything that might make the state withdraw his parole."

"You can count on it," he said, tightly.

"And tell Blazer. He was planning to put a deputy outside my door tonight." She took a shaky breath. "Tell him that deputy better be a damn good shot."

"Harper, wait. Are you sure you should go home? Can you stay somewhere else?"

"Where, Luke?" Her voice quavered. "I could stay at Bonnie's but he would kill Bonnie to get to me. I could stay at a hotel and he'd have me alone in a room on the sixteenth floor. Where am I supposed to go? I can't sleep at the police station."

"I don't like you being alone out there," he said.

"Me neither." She swallowed hard. "But if Dowell just killed an FBI agent, nowhere is safe for me."

There was a brief pause before he replied. "I'll talk to Blazer as soon as we hang up." Through the phone, she could hear the rough edge to his breathing. "Harper, don't worry. We're going to get that son of a bitch."

In the silence after he hung up, Harper stood for a long time in the empty hallway with her back to the wall, thinking about the predatory man she'd seen on the street and the tall, quiet FBI agent who'd tried to save her.

3 0

By the time Harper left the paper that night, the weather had begun to turn. The wind was picking up. The night sky had a greenish hue that drained the color from the city.

A smattering of rain fell as she walked out to her car. The security guard stood at the edge of the street, keeping watch. A blue-and-white Savannah patrol car sat behind the red Camaro, its engine loud in the quiet street.

Harper jumped into the driver's seat, starting the engine with a roar.

The patrol car accompanied her as far as the city limits, dropping back right when she turned onto Highway 80. After that, for an unnerving few miles, she was alone. But, just before she hit the marshes, a Chatham County sheriff's deputy appeared in front of her, rolling slow. As she neared, he sped up and stuck with her the rest of the way. When she pulled into the driveway at Spinnaker Cottage, he backed into the entrance and parked there, facing the street. Effectively blocking anyone from getting in or out.

As she walked from the car into a slow, steady rain, Harper lifted her hand and saw the faint movement as the deputy responded.

She hurried up the steps to the porch, finding Zuzu, high and dry on the chair, waiting. Harper scooped her up and unlocked the door. Inside, she looked around, her gaze lingering on the blue chair where Lee had sat not twenty-four hours ago.

Unexpectedly, the room blurred.

Why had he come here last night? Had he somehow known he wouldn't make it through this? Was he planning even then to confront Martin Dowell in that hotel room?

Every word he'd said to her seemed weighted with meaning now.

"Maybe I'm as obsessive as Martin Dowell. But I need to finish this case. . . ."

"Well, your case is over now," she told the chair, her voice breaking.

Forcing back tears, she stalked around the house, checking each window as she went—all were locked tight.

In the kitchen, she got the gun out of her bag and set it on the counter before grabbing the tall, slim bottle of Jameson whiskey from the cupboard and pouring herself an unhealthy measure. She drank it down fast, and drew in a long breath.

She needed to calm down. With the deputy outside and every cop on the coast keeping an eye on her, she had to be safe.

But maybe she was now underestimating Martin Dowell, too.

Setting the glass down with a bang, she ran back to the front door and pulled the sofa in front of it, using her weight as leverage.

When she'd finished, she stood, hands on her hips, looking for anything else she could do. Crouched in the bedroom doorway, Zuzu watched her doubtfully.

Harper realized she'd forgotten to feed her. Guilt washed over her. None of this was the cat's fault.

Returning to the kitchen, she took a can of food from the shelf and emptied it into Zuzu's bowl. She checked that her water dish was full, then picked up the gun and slid down to the floor to watch as the gray tabby ate, her whiskers tucked back delicately.

"I'm sorry about all this," she whispered, resting her head on her knees. "All you wanted was a safe place. I let you down."

In her pocket, her phone vibrated. Luke's name was on the screen. Harper answered without getting up. "Hey."

"I'm outside your place," he said. "Can I come in?"

She nearly dropped the phone. "What? *Now?*"

"Yeah. Sorry I didn't call first. It's been crazy."

She was already scrambling to her feet. "Hang on," she said. "I just barricaded the door. Give me a second."

She heard him say, "You did what?" But she was already dragging the sofa back.

When she opened the door, Luke was on the small porch, his hair damp from the rain. His eyes swept her face, as if looking for damage.

Stifling a sob at the back of her throat, Harper stepped toward him. When he folded her in his arms, she let him. His chest was solid and familiar beneath her cheek. His arms held her tightly.

"You shouldn't have come." Her words were muffled against his jacket, and she made herself let go. "But I'm glad you did. Do you want a drink?"

He nodded.

"Whiskey okay?" She was already walking to the kitchen.

"Better than okay."

She poured them each a glass, and they stood in the small, windowless kitchen, leaning against the counters listening to the rain patter against the windows. Luke's eyes flicked from the bottle to the gun lying next to it.

He drank half of his shot before looking up at her. "It was Dowell," he said. "He slipped the state police last night. They don't know what time, exactly. Sometime between midnight and six A.M., he left the hotel where they've been keeping him, cut off the ankle bracelet, and threw it in a dumpster. Blazer's furious. The FBI's involved, after the murder tonight. But Dowell's got a head start." He shook his head in disgust. "Now that the shit's hit the fan, the state cops are backtracking and making excuses. But it's too late. Dowell's on the run."

Harper felt gut-punched. This was every bit as bad as she'd feared.

It was hard to think through the low roar of panic filling her ears. "When I saw him tonight, he wasn't alone." Her voice was thin and tight. "He was with a younger man. Maybe in his forties. Taller, thinner."

"That's almost certainly his son, Aaron. The FBI thinks the two of them planned this whole thing together. Aaron helped him escape. He's a chip off the old block." Luke looked down at the amber liquid in his glass. "We collected blood at the scene and ran it. Preliminary tests say it's a DNA match for Dowell."

"How bad is he hurt?" she asked. "Was there a lot of blood?"

"Enough." He met her eyes. "Your guy put up a hell of a fight."

"Dammit." She covered her face.

Taking the glass from her nerveless fingers, he set it on the counter, and pulled her close. She knew she shouldn't let him. But he was always the one she went to when she needed to feel safe.

He stroked her hair. "We're doing everything we can. This place is Fort Knox. County's on board, too. You'll be protected."

"He'll get to me," she whispered, her voice muffled. "He'll find a way."

"He's out of his territory," Luke reminded her. "This isn't Atlanta. Every cop in town is looking for him. The FBI is tracking him. He can't hide for long." Taking her by the shoulders, he waited until she looked up at him. His eyes were deadly serious. "We'll get him, Harper. I promise."

She knew he'd come all the way out here in the pouring rain on a night he was unlikely to get any sleep just to tell her that. The thought filled her with so much gratitude she couldn't speak.

Standing on her toes, she pressed her lips against his cheek, the slight bristle of his whiskers soft against her skin. "Thank you," she said.

She felt him tense. His hands slid up her arms, holding her close to him.

She leaned back to see his eyes darken as he stared back at her. The moment seemed to slow. And then his lips were on hers. She could taste the salt of her own tears and the soft, familiar sweetness of him.

God, she wanted this. To forget. To be safe. To be with Luke the way they used to be.

She ran her hands up his chest, tracing the hard outline of his muscles, until she found his neck and pulled him down, deepening the kiss.

"Luke . . ." She breathed his name against his lips. Pushing him back against the cheap cabinets.

His fingers tightened against her hips. In one, smooth move he lifted her until she was sitting on the countertop, her back to the cupboard, her legs wrapped around his waist, her arms around his neck. His hands were under her top, touching the warmth of her skin.

"Wait." She cupped her hands on his cheeks, gently lifting his face, so she could look into his eyes. "We can't," she said. "Sarah."

He flinched at her name. There was a long pause. And then he said, "I know."

Still, neither of them pulled away.

"What is it with us?" His voice was low and bewildered. "I've tried everything to let you go. But I keep coming back."

Harper thought of Dells. Of kissing him by her car. It had been a good kiss. But it hadn't felt like it did with Luke. Luke felt like home.

She could feel his heart, beating as fast as hers. "You're the only one I want," she said, simply. "I try to date other men but I keep coming back to you. I don't know why. I know it's impossible. Except, then I see you and I forget what impossible is. But I can't have you. Can I?"

He hesitated. "The only thing that matters right now," he said finally, "is that you survive."

It was the wrong answer. She twisted to get away, but he held her tight. "Wait, Harper. Dammit." His face flushed. "Let me finish what I'm trying to say."

Reluctantly, she stilled.

"You need to live first," he said evenly. "And then we have to figure this out. If we keep finding ourselves here, there has to be a reason, right? So whatever I thought I was doing with Sarah to put you behind me, it's not working."

Harper could think of a whole lot of arguments against almost everything he was saying, but she couldn't bring herself to say them now. Besides, what good would it do? Things were what they were. He wasn't wrong.

Besides, she'd tried to put him behind her as well. And failed.

"Okay," she said. "I accept that."

He watched her for a second, and then moved back. She slid down from the counter, feet thumping on the floor. Picking up the whiskey he'd set down a few minutes ago, she finished the shot and then lifted her head.

"Now. Let's talk about Martin Dowell."

31

Luke stayed another hour. He would have stayed all night, but everything between them was confusing enough. Sex would have made it worse.

"I'll sleep on the couch," he insisted. "I don't like you being alone."

"I'm guarded up to my eyeballs," she said, gesturing in the direction of the patrol car in the driveway. "You can save me again tomorrow. Right now, go home and get some sleep."

Still, he lingered in the doorway, darkness and rain behind him.

"That thing we talked about," he told her. "I was serious."

"Me too," she said.

When he was gone, she tried to get some rest. But the rain lashing against the windows and the wind roaring off the sea were the perfect formula for insomnia.

The next morning, she prowled the apartment restlessly, exhausted and hyperalert, listening to rain batter the roof, while fielding occasional calls from Baxter, who knew the basics, and DJ, who didn't, but still felt bad about the way she'd learned of Lee Howard's death. Even Lieutenant Blazer called. He had nothing new on Dowell, but insisted that she notify police dispatch when she was heading into Savannah.

Baxter told her not to come in to work. "If you're safer out there, stay out there."

The idea of not working sent panic rising in Harper's throat.

"It's not safe anywhere," she insisted. "And I've got work to do."

She showered and dressed for work, and then paused in front of the closet.

The shoulder holster was right where she'd shoved it the other day, on the top shelf. Slowly, she took it down, and pulled it on. She lifted the pistol from her bag, and snapped the clip into place. The metallic click was strangely satisfying.

After checking the chamber, she slid the gun into the holster under her arm and secured it. She pulled a light jacket on over the top.

"I can do this," she told herself.

There was no way Martin Dowell could stay on the loose for long. Luke was right: This wasn't his territory. He didn't have the same contacts here he did in Atlanta, and half the law enforcement in the state was searching for him. Eventually, they'd find him. All she had to do was keep her head down. And live through this.

For some reason the lyrics to "Revolver Road" went through her mind, sung in Allegra's pure voice. *Now the night grows dark and the hour grows cold. Meet me on Revolver Road.*

She thought again about last night—the conversation in the bar. She was convinced she knew who the killer was, but it seemed less important than it had last night. Still, she'd have a word with Baxter.

She headed for the door, dialing the number the lieutenant had given her for police dispatch as she walked.

A woman's voice answered, "Traffic investigations."

"This is Harper McClain. I'm heading in now."

"Come in via Abercorn Street," the woman told her crisply. "A patrol unit will be waiting there."

Outside, the rain was still falling hard. The weather system seemed to be settling in over the coast. Flooding was predicted. She dashed across the muddy drive to the Camaro, feet splashing as she waved at the patrol car.

Over the drumming of water against metal, she faintly heard the deputy start his engine. She backed in a half circle and pulled up behind the patrol car. The county deputy led her across Tybee's quiet streets, escorting her all the way to the far edge of the rain-soaked marshes, watercolor gray in the misty light. He peeled off a mile or two before she reached the city and turned back, leaving her alone.

As the dispatcher had instructed, she headed for Abercorn. Right as she reached it, a police motorcycle unit pulled out in front of her, gesturing for her follow.

On the dash, the scanner crackled into life, "Traffic unit one-five-seven."

"TU one-five-seven go ahead," the dispatcher said.

"Package collected. En route to agreed location."

"Copy that," the dispatcher said.

The package gripped the wheel, following the motorcycle as it splashed through streets that were beginning to flood.

The rain was starting to take its toll in other ways, too. Some tree branches bent so low from the weight of water that the long fronds of Spanish moss touched the ground. The motorcycle cop nimbly avoided the worst streets, leading her to Bay, where traffic was moving quicker.

Normally, she parked in the lot behind the newspaper building during the day—the street meters out front were cripplingly expensive—but the cop gestured for her to pull over directly in front of the main entrance. A guard stood waiting outside, water dripping from his hood.

The traffic cop stopped, his engine growling, and waited while she emerged from the car and hurried inside with the guard. As she walked, Harper cast quick glances down the street but spotted no barrel-chested, gray-haired men.

Then the guard closed the door and the street disappeared.

Even though she'd only been outside for seconds, water dripped from her hair into her eyes as she ran up the stairs, her scanner buzzing with fender benders, downed branches, and other rainy-day chaos.

The newsroom was humming with activity.

On a high from having his name on a front-page story that had been picked up by the wire services, DJ ran to intercept her.

"You okay?" he asked, searching her face.

"I'm fine, I promise," she said.

She wasn't at all certain it was true, but he took her at her word.

"Baxter wants me to work with you for the rest of the day. She says it's going to be busy and you'll need the spare hands." He was jittery with energy.

"Welcome to the dark side." Harper set her scanner on her desk.

"Where do I start, boss?"

Picking up the newspaper that lay on her desk, she flipped it over to the Lee Howard story, and thumped it with her finger. "Follow up on this. Find out more about the victim: call the Atlanta FBI office, see if you can get his biography or a photo, doesn't matter how old. You might be able to get that from the motor vehicles office. Find out about his record, any commendations. And his family. Was he married? Kids?"

It was a job she normally would have done herself, but she couldn't face it.

"Gotcha," he said. He spun back to his computer, fumbling with the phone in his haste.

He was getting down to work when Baxter appeared from the back room. Spotting Harper, she strode across the newsroom, blazer flying.

"You're alive," she said.

"For now," Harper replied, grimly. "DJ's looking into Lee Howard," she said. "We've got to decide how much to report about Dowell."

"Well, he's on the loose and he's a convicted killer evading parole," Baxter said. "That should do." She gave Harper a penetrating look. "Are you sure you're up to this."

"I can handle it," Harper said, curtly. "What about the Rayne case? The housemates were at each other's throats last night at the bar."

Baxter made a dismissive gesture. "If one of them confesses to murder we'll find space for it. For now, Dowell's our big story. Keep your mind on that."

It wasn't hard to do. News of Dowell's escape was getting around. The state police issued a defensively worded statement claiming that Dowell had been working with them on a high-level investigation. They also released a more recent image of him than any Harper had been able to find. It was clearly and without question the man she'd seen on Bay Street the night before.

When Harper called Blazer for an update that afternoon, he was confident they'd find him. "His face is all over the TV news," he told her. "He can't hide forever."

The problem was, he could hide for now.

The Dowell case kept her busy but whenever she had a break, she called Cara's number. Each time it went straight to voice mail.

She wondered where the actress had gone after leaving the Library Bar the night before. Surely not out to the house at Tybee. Not after those scenes.

There was no point in contacting Hunter or Allegra—the two of them clearly viewed her as untrustworthy now. She'd have to wait until Cara got in touch.

When her phone rang at around three o'clock that afternoon, she snatched it off the desk. But it wasn't Cara's name on the screen. It was Paul Dells.

Harper didn't answer right away. She was sorry, now, that she'd gone on that date.

Maybe she was being foolish. Dells had money, charm, and wit. She liked him. The only problem was, whenever she tried to imagine herself dating him, it just didn't work. She couldn't see herself dressing up to go to expensive restaurants with him. Having him always choose the wine. Meeting his friends, with their designer clothes. Talking about anything except murder. It just didn't work. She'd never fit into his life. There was too much blood on her shoes.

But she knew in her heart that wasn't the real the problem. The real problem was, Dells wasn't Luke.

With a sigh, she stood up and headed out of the room for some privacy and hit answer.

"Hey," she said.

"Hey yourself," Dells said. "I've got some leads on furnished apartments downtown. I thought we might go look at them this afternoon if you don't mind getting wet."

"I can't today," she said. "I'm working on a story. I won't get out of here until late."

He wasn't put off. "Tomorrow then. Before you go to work. Meet me for lunch."

Harper braced herself. "Look," she said, slowly, "I have to tell you the truth. I don't think now is the time for the thing we started the other night."

There was a pause.

"I see." His tone cooled. "You've had second thoughts."

"I have." She drew a breath. "Paul, I like you a lot. And I think this is probably a terrible decision. But I honestly don't see how it would work. We're too different. Besides, right now, my life is such a mess—"

"You don't have to make excuses," he cut her off, crisply. "I understand how this works. I've done it enough times myself. You don't owe me anything. But, the offer on the apartment stands separately from all of that. For your own safety. I can email you the addresses and arrange for you to go on your own."

He was being so reasonable, but she didn't miss the hurt underlying his words, and suddenly she felt guilty, and she wanted nothing more than to get off the phone and back to work.

"Thank you for everything," she said, hurriedly, "but right now I'm fine."

"McClain, don't make rash decisions because of what happened between us," he insisted. "Nothing matters as much as your safety. Anything you need, call me."

He'd gone back to using her last name and for some reason it stung.

"Paul, I am sorry about this," she said. "I warned you from the beginning I wasn't sure I was ready."

"Don't worry about me, McClain. I'm a big boy. Just watch yourself out there. Oh, by the way. This dead FBI agent. Does it have anything to do with Martin Dowell?"

Harper hesitated only briefly. But he was Channel Five now. And that's all he was.

"I don't know," she said. "Ask the detectives."

It was a long day on no sleep. By nine o'clock, she sat at her desk with her head resting on her hand, watching the rain pour down the windows, thinking about Lee Howard's lifelong guilt. And how it had cost his life.

In the mist and the dark, the Savannah River was invisible. She could see no farther than the street directly below. The old stone warehouses had faded into ghosts of themselves. Parts of the city were flooded now, but the highway out to Tybee was still clear. The marshes were good that way—a giant sponge, absorbing the rain. If this kept up, though, even the wetlands could be overwhelmed. The island would be cut off.

Everyone at police headquarters had been running their tails off all day dealing with the weather. But she couldn't go home without knowing the latest about Martin Dowell.

She stood up so suddenly, DJ glanced at her in surprise. "I'm going to police headquarters." Picking up her scanner, she weighed it in her hand, then handed it to him. "Keep an ear on this." She grabbed her bag. "I'll have my phone with me. Call me if you hear anything."

"Code four in particular," he said.

She shot him a look. "Learn the other codes, DJ."

"I have a list," he called after her, but she was already halfway across the newsroom.

Downstairs, she stood impatiently by the door waiting for the guard to go outside first. He donned a raincoat, then splashed out in grim silence, looking both ways before motioning for her.

Harper ran for the car, keys in her hand. She moved fast but she was soaked by the time she got in. The rain was relentless.

This time, she didn't call the police to let them know she was on the move. They'd find out soon enough.

Still, as she crawled through the city streets, avoiding the lanes she knew by now were submerged, she watched the rearview mirror intently. Nobody was behind her. The streets were deserted. Even the tourists were staying inside.

She parked in the fire zone close to the sturdy brick police building and dashed through the pouring rain for the door, her boots sloshing through the water, the gun pressing against her ribs.

Dwayne looked up from the front desk as she walked in. "Lord. Look what the cat dragged in," he called as she dripped across the lobby on the flatted cardboard boxes someone had placed atop the old linoleum flooring to soak up the water.

Harper didn't smile. "I need a word with Luke Walker or Daltrey," she said.

Dwayne had known her since she was twelve. He heard the edge to her voice.

"They're both upstairs. Hang on." He dialed quickly. "Detective, I've got Harper McClain down here." He listened and said, "You got it." When he hung up he gestured at the security door. "She says go up."

After he released the security door, Harper hurried through, her boots skidding on the floor as she raced down the dark back hallway that always smelled damp even on the driest day, and was worse than ever now, and up the wide, scuffed stairs to the next floor. When she reached the landing, Luke and Daltrey were already walking toward her.

"Is there any news?" she asked. "I've been going crazy sitting in the office."

Luke's worried expression told her the answer even before he spoke. "We've got nothing."

Seeing her face fall, Daltrey explained, "The storm's slowing everything down. Martin Dowell's got too much sense to go out in this. He's holed up somewhere."

"We've got warnings out statewide and into South Carolina and Florida as well," Luke told her. "If he moves we'll find him."

Biting her lip, Harper nodded, slowly. But she couldn't seem to catch her breath. How was she was going to make it through another night sitting with a gun, waiting to be killed?

"He doesn't care about warnings," she told them. "We're giving him too much time."

Hearing the panic in her voice, Luke stepped toward her. "We *will* get him, Harper."

"I know you will," she said, but her voice was uneven.

Luke glanced at Daltrey. "I don't like her being alone out there tonight. What does Blazer think?"

"He thinks she's safer out there than she would be in the city," Daltrey told him. "There's a county unit sitting outside her door all night."

Still, he shook his head, every muscle tight as a wire. "I still don't like it," he said. "I'm going to talk to Blazer."

Daltrey leveled a warning look at him. "You do you, Walker. But the lieutenant has a plan, and he believes that plan is working."

"Luke, don't." Harper reached out, and then stopped herself. Her hand fell back to her side. "I'll be okay."

Luke held her eyes for a moment, and then nodded reluctantly.

She wondered whether he'd show up at her door again tonight. And if he did, whether she'd be strong enough to send him away twice.

Daltrey's phone buzzed. She glanced down at it, and then turned to Luke. "We need to go. The coroner needs to talk to us."

The three of them walked down the stairs together in somber silence. At the front door they stopped.

"Call dispatch before you go home tonight," Daltrey told Harper. "Take the escort."

"I won't forget," Harper said.

As Daltrey pushed open the door and walked into the wall of rain, behind her back, Luke caught Harper's hand for just a moment, out of sight.

"Dowell's going to make a mistake," he assured her. "They always make mistakes."

As Harper walked to her car, she hoped he was right.

Because it seemed to her that Martin Dowell kept proving everyone wrong.

32

After leaving the police station, Harper drove cautiously back toward Bay Street. Three times she had to slam on the brakes to avoid oak branches blocking the road. She'd just stopped at a red light when her phone rang. Sure it was Baxter wondering where she was, she pulled it from her pocket.

But it wasn't Baxter. It was Hunter.

"Harper, thank God." His voice had a high, nervous pitch. She could hear the wind through the phone, howling like someone in pain.

The fine hairs on the back of her neck rose. "What's wrong?"

"You've got to get out here." He gave a gasping, unfunny laugh. "I thought we were fine, you know? I thought we'd get through this. But we won't. Cara's lost her mind."

The light turned green but Harper stayed where she was, windshield wipers thumping hard. "What's happening?"

She could hear muffled sounds through the line. Raised voices. Someone—Allegra?—was crying hysterically.

"*Stop it,*" Hunter shouted so loudly it made Harper jump. "Put down the gun."

Then very clearly, Cara's voice, screaming, hysterically, "He trusted you. And you—"

Someone covered the receiver and she couldn't make out the last words.

"Just hang up!" It was Allegra's voice. "Hang up and help me!"

The phone went dead. Harper stared at it for just a moment, then shook herself and dialed Luke's number.

He answered on the first ring. "You okay?"

"I just got a call from Hunter," she said. "He told me to come out there. They're fighting. Cara was screaming in the background. It sounded like she was accusing Hunter of murder. They said something about a gun."

"Hang on a minute," he said, tersely.

She heard him relaying this to Daltrey, who gave a short reply.

"We're on our way to the coroner's office right now," he said. "I'll call Tybee P.D. and get a local unit out there."

"I'm going, too," she said. "I need to see what's happening."

"Harper, don't do that," he said. "It's too dangerous."

"It's my job," she reminded him, although she knew Baxter wasn't interested in this story. "I'll call dispatch and let them know. I promise I'll be careful."

"The roads are a mess. Half the streets are flooded."

"The Tybee highway's still clear," she said, stubbornly.

There was a pause. When he spoke again he'd clearly realized there was no point in arguing.

"For God's sake, be careful," he told her. "If it gets much worse they'll close that highway. You could get stuck out there."

"I will."

As soon as she hung up, she switched to hands-free and called police dispatch to let them know where she was going. They directed her to a nearby street for an escort.

The next number she dialed was Miles's. "Get out to Tybee," she told him. "There's trouble at Xavier Rayne's house."

"Ah, hell," he complained. "They couldn't wait until there's a nice little hurricane to do this?"

"They just called me, screaming about a gun. I'm heading out there now." He didn't say anything, but she could sense his reluctance. "Something's going to happen out there tonight, Miles," she insisted. "I can sense it."

He heaved a sigh. "Fine. I'll head out there."

Baxter, when Harper called her a minute later, was even less impressed. "We've got a dead FBI agent to deal with and you're going to babysit a movie star?"

Harper was nearing the marshes by then and the phone began to break up, the signal crumbling from distance and bad weather.

"This is it, Baxter." She raised her voice to be heard above the crackle. "I can feel it. Someone's getting arrested tonight. Just hold the front page until you hear from me, okay? Baxter?"

The phone was dead.

Harper didn't know if the editor had hung up on her or she'd lost the signal. The wind was blowing the car so hard it shimmied. Driving required all her attention now.

This time, no county patrol car met her on the marshes to escort her across. All the deputies were probably too busy dealing with the storm. The road was deserted. Water blew across it like shallow ocean waves. The car's wide tires sent wide sheets of spray high in the air.

If anything, the weather grew worse as she neared the coast. Even with the wipers at top speed, she could see the highway only in flashes before it disappeared beneath streams of water again. She slowed to twenty miles per hour, and gripped the wheel so tightly her hands ached.

When she finally reached the bridge onto the island, she let out a long, relieved breath. At the first intersection, the traffic light had come loose and swung by a wire, buffeted by the wind. The light was flashing red.

Danger.

Her phone rang as she was navigating cautiously around a fallen tree that had blocked much of the road. She hit answer without looking at it. "McClain."

"Harper, it's Luke."

He said something else, but the signal was terrible. The sound broke apart before she could catch it. "What, Luke?" she raised her voice. "I can't hear you."

"Tybee Police . . . busy . . . can't . . . won't . . ."

"You're breaking up, Luke," she said.

"Soon . . . careful." His voice disappeared.

Harper hit recall, but the phone had no signal at all. She thought she'd got the gist anyway: The local police were tied up with storm damage and couldn't get to the house right now. She'd be on her own. And she wouldn't be able to call Savannah if she needed help.

The realization made her stomach tighten. If her suspicions were right, there was a killer in that house. But she couldn't go back now. Not without knowing the truth.

When she neared the turn for Admiral's Row, everything was strangely dark. Not a flicker of light came from any window. Every streetlight was out.

A power line must be down, she thought as she turned cautiously into the narrow street. Her headlights were blinding in the pitch-black night. The darkness gave the island an abandoned feel, as if everyone had fled in a panic, leaving behind cars and homes full of belongings. It was eerie.

The trees swayed violently, casting skittering shadows. A frond broke loose from a palm and shot across in front of her car, making her jump.

Harper pulled up behind number 6 and cut the engine. The century-old house sat in absolute darkness, its windows closed and opaque.

Nervousness sent a shiver down her spine. She could feel danger around her. Taste it in the air like salt water.

Putting a hand on her side, she touched the hard metal of the gun and hoped to God she wouldn't have to use it.

Then she grabbed the door handle and pulled it. The second she stepped out of the Camaro she could hear nothing except the enraged roaring of the wind. She fought to close the door, leaning her weight against it until it finally latched.

Squinting against the rain, she bent forward and ran to the house. At the top of the low steps, she knocked twice, hard.

No one answered.

The wind lashed wet strands of her hair into her eyes as she knocked again, harder this time, shouting into the howl of the storm, "It's Harper. Are you in there?"

The storm was so loud she almost missed the sound of the gunshot.

Crouching low, she spun around just as Cara stepped out of the darkness, a gun glittering silver in her hand.

Her billowing white dress and flying pale hair gave her the appearance of a vengeful angel as she strode purposefully toward the house.

Harper froze, uncertain whether to run away or try to stop her. In the end, though, Cara made the decision for her, pointing the gun at her chest. "Get out of the way, Harper. I'm going to kill her." Her voice was steady, but the hand holding the gun trembled visibly.

Harper didn't have to ask who she was talking about.

"Don't do it," she pleaded, holding up her hands. "You don't have to do this."

The actress shook her head, rain streaking her face like tears. "She thinks she can just take whatever she wants. Destroy whatever she wants. Because her life has been *hard*?" She took a sobbing breath. "They both betrayed Xavier and they lied to me. I lived with them and they were *murderers*. They have to pay."

At that moment, the door flew open. Hunter stepped out into the rain and took in the scene.

"Jesus Christ, what is this?" He gestured to where Harper was huddling—hands held out as if they could protect her from a bullet. "You're going to shoot Harper because you're mad at Allegra?"

"I'm not hurting Harper." Cara raised the gun toward him. "But I will hurt you if you try to stop me. Where is that cowardly bitch?"

"You can't do this." Pale but determined, Hunter didn't flinch when she jerked the gun at his head. "Killing Allegra won't bring him back."

"Stop protecting her," Cara snapped. "You're pathetic, you know that? You protect her like she's a little kid. She's a murderer. She's a cheat. She's insane."

"*She's* insane?" Hunter was incredulous. "You're standing in the middle of a storm waving a gun at me and a newspaper reporter and Allegra's the crazy one? Put the gun down, Cara. Let's talk about this."

"There's nothing to talk about." She held the gun steady. "The best thing about prison is that I won't have to listen to you anymore."

The wind gusted, pushing her with such force she stumbled, swinging the gun. Harper flinched until she regained control. She could barely stand. If she didn't kill someone on purpose she might kill them by accident.

She had her own gun, of course. But two guns being waved around wouldn't make anything better.

Taking a deep breath, she stepped forward slowly and held out her hands. "Cara, put the gun down. Let's just talk about this."

The two of them looked at her as if they'd forgotten she was there.

"You don't have to kill anyone," she continued. "Tell the police what you know. Or tell *me* what you know. Let the law do its job."

Cara gave a dark laugh. "I've been waiting days for the law to do its job. It's done nothing. And all along I thought some crazy fan killed my boyfriend. Then I figured it out. Do you know what happened, Harper?" She twitched the gun at Hunter. "Did he tell you?"

Hunter started to argue, but she raised the gun to his head.

"Shut up," she ordered. He closed his mouth again.

"Xavier's two best friends killed him," Cara said. "Didn't they, Hunter?"

"No," he said firmly. "No, they didn't."

"Don't lie!" she shouted, squeezing the gun convulsively. "You know what you did."

Giving up on mediation, Harper looked around for escape. She took a step away as the two argued. And another, until she was off to one side—far enough that Cara couldn't keep the gun trained on both Hunter and her. The actress didn't seem to notice—she was focused on him, now.

"I'm not lying," he insisted. "You don't know the whole story."

"Sure I do." Cara's voice was bitter. "My friend Allegra slept with my boyfriend. She was in love with him. You knew all about it, and decided not to tell me. But I knew something was going on and I demanded to know. Xavier told me he'd been seeing someone else. He promised he'd never sleep with her again. He said he didn't love her, that he loved only me. The only thing he didn't tell me is that it was Allegra." Her voice broke. Harper couldn't tell if she was crying—the rain was falling too hard. "Then she killed Xavier because her feelings were hurt. Get out here, Allegra, you *murderer*." She screamed the last words at the impassive white building behind him.

Harper waited for Hunter to tell her she was wrong. But he didn't. He just stared at her, his glasses speckled with rain.

"Why are you protecting her?" Cara demanded. "Why won't you just turn her in?"

"She's only nineteen, Cara, for God's sake." Hunter seemed to think this explained everything. "She can't go to prison for the rest of her life."

Cara's lips twisted. "I was nineteen once. Nobody died."

Something shifted in the shadows behind her. At first, Harper thought it was just branches swinging. But gradually she made out the shape of a man hidden behind the trees, moving slowly. In his black uniform, he was almost invisible until a flicker of lightning lit up the street and for an instant she saw his face. It was Tom Southby, the officer she'd met the night Xavier Rayne was killed. His eyes were fixed on Cara.

"Allegra!" Cara screamed, pointing the gun at the house. "Stop hiding."

"Fine. I'm here." Allegra appeared in the doorway. She looked tiny next to Hunter, almost childlike. Her brown eyes held Cara's with unnatural calmness. "Just put the gun down. I'll tell the police the truth."

Cara clearly hadn't been expecting this. "I don't believe you," she said, but she sounded uncertain.

"You're going to tell them anyway, and they'll figure it out." She glanced at Harper. "And Harper knows now so what's the point?"

"So, you admit you murdered him," Cara said.

"It was an accident. I was angry." Allegra stepped closer to Hunter. "I didn't want to hurt him."

"That was no accident. You dumped him in the ocean." Cara's voice trembled. "That took effort."

"It's just . . . he was abandoning me like everyone always abandons me." Allegra stifled a sob, pressing her fists against her eyes. "I wanted him to stay with me. That's all. I wanted him to care. I didn't mean to hurt him."

"You're a lying little murderer." Cara's voice grew cold. "You killed him because he hurt your feelings. And you have to pay." She steadied the gun.

Southby jumped from the darkness, landing hard on her back. The blow knocked her off her feet. The gun went off, the retort loud but fleeting, dulled by the wind.

Harper threw herself down.

That was when she heard Allegra cry out. "No!"

Harper lifted her head. Hunter was sliding slowly down the stairs. He clung to the narrow bannister with both hands, but seemed suddenly too weak to grip it.

As she stared in horror, he gave her a look of puzzled disbelief, before collapsing in the mud at her feet.

3 3

Still held in Southby's fierce grip, Cara gave a howl of despair that sent goosebumps up Harper's arms as she knelt at Hunter's side, putting an arm beneath his thin shoulders.

Trying not to panic, she pressed her hand to his neck, feeling for a pulse. It was there, fluttering beneath her fingertips. But his skin was so cold.

Behind her on the front steps, Allegra was hysterical, screaming, "*No, no, no.*"

Hunter blinked slowly. His lips moved, but no sound came out. A dark stain spread inexorably across the right side of his shirt. It was hard to tell where he'd been shot—it could have been anywhere from the shoulder to the chest.

"Allegra, get me a towel or some cloth," Harper ordered.

The girl didn't seem to hear her. She was white as milk, staring at Hunter.

"*Allegra.*" Harper raised her voice. "Get me a towel."

Her firmness got through. Giving her a startled look, the girl turned and fled.

Southby talked quickly into his radio before hurrying to her side, leaving Cara where she'd fallen. "How bad is it?"

"Bad," Harper said, quietly. "Ambulance?"

"On its way, but this storm . . ." He didn't complete the thought, but he didn't have to.

Carefully, Harper began to open Hunter's shirt.

"Help me . . ." he whispered.

"You're going to be okay," she said, but she could hear the doubt in her own voice.

Her wet fingers slipped on the buttons and she swore under her breath, ripping the shirt open. Blood mixed with rain on his thin chest and ran in dark rivulets between his ribs. The hole was just below his shoulder.

Allegra dashed out of the house, clutching a white towel like a surrender flag. Snatching it from her, Southby wadded it up and pressed it firmly against the wound, holding it in place with both hands. In the distance Harper thought she heard a siren wail, but the wind blew the sound away.

"I didn't want to hurt anyone," Hunter whispered, looking at Harper. "I've been so scared."

"I know," she said gently.

Kneeling in the mud beside him, Allegra clung to his hand, her eyes wide with fear. "Don't die," she kept whispering, over and over. "Don't die."

Harper rested a hand on Hunter's good arm as Southby kept steady pressure on the wound. "Allegra shot Xavier, didn't she? She came to you for help. You pushed him out into the ocean. To protect her."

Hunter's eyes almost closed, then opened again. A tear escaped and ran down his cheek, mingling with the rain. "She's just a kid." A whisper, lost in the storm.

A few feet away Cara sobbed brokenly, her perfect white clothes stained with mud, her hands cuffed behind her back.

At the end of the road, the flashing blue lights of the ambulance lit up the night. Relief loosened the tightness in Harper's chest.

"Hang in there," she told Hunter. "You're going to be fine."

Miles arrived just as the paramedics were loading Hunter onto a stretcher. By then, Southby had separated and handcuffed Cara and

Allegra, and secured the house. He did a damn good job on his own, Harper thought, bagging the gun, taking her statement. Working methodically.

"I think I underestimated you," she told him, as she watched him lock the mansion's front door and seal it with crime tape.

"Everyone does," he said. But he smiled.

A paramedic gave Harper wipes to get the blood off her hands. "Works better than soap," she assured her, before hurrying back to the ambulance.

While Miles got busy taking pictures, she kept trying to call the newsroom, but her phone had no signal.

"It's the storm," Southby told her, rain dripping from the plastic cover on his hat. "Cell tower's out."

Harper glanced at her watch. It was nearly eleven o'clock and Baxter had no idea what had happened out here, or that the paper had an exclusive front-page story on its hands.

She ran over to where Miles was checking shots on his camera. "I'm heading back to Savannah. How much longer will you be out here?"

Clutching his Canon in one hand, he looked around, frowning. "Ten minutes? Maybe fifteen?"

"Okay. I'll see you back there." She hurried away, boots splashing in the water.

"Drive carefully," he called after her. "The road's starting to flood."

It was a relief to get into the car and turn the heater on. Harper hadn't realized how cold she was until she began to get warm again. She was soaked to the skin.

The winds had let up a little, but the rain was still falling hard when she crossed the bridge off the island and into the marshes. In her mind she kept going over the night's events, hearing Cara's terrified scream, as if she'd been shot instead of Hunter.

She could see now how she'd pieced it all together last night at the Library. When Allegra dedicated the song to the love of her life, Cara had known her well enough to know she'd meant it. From there, she'd figured out the rest. Everything she hadn't wanted to see unfolded in front of her.

Harper wanted to believe Allegra when she'd said she hadn't meant to kill Xavier. She didn't know why she'd taken a gun to the beach, though. Maybe she wanted to scare him. Maybe, like so many people, she simply underestimated the power of a bullet.

But the law wouldn't care. Not enough to keep her out of prison.

She'd gone about four miles when she first noticed the headlights in her rearview mirror. At first, she thought it was Miles, heading back to the paper earlier than he'd expected. He always drove so fast.

The next time she looked up, the lights were much closer. As she watched them she felt the first stirrings of unease.

The vehicle was too big to be Miles's Mustang. It looked more like an SUV. Perhaps it was a police car, she told herself, or an ambulance. Nobody else was out in this weather.

Whoever it was, they were moving fast. The golden glow of the head-lights soon filled the mirror.

Nervously, she sped up, but the lights continued to approach at the same relentless rate. She considered slowing down and motioning for it to pass, but couldn't make herself do it. Every instinct told her to get away.

Swearing under her breath, she pressed the accelerator to the floor. Almost immediately, the low-slung Camaro hydroplaned, its tail swing-ing sickeningly left-right, left-right, until she eased up again.

Sweat beaded her forehead. There were no turnoffs out here. No side roads. No one to help. Just the flat, empty marshes, invisible in the dark-ness around her.

She stared at the headlights in the rectangle of glass, willing it to back off. To go around.

Instead, with an animal-like roar, it accelerated, slamming into her car.

The jolt sent the Camaro skidding wildly.

Gasping, Harper gripped the wheel so hard her arms hurt as she wrestled the car straight again. Desperately, she shoved the accelerator down, fighting the hydroplane. Her hands white-knuckled the wheel.

But the SUV had more weight than the Camaro. It could get a grip on the road as it roared up at her again, slamming into her again, harder this time.

In an instant, everything turned into a nightmare.

The steering wheel spun beneath Harper's hands as if some invisible, powerful creature had taken control of it.

The car seemed to float in dizzying circles, and then there wasn't asphalt beneath the tires but grass and mud, and the Camaro was juddering and whirling and she was slammed against the door.

She could hear herself sobbing, as if from far away.

With awful silence, the car tilted on its side and then flipped over. The top became the bottom. The sky became the floor. Again. And again.

And then there was nothing.

34

The first thing Harper knew was pain. She didn't know where she was. All she was certain of was that she was cold and everything hurt.

With effort, she opened her eyes, but it made no difference. She saw only blackness.

Someone whimpered and it took her a second to realize it was her.

Her thoughts were hazy as the previous moments slowly took shape. *I've been in an accident,* she told herself. *I'm alive.*

Something cold dripped down the side of her face; she wondered distantly whether it was water or blood.

Gradually, the fog of shock lifted and she remembered it all.

Martin Dowell. It had to be him. He'd found her. And he was out there somewhere. Waiting for her.

The realization was like a slap. Her thinking cleared.

The airbag had deflated and she shoved the delicate fabric away from her face. All the windows had shattered, and rainwater was pouring in, drenching her.

Everything seemed to work but something was wrong with her left arm. She kept trying to move it but it wouldn't cooperate. When she shifted it with her right hand, the stab of pain made her breath hiss between her teeth.

She reached out for her phone but it wasn't on the central console anymore. The console, the passenger seat—everything was covered in broken glass and mud. Her bag, her phone—she had no idea where anything was.

And it was so dark.

Twisting her body, she fumbled for the door handle with her right hand. The handle gave but the door opened only an inch before jamming in the mud.

Harper sat back in her seat, panting from the effort. She couldn't stay here, not if Dowell was looking for her. She had to get out. She had to run.

Gritting her teeth against a pain so intense it made her sweat, she swung herself sideways, hanging on to the wheel with her good hand and kicking the door, forcing it open another inch. And again. And again.

But it wouldn't open far enough. The mud was too high, and the car was too low.

She'd have to find another way.

Pulling her jacket sleeve down around her good hand, she swept jagged shards of glass from the window frame. Using her right hand to lift herself up, she slowly, painfully, swung her legs out the window.

Taking a deep breath, she tried to jump away from the car, but she was too weak to make it and instead landed in an ungainly pile in the ice-cold water. The pain was so excruciating she cried out.

She lay on her back, rain lashing her face like thousands of tiny stones. Her breathing was raspy and labored. Every single breath hurt. She thought she might have broken a rib. She knew she had to move, but she was so *tired*.

She couldn't do this. She was done.

Hot tears burned her eyes, and she took in a painful, shaky breath.

I never thought it would end like this, she thought, hopelessly. *In the mud. In the rain. Alone.*

Through a blur of tears, she saw a single beam of light cutting through the darkness. For a split second, she thought someone was coming to save her. But then she realized it wasn't a helicopter or a police car.

It was one of the Camaro's headlights, glowing like a beacon.

The car was crushed on all sides, axle deep in mud, and *shining*.

A gunshot cracked across the marsh, as loud as cannon fire.

Drawing in a sharp breath, Harper rolled over, dragging herself up onto her knees.

"Where you hiding, girl?" The voice came from the darkness. It was oddly familiar. Southern and comfortable, like family.

And it was close.

The rush of adrenaline gave her strength. She had to move. That light couldn't give him better directions. She had to get away from the car if she wanted to live.

Groaning under her breath, she lumbered to her feet like a beaten boxer, punch-drunk and stumbling. Her left arm swung loose, as if it belonged to someone else. It didn't hurt anymore but it felt wrong, hanging like that.

Clutching it with her right hand, she stumbled away from the voice, away from the car, away from the light.

Instantly, another gunshot crackled through the black night.

She ducked but kept going, wondering if she'd even feel it if the bullet hit, she was already in so much pain. Her feet splashed through the water.

A few yards away, a flashlight swung around the marshes, seeking her.

"I don't want to kill you." The voice echoed above the rain. "I didn't want to kill your mama. But I've got to do this. I made your daddy a promise, and I gotta keep it."

Gritting her teeth, Harper kept moving, more cautiously now, trying to be quiet.

"He betrayed me," the voice continued, as the light searched the flat landscape. "And there's a price for that."

The water was getting deeper. It was up to her knees. But Harper kept moving in a slow, limping run, clearing the rain and mud out of her eyes with her fist, then grabbing on to her arm to stop it flopping like a dead thing at her side.

She knew enough about shock to know she needed to get warm and dry soon, or that alone could kill her, but before she could think about it much, another gunshot split the night—this one sounded closer.

She ducked and lost her balance, tripping over something solid and low, and went sprawling.

For a second, her head was underwater. Panicking, she thrashed until she realized the water wasn't deep and pulled herself up, spitting mud and fighting the urge to cough.

She knew she couldn't go much farther. Her breathing was getting worse and she'd begun to shiver violently.

When she looked around, she found this wasn't a bad place to hide. She was surrounded by high grass, which shielded her. From this location, she could see the Camaro, about thirty yards away, resting at an unnatural angle, its lone working headlight pointed mournfully at nothing. Beyond that, she could just make out the shadowy shape of an SUV, parked on the highway, about a hundred yards from her hiding place.

Between her and the battered Camaro, a flashlight moved unsteadily as Dowell picked his way through the deep mud.

Harper peered into the distance on all sides but there were no other signs of life. There was no indication that his son was with him.

It was just the two of them, alone, in the dark.

Maybe she could wait him out? But even as she thought it, she knew it wasn't likely.

If there was one thing she'd learned about Martin Dowell, it was that he was a patient man. Only one of them was walking out of this marsh alive.

Something brushed her leg and she scrambled back, nearly landing on her back in the water again. Her heart hammered against her ribs. There were alligators out here.

If Dowell didn't get her, they might.

Somehow, she had to get away. But, how? Every time she moved, he fired.

It didn't matter, she decided. She had to try. If she could get far enough away from him, she could get through the marsh to the road and find help.

It was the only option.

She waited until the flashlight was pointed away from her. Then, cautiously, she stumbled to her feet and began to limp away from the car. She moved slowly but each step seemed to echo as loudly as a shout.

She'd only gone a few feet when she heard that grating voice again. "I know you're there, girl. I can hear you splashing. Come on, now. Let's talk this through."

Harper bit her tongue. The one thing she absolutely couldn't do was say a word. She might as well pin a bull's-eye on her forehead. When a moment of silence had passed, she stumbled on, her feet sinking into the mud. Her lungs weren't working right, and pulling her feet out of the muck took all her strength. In a few minutes she was winded.

Her left arm had begun to ache fiercely and she reached over to hold it steady. As she did, her hand brushed the hard lump against her side. It took her a second to realize what she was feeling.

The Glock.

In her panic, she'd forgotten all about it. Of course, she couldn't be certain it would work. She'd been in water—it must have gotten wet.

Still, what if it did?

Reaching inside her jacket, she carefully unsnapped the clasp holding the gun in place and pulled it out.

Thanking whatever gods had seen to it that she broke her left arm instead of her right, she held the pistol steady.

"Come out, girl," Dowell cajoled from somewhere near the car. "I've waited long enough. Every second I spent in that prison, I thought of this moment. Seventeen years I waited in that cell. It's time."

Harper was warmed by a surge of hatred. There were so many things she wanted to say to him. So many angry, true things.

But she stayed silent, the gun in her hand, and angled herself toward his voice.

If he came for her, she'd get him first.

As she waited, beneath the steady rush of rain, she noticed a new sound. It was far away, but getting closer.

She turned toward the road. A car—its headlights like long golden blades—appeared from the Savannah end of the highway, far away but moving straight toward them. Harper's heart leaped.

If she could get to the road she could flag it down. Get help. Live.

But as she calculated her chances, her hope ebbed. She was too far away. She'd never make it. Dowell would see her.

She watched with bitter longing as the car swept down the road toward Tybee. It was going to pass right by them, never even realizing what was happening.

Just as she was beginning to despair, the car slowed. The driver must have noticed the SUV. Maybe seen the Camaro's headlights. Whoever it was, they must have realized there'd been an accident.

By the time it reached the SUV, it was barely moving.

Then, miraculously, the car stopped.

Harper held her breath. Dowell had gone quiet. Had he seen it, too?

For a long moment, nothing happened. The headlights stayed on. The car didn't move.

Finally, the engine switched off.

The wind had died down. Across the acre of marshland, she heard the sound of car doors opening and then closing hard.

Dowell must have heard it, too, because she heard him mutter, "Goddammit."

His flashlight went out.

Hope rushed through Harper like heat. She longed to scream for help but he was too close. He could shoot her and have plenty of time left over to shoot whoever just got out of that car. So, she said nothing. And waited.

Above the sound of the rain, she heard Dowell stumbling through the water. He seemed to be heading toward the wreckage of the Camaro.

Harper strained her ears. What was he up to?

Near the road, the cold, white beams of two flashlights flickered on, moving steadily toward the wreckage of the Camaro.

"Harper?" a voice called out across the marshes.

Her heart stopped.

It was Luke and Daltrey, looking for her. Joy quickly turned to fear, however. They had no idea what they were walking into.

As she studied the terrain, she realized with horror what Dowell was planning. By moving closer to the Camaro he'd positioned himself right where they were heading.

If she called out to them, he'd kill her. If she didn't, he'd kill them.

It was a trap.

Swiping the rain and mud from her eyes, she watched the flashlights moving toward the damaged car in tormented silence.

She couldn't let them get hurt.

She drew a breath and shouted, "Luke! Dowell's out here. Be careful—"

The sound of a gunshot cut off the last word. Dowell was a hell of a shot. He missed her by inches. She thought she felt the heat of the bullet as it passed.

She dropped down low, holding the gun above her head to keep it dry.

Another shot cracked through the night.

Both flashlights blinked out.

A beat passed.

"Martin Dowell." It was Daltrey's voice, dripping with authority and contempt. "We are Savannah police officers. Give yourself up. It's over."

From somewhere in the dark, Dowell laughed, an awful, unfunny sound. "I've got an idea—how about you come and get me, girl? I'll show you how that FBI agent died. I know you've been wondering."

"Dowell, there's nowhere to go." Luke acted like Dowell hadn't spoken. "There's nothing out here but alligators and mud. "

"Now, that simply ain't true," Dowell replied gleefully. "There's also Harper McClain out here. Isn't that true, Miss McClain?"

Harper leveled her gun in the direction of his voice and said nothing.

"Just walk out of here now, with your hands where we can see them, and you get to live," Daltrey said. "I assure you that's the best option you have right now."

There was a long silence, and then, without warning, Dowell let loose a spray of bullets in the direction of the detectives' voices.

He was shouting something but Harper couldn't make out the words above the deafening sound of gunfire.

In the silence that followed, she heard the distinctive metallic sound of a clip being ejected and a new one being inserted.

Fifteen more bullets, she thought. *Fifteen more chances to kill.*

He would get them eventually. They would try to catch him off guard and they would fail and he'd kill them.

She couldn't let that happen. She had to act. He was close enough to her that she could hear his labored breathing. She had the best chance to bring him down.

Besides, it was her he wanted.

"Dowell," she called without moving, letting him gauge her voice. "Stop shooting. I'll come with you if you let them go."

There was a pause.

"You had a change of heart? What's caused that now?" His voice was suspicious.

She thought fast. "I can't stay out here any longer," she said, making her voice weak. "I've pierced a lung. I need help."

"Come over here, then." His voice held lazy interest. "Let's finish this thing."

Harper moved in the water, just enough to attract his attention, but remained on her knees, the gun held steadily in her good hand.

"I've got a broken leg," she said. "I can't walk anymore."

For a second, he didn't reply. Then, the sound of splashing as he began wading toward her.

Her pulse began to race.

"Where the hell are you?" His voice was closer.

She could see his shadow now, no more than twenty feet away. Short and sturdy, silhouetted against the Camaro's fading headlight.

One last time that car was trying to help her.

In one smooth move, she raised the gun, using all her strength to hold it steady with one hand. She pressed her finger firmly on the trigger to release the safety. Felt the mechanism shift.

She exhaled. And pulled the trigger.

The noise was deafening. With no strength and no left hand to brace her, the recoil knocked her over. She landed flat on her back in waist-deep water. The gun slipped from her fingers.

She fought to get up, scrambling frantically to find it in the mud with her one good hand. When she looked up, Dowell was stumbling toward her, holding his own gun.

Sobbing, Harper fought to get away, but her legs wouldn't cooperate. The deep mud clung to her knees, pulling her down.

Dowell stood over her. His eyes were glazed. The gun wavered in his hand. Harper flinched, waiting for the shot.

Instead, his knees buckled and he toppled forward, landing heavily on top of her, pushing her down under the dark water. Caught off guard, she fought to push him off, but he held on tenaciously, holding her down, his fingers like snakes against her body.

She tried to cry out but the sound was lost in the water and mud filling her mouth.

As the last of the air left her lungs, it occurred to Harper that he finally had what he wanted. She was going to die.

Then, with shocking abruptness, Dowell was gone, the weight of him lifted from her chest.

Freed, Harper struggled to the surface and took a gasping breath. Seconds later, a hand grabbed her by the jacket, pulling her up and dragging her to a patch of grass.

"You okay?" Daltrey asked, bending over as Harper sank to her knees, coughing muddy water from her lungs. She spat, trying to clear the metallic taste from her mouth.

A few feet away, Luke stood grim-faced over Dowell's body. The man lay on his side. His hands were cuffed, and he wasn't moving.

"Is he alive?" Harper rasped the question through frozen lips.

"Barely." Daltrey shone her flashlight into the darkness around them, her face alert. "Was he alone?"

"I th-think so." Harper was shivering so hard the words came out in pieces. She'd never been this cold before. She felt strange—distant from her own body.

Luke waded over to them and crouched down next to Harper. His eyes searched her face. "You okay?"

She shook her head. She had never been less okay.

"We should search the area," Daltrey told him. "His son could be out there."

He didn't take his eyes off Harper. "She's in shock. We need to get her somewhere warm," he said. "Backup's on the way. Let them search. Anyway, if he's out there for long, the gators'll get him."

He tried to pull Harper to her feet, but as soon as he let go, she sagged back toward the ground. Her legs had given up. There was no strength left in her.

Swearing softly, he slipped an arm beneath her shoulders and swept her into his arms, lifting her like a child.

"Hang in there," he told her, and began striding across the marsh toward the road.

Faintly, above the sound of the rain, Harper heard sirens wailing. Far away, flickering blue lights lit up the sky.

She rested her cheek against his chest, where it fit like a puzzle piece put in the right place at last, and closed her eyes.

It was over.

35

The next morning, Harper sat propped up in her bed on the fourth floor of Savannah Memorial Hospital, holding the extra-large coffee DJ had smuggled in. She leaned over to look at the newspaper he was holding. The main headline read SUSPECTED MURDERER KILLED IN MARSH SHOOT-OUT.

Beneath it was a picture of Harper's Camaro, deep in the mud, the headlight still shining a warning. It was juxtaposed with an old photo of Martin Dowell, square-faced and scowling. Next to that was a shot of Harper that Miles had taken last autumn, her auburn hair backlit by the sun.

The first paragraphs read:

Convicted murderer Martin Dowell died of a gunshot wound after attacking *Daily News* reporter Harper McClain on Highway 80 in the marshes near Oyster Creek during the height of the storm.

Dowell, who had been recently released after serving 17 years for murder, had been under the supervision of state police, until he removed his monitored ankle bracelet and disappeared two days ago, with the help of his son, Aaron Dowell.

McClain said he forced her car off the road and held her at gunpoint. He told her he'd come "to finish what he started" before firing at her repeatedly as she fled on foot.

McClain, who was also armed, shot back, striking Dowell in the chest.

He later died in the ambulance, en route to the hospital.

Police say they are investigating whether Dowell might have ordered the murder of Alicia McClain, mother of Harper McClain, in Savannah 16 years ago from his prison cell.

McClain has not been charged with any offense, although police said the case will be investigated.

Aaron Dowell is still missing.

She'd read enough. Shifting the paper, she glanced at the article taking up the right-hand side of the page under the headline THREE AR-RESTED IN MUSICIAN'S MURDER.

Both stories were bylined "DJ Gonzales, Miles Jackson and Emma Baxter."

"So Hunter's going to be okay?" she asked, scanning the article.

"Yeah. They think he'll make it." DJ was sitting on the green vinyl chair next to her bed. "It was such an insane night. Baxter had to tear up the front page at midnight. Everyone helped. Miles was interviewing the cops while I was interviewing you." He squinted at her. "Has Miles *ever* written a news story before?"

Harper shook her head, wincing as her fractured ribs shifted.

"Everyone was throwing each other lines, reading over each other's shoulders." He beamed at her. "It was like a movie."

"I'm sorry I wasn't there." She said it with real regret.

"So . . . how bad is it?" He gestured at her arm, encased in plaster.

"Oh, it'll heal." She thumped her knuckles against the cast. "Broken in two places, but they pieced it back together. Two fractured ribs."

She kept her tone light but DJ's smile faded. He reached across the blankets and rested his hand on hers. "Hell of a night," he said.

A memory of freezing water, darkness, and gunfire flashed through Harper's mind, and she shuddered. "Yeah."

Picking up his coffee, DJ looked around the bare, white room, with its bottles of hand disinfectant and official notices on the wall. "So, how long are they keeping you here?"

"I get out today, on good behavior."

"I'll tell Baxter. She's been worried about you, even though she pretends not to care." He paused before adding, "By the way, she told me about the layoffs."

"Oh." Harper gave him an apologetic look. "I should have told you. Things were so crazy."

"Yeah, don't worry about it. There's something I didn't tell you, too." He looked down, his fingers tapping nervously on the chair arm. "Paul Dells offered me a job at Channel Five."

Harper shouldn't have been surprised, and yet she felt as if he'd slapped her. She didn't know when, but at some point DJ had become essential to her. She couldn't imagine the newsroom without him.

But all she said was, "He did?"

"Yep." His eyes searched hers. "Baxter told me he offered you one, too."

They studied each other across the pale blankets.

"What did you tell him?" Harper asked.

"I told him I already had a job." He said it with some regret.

Relief flooded her chest with warmth. "I told him the same thing."

"We're such idiots," he said.

They grinned at each other.

Maybe it was the pain medication, but suddenly she wished she could hug him.

Instead, she said, "You're good people, DJ."

Reddening, he rubbed his nose furiously before saying, "Right back at you."

"Looks like we'll be running the paper alone soon," she mused. "Won't be anyone left but us."

"Yeah." He smiled at her. "I think we can handle it."

With a sigh, he stood up. "Well, I better let you get some rest. I've got about a hundred articles to follow up on. Your beat is hard work." He patted her bed as he headed for the door. "Get back to the office soon. I can't do this on my own."

When he'd gone, she sagged back against the cool pillows. She would never admit it to him, but even that short visit had exhausted her. Every movement hurt. Her eyes fluttered shut.

She'd barely been alone since she got to the hospital. Bonnie had spent the night in the chair next to her. She'd only gone home a couple of hours ago to shower and change.

At some point in the night, Baxter had come in to check on her. It must have been two in the morning by then. Harper had been so drugged up, she couldn't fully open her eyes.

The editor told her Dowell was dead. "He died before he reached the hospital," she'd said, standing beside the bed. "The police are out looking for his son."

It had taken effort for Harper to form words, but she had to be sure she understood. "He's really dead?"

Her lips tightening, Baxter had rested a hand on the bed rail. "Really dead. He's never coming back."

The rest of the editor's visit was a blur. At one point, she thought she heard Baxter say, "Someday, I'd love for you to write a story that doesn't end with you in the hospital."

By then, though, Harper was falling back into a deep sedated sleep. She dreamed that she and her mother were back in the light-filled kitchen of the little house where she'd grown up. Standing in front of an easel, her mother was painting a field of white daisies, her brow creasing with concentration as she added slender green stems to each flower.

"It's over, Mom," Harper had told her, eagerly. "It's finally over."

In her dream, her mother had looked over at her and smiled; then the light in the room had blazed like a fire.

When Harper woke up, it was day, and she felt at peace.

After DJ left, she must have slept again. She didn't know how long she'd been out before someone knocked at her door. Her eyelids were heavy, and she lifted them slowly, expecting a nurse.

Luke stood in the doorway.

"Hey." She tried to raise herself up, but flinched when that brought a stab of pain.

He crossed the room in three steps, bending over her to straighten the pillows. He'd showered and shaved; she could smell the sandalwood shower gel he used. But it didn't look as if he'd slept. Shadows under- lined his eyes as he lowered himself onto the edge of the chair.

"How're you feeling?" he asked.

"About a hundred years old, but I guess I'll live. How's it going out there?"

"Florida State Police pulled Aaron Dowell over a couple of hours ago on Interstate 10, driving a stolen car." He gave her a look of pure satis- faction. "He's in custody. He's going to be charged in the murder of Lee Howard. We found a knife in his possession that could be the murder weapon. It's being analyzed now."

Harper let out a long breath.

Luke squeezed her good hand. "I knew you'd want to know."

"Thank you," she said, holding his gaze. "And for being there last night. You and Daltrey saved my life."

"Don't thank me," he said, gruffly. "I'm just sorry you had to go through that." He looked down, his brow knitted. "Last night scared the hell out of me," he said. "Seeing your car like that . . . I thought for a second . . ."

His voice faltered. He lifted her hand to his lips.

"Do you have any idea how Dowell found me?" she asked.

"We think maybe he staked out Xavier Rayne's house. If he'd seen your articles, he'd have known you'd come out there at some point."

Harper tried to imagine Dowell watching everything unfurl outside the house. Cara holding the gun in a shaking hand. Hunter sliding down the steps, color draining from his face.

"I'll give him credit—it was a good time to go for you," Luke said. "That storm was so bad, the highway was closed. The chief banned all nonemergency travel out of the city. We only got permission to go when Tybee Police called in about the shooting. That's where we were headed when we saw the SUV parked on the side of the road. At first we thought someone had broken down. Then we spotted what was left of the Camaro." He drew a breath. "We put it together pretty fast after that. We knew you were out there somewhere, and he had to be out there too. The rest you know."

"Luke, what's going to happen to me?" She searched his eyes. "Are you going to investigate me?"

He went quiet. "There'll be an investigation," he said, finally. "I won't have anything to do with it because . . ." He didn't have to finish that sentence. "It doesn't matter. You're going to be fine. You stopped a killer from killing all three of us. No prosecutor in Georgia will want to try that case. If some fool tries, you'll win."

Harper thought of all that Dowell's vendetta had cost. This had to be the end of it.

"I hope you're right," she said.

He leaned forward, resting his forearms on his knees. "Look, there's something else we need to—"

"Miss McClain, how are you?" A nurse bustled in, interrupting him.

Jumping to his feet, Luke retreated to a corner of the room as the woman checked Harper's blood pressure and oxygen levels. After pushing various buttons on a number of machines, the nurse headed for the door, saying cheerfully, "I'll be back shortly with your pain meds."

When she was gone, Luke stayed by the window, staring out.

Harper looked at the side of his beautiful face—the worried crease in his brow. "Hey," she said. "What were you going to say?"

He hesitated before turning to face her. "It's nothing. We can talk about it when you're better."

The moment felt weighted with all the unspoken words and misunderstandings that had driven them apart for years, and she willed him to say something true, just this once. Anything at all.

He cleared his throat, his eyes skittering around the brightly lit room.

"This isn't the right time, or the right place." His face was hard, as if the words were costing him. "But, last night, seeing you, half dead. I learned something. Something I should have learned a long time ago." He met her eyes. "I love you, Harper. And I don't know what to do about that."

She reached out for him. "I don't know what to do, either," she said. "But, I love you, too."

He took her hand and bent down, his lips gently brushing hers.

"We can't ever have a normal relationship," he said, his breath warm against her skin. "Our jobs won't let us. We can't do this."

"I know," she said. "But I don't want to live without you."

He straightened, looking down at her with those watchful blue eyes she'd loved since she was twenty-one years old, and he was a rookie cop, and she a rookie reporter. That was seven years ago. So long to wait.

"We'll figure something out," he said.

Not trusting herself to speak, she nodded.

The nurse bustled back in, humming to herself.

Luke stepped back again. Glancing at the nurse, who held a tray of medicines, he said, "I better get moving."

He crossed the room, his shoes silent against the linoleum, and paused in the doorway.

"By the way, what are you going to do about the car?"

Harper hadn't had a chance to think about that yet. The Camaro was totaled.

"I don't know," she admitted. "I guess, get a new one? Somehow. With no money."

"I might be able to help," he said. "Give me a call when you're out of here. I'll hook you up."

It was so Luke. *I love you. Let's get you a safe car.*

When he was gone, the nurse came over with the pills and a cup of water and glanced at the empty doorway.

"Now that's a good-looking detective," she observed.

Harper smiled as she took the cup from her. "Yes, he is."

THREE MONTHS LATER

Bonnie walked out onto the porch holding two glasses of wine. She pushed the door shut with her foot and crossed to where Harper sat. "I really like this place," she said, holding out a glass. "Once you're settled you're going to love it. I can tell."

Harper looked around doubtfully and took a sip of wine. "I guess I'll get used to it."

"You will." Bonnie sat down across from her. "It's so great seeing your stuff out of storage again. Though why you had to move on the first hundred-degree day of the year . . ." She leaned back in the chair, propping up her feet. "Still, it's worth all that sweat for this."

The night air was velvet soft, perfumed with the scent of the honeysuckle that tumbled over the fence from the garden next door.

"It's probably just a relief to have me out of your house," Harper said, giving her a look.

"Never. I loved having a housemate." Bonnie relaxed back against the high seat back. "It's too quiet without you there. I might get a dog."

Harper snorted. "I love that I can be replaced by a poodle."

"Not a poodle," Bonnie said. "A German shepherd."

Sipping the cold wine, Harper looked at her new home. Made of a pale, rose-colored stone, the building on Huntingdon Street was hulking and sturdy, with a high peaked roof and a fanciful curved front porch. Inside, the apartment was big, with original wood floors that showed their age, and windows big enough to step through without bending.

It wasn't a bad place to end up. It felt good. It felt safe.

A stack of flattened boxes lay at the foot of the front steps, waiting to be taken to the recycling center. Her new car was parked a few feet away. Like the house, the black Dodge Charger still felt strange to her. Luke had, as he'd promised, helped her find it. It had been seized from a drug dealer and sold by the police at a steep discount. She'd paid for it with the car insurance money.

She and Luke were still figuring things out. As he'd promised, he'd broken up with Sarah. But nobody on the police force could know that the two of them had resumed seeing each other. It had to be secret. Possibly forever. And she had no idea how that would work.

Right now, though, her heart leaped every time he called at midnight to see if she was coming to his place. She loved the novelty of waking up next to him.

For the moment, that was enough.

"I can't believe we got everything unpacked in one day." Bonnie stretched her tanned legs, propping her feet up on the stone bannister a few feet from where Zuzu sat hunched, studying her new kingdom with open suspicion. "Billy was so nice. My landlord wouldn't pick up a box to help me if my life depended on it."

"Billy's one of a kind." Glancing at her, Harper said, "Hey, thanks for all the free labor." She held up her glass. "I hope we don't have to do that again for a very long time."

"I'll drink to that," Bonnie said.

Harper massaged her left shoulder gingerly. It ached a little—carrying boxes was the biggest workout she'd given it since the cast came off.

"How are things at the paper?" Bonnie inquired, setting her glass down. "Is everyone settling down since the layoffs?"

It had been a tough couple of months at the *Daily News*. Seven writers had been laid off, along with sportswriters and people in the advertising office. The newsroom felt increasingly hollow. But those who remained—

eight news reporters, two lifestyle writers, and five sportswriters—were forming a tight group. One writer had been promoted to junior editor, meaning Baxter no longer had to work fourteen-hour days. It also meant she wasn't there every night. But Harper was getting used to that.

DJ had been given a split beat, writing about the courts and helping Harper cover the police.

"Baxter did the best she could with a bad situation," Harper said. "DJ's happy as a clam, charming all the lawyers. Winning over the cops."

"What about you?" Bonnie asked. "Are you sleeping better?"

Harper hesitated. She still had nightmares of bright headlights, and the shriek of metal. But things had been getting better since the district attorney decided not to file charges against her. Some nights she slept dreamlessly.

She and her father had spoken only once since the night she killed Dowell. A stiff, uncomfortable conversation that felt like good-bye. Maybe she was ready to move on from her childhood. Ready, at last, to let go of the demons that had haunted her all her life.

"I'm a little better," she said. "But, you know. Baby steps."

Bonnie watched her, a tiny crease forming between her eyes. "This is a strange question but, do you ever think about doing anything else? I mean, you've been shot. You've been stalked. Doesn't the violence wear you down?"

Harper looked down the dark street. Somewhere in the distance a siren wailed, and her heart quickened in response, as if she were intrinsically connected to that sound. As if it were in her blood.

After all these years, maybe it was.

"This is my job," she said. "I don't think I'll ever do anything else." She smiled, lifting her glass. "Anyway. Someone's got to do it."